The Kingdom of Keys

By

Brian Moloney

ISBN-13: 978-0692435151

ISBN-10: 0692435158

Keymaker Publishing

Email: freelanceretort@gmail.com

Cover Photography by Joelle Wilson

Brian Moloney

Dedication

To those special people, past and present, for taking the time to read my endless drafts and providing not only encouragement, but the optimism and enthusiasm I found so hard to muster in myself over the last 20 years. The ones who always picked me up, pointed me in the right directions and said: *"Just start walking and don't look back...."*

And especially to Betsy, whose endless patience, understanding and constant good humor, allows me to open the door and follow my dreams, every day...without hassle....*for the most part...a lot of the time...pretty much...sort of....*

Thanks to all...this one's for you.

Prologue

The boy couldn't recall when he'd first noticed the peculiar looking key.

Thinking back, it might have been that cold, windblown night, late last year. Even now the icy chill of the rattling panes still shivered deep inside his bones.

Of course, he knew—*he thought*—it was—*probably*—just a wayward shaft of moonlight that had sparked its tarnished skin, fluttered in the dark and caught his wary eye.

But, the dust, that strange, peculiar dust. The ancient key was buried in what seemed to be a mountain of...*that dust*....

The boy didn't dare disturb that powdery shroud...let alone dream remove the key and unlock the door...on whose forgotten ledge it lay.

Yet, somehow, still, he knew...this key...*this simple skeleton key*...could change everything. And he knew it was meant for him.

"The key...always the key...."

Until that night, the boy had always defined his fantasies with reality.

But, on that night...fantasy *became* his reality....

* * * * * * * *

Brian Moloney

Chapter 1

Click, click...click, click....

Outside, steel gray skies had surrendered to the first *real* cliché of spring. Seventy-two degrees and a high sun melting away the last remaining cobwebs of winter.

Click, click...click, click....

Inside, behind closed doors and windows, propped up on a mountain of pillows, a young man lay lump-like on his bed.

Click, click...click, click....

"And this amazing hair in a can product can only be purchased through this amazing once in a lifetime amazing TV offer...."

Click, click....

"Beware the full moon; it carries the sign of the wolf. It can mean only death."

Click, click....

"And that's the latest rap-a from Italian Ice, `I Hatesa My Mommas Pasta, Lotsa...' Remember you saw the world premier right here on Rap-TV!"

Click, click....

Sixteen year old Toby Pierce was in channel surfer's heaven. Only problem was, like the man said, there were *fifty seven channels and nothing on.*

Actually, now, it was more like *three hundred and fifty seven* channels, plus, on demand, along with on-line-streaming, which made it even worse. But, in fact, it didn't *really* matter at all because Toby wasn't in the mood to watch *anything*; he was just killing time.

Lately, that's all he seemed to *ever* do, all he seemed to *want* to do. He was the *Terminator* of time killers and, best of all, he didn't have to move from his bed to do it, which was just fine with him, considering his legs felt like iron anchors, sinking deeper and deeper into his mattress of muck.

BOOM...!

The bedroom door crashed open, followed closely by Mom exploding into the room.

"Toby, what on earth are you doing indoors on the most gorgeous day of the year...with all the windows and blinds closed, no less?"

Mom was at her best, swirling *"Road Runner"* like through the stuffy room, picking up dirty laundry, pulling up blinds and opening windows, all in one complete eye blurring motion...*beep...beep!*

"Ah, Mom, you're blinding me with all that sunlight. And that air...it reeks of mold and pollen. I can feel my bronchioles closing up as we speak. My asthma's kicking in."

"What asthma? You're the healthiest person I know. Why aren't you outside with your friends doing something...something *youthful*...or something?"

"Come on Mom, your killin me here, can't you see I'm like totally engrossed in this show?"

Mom stopped and glanced toward the screen. "Oh, I see. I didn't realize your favorite program, on the migrating and mating habits of hump back whales, was on. How silly of me. I know you never miss an episode. In fact, didn't I buy you the Blu-ray collection last Christmas? I believe they had a special at the fish market, as I recall."

"Mammals, Mom, whales are mammals, not fish. And besides, I think you're thinking of that *fishy* version of `The Little Red Christmas Ball', you got me."

"I thought it was a cute little story, and besides, what do you mean by `*fishy*'."

"I don't know. I was just trying to be topical. Anyway, I'm watching TV."

"You're not watching, you're flipping. Honestly, I don't know what you'd do without that remote. Look at it; you've just about worn the buttons down to the nubs. You know, in my day we had to *actually* get up and change channels. Can you imagine?"

"Mom, *in your day*, there only *was* one channel."

There was a brief pause as Mom tried to swallow a giggle. Fearing the battle lost, but refusing to surrender, she lashed out and pillow-whacked her son on top of the head.

"Okay, buster, you've *really* crossed the line, now. The TV goes off, and *you* are going outside to, heaven forbid, get some fresh air and a healthy glow on your poor colorless cheeks." Mom reached down and without ceremony, unplugged the TV.

"Ah, Mom, *nooooo*—" Toby moaned, but to no avail, his precious remote was rendered useless.

"And don't give me that devastated *big blue eye* routine, either, young man. Someday you'll look back and thank your poor old Mother for this." And with that Mom spun and vanished from the room...*beep...beep!*

"Someday you'll respect my big blue right to sink into utter blobdom!" Toby shouted after her.

Toby Pierce *was* graced, or cursed, he sometimes thought, with deep, *piercing* eyes that well befit his surname. Vibrant blue irises, accentuated by a set of stark black pupils that appeared to bore a hole right through to the very soul.

Standing out on an otherwise unremarkable face, framed with a shaggy growth of thick, sandy hair, his eyes immediately made an impression on people—people who almost always felt they had to comment.

"My, what startling eyes! What I wouldn't give to have a pair of eyes like yours," was how it usually went.

Over the years, Toby patented some lame responses, such as, *"Thank you very much, but I think I'll keep them for a while. I can't see how I could possibly give them up. Be seein ya around...."* Corny stuff like that; anything, just to change the subject.

The thing was, no one was really sure *how* Toby came to inherit the unusual orbs, seeing as both his mother and father possessed rather dark, soulful eyes of brown. His grandmother thought it might have been a maternal great grandfather's brother, from the old country, wherever that was.

And wherever that was, like most things these days, was not important to Toby, who chased away the thought with a sigh and melted further into his fortress of pillows.

After a while, he reluctantly allowed his gaze to drift onto the *"Door to Nowhere"*. He scanned the thin irregular crack that ran through its center and wondered if it had gotten a little bit bigger lately. *Who cares...?*

From somewhere, the phrase that had been lately weaving in and out of his mind echoed in the silence and reminded him who cared.

"The key...always the key...."

The *"Door to Nowhere"* was just that: a useless door that once upon a time, long before his time, had led into an adjoining bedroom, but now, led nowhere. Toby imagined that one ambitious weekend, the house's previous occupants had decided: *"Wouldn't it be a great idea to seal it over!"*. Something about creating more wall space in the other room; maybe to hang a picture of Great Aunt Gladys.

Soon, afterwards, the *"handy dandies"* after plastering over the opening, lost their enthusiasm - he surmised - as quickly as they found it and never actually removed the *door* itself, crack and all, on this side of the sealed over wall. Apparently, they just locked it up and threw away the key.

On the day - almost a decade ago - that Toby's family moved in - *it seemed like it was yesterday* - Toby's Dad said something about the useless door being a testament to *"Suburban Do-It-Yourself Home Improvements"*, and promptly christened it: the *"Door to Nowhere"*.

Well, like any self-respecting little boy, especially one with a turbo charged imagination, Toby was immediately fascinated by the *"Door to Nowhere"*.

"Where does it lead...why's it always locked...why doesn't anyone have the key?"

His Dad, never at a loss for tales, would reply, *"Well, Buckaroo, the Door to Nowhere is* really *the secret passageway to the* Kingdom of Keys; *a special place where* all *the keys to our* future *are made."* And, as always, Toby would sit, wide eyed, while his father spun the yarn.

"Everyone in the kingdom, when it's their time, is given a small sack, filled with keys. Each key opens different doors, differently, and behind each door lays a different adventure. The trick is in the `knowing': which key...what door."

Later on, Toby - a fine storyteller himself - wouldn't hesitate to mesmerize his friends with the tale, boldly proclaiming,

"Someday, I'm gonna find the key and open the Door to Nowhere. Then I'm off to the Kingdom of Keys!"

His friends would gasp and nod their heads, then, half-heartedly, beg to come along.

Of course, like all *"really good"* fantasies, this one came with a price tag, and Toby paid for it with many a sleepless night.

But he didn't really mind. On most of those occasions he'd happily lie in bed, studying the door, searching for its secrets and marveling at the magical adventures that stood just a few feet away.

If only I had the key.

In the end, those sleepless nights gave way to countless dreams, followed by a wealth of morning suns. Now, it seemed only remnants of those magical adventures remained, and even those were filed in a dark forgotten corner, lost forever, somewhere under *ancient history.*

Yet Toby could still hear his Dad on that rainy afternoon as they sat and listened to one of the dusty, old records from his treasured collection of sixties rock 'n' roll. Relics from the past, his dad had called them, which he insisted could never be duplicated on today's "digital doo dads".

"What do you say, son. I was thinking of finally closing over that old Door to Nowhere...this time, the right way."

Toby immediately tossed aside an old folk singer's album cover he'd been studying and sat up, straight as an arrow. *"Sure Dad, let's do it. Can I help?"*

"I was counting on it, Buckaroo. That is if you're not afraid of falling into the Kingdom of Keys.*"*

"Kingdom of Termites *is more like it,"* Toby replied.

Dad smiled, proud of his son, *"Great, we'll get started next weekend"*...not knowing then, he'd leave the house a few days later and never return. Just one of those unexpected plot twists that sometimes occur in *real* life, which a twelve year old boy is never really prepared for.

Toby dealt with his father's, *unexpected passing* - as the euphemistic choir liked to sing - in a foggy, detached sort of way. He told himself it was okay, just *kind of a detour* on the safe, straight and narrow highway he'd been traveling all his life. He figured after a while he'd link up with the main road again; soon, very soon. But now, nearly four years later, it seemed as if the detour was taking detours of its own.

Another sigh broke his thoughts and dragged his gaze away from the door. Now his eyes burned a hole through the ceiling, trying to formulate a plan to get Mom off his case.

When he ran out of formulations, he concluded the inevitable and in his best Shakespearean announced, "To be...or not to be. Alas, I fear I have no choice. I must venture out into the land of the living," and, somehow, he mustered a reserve of latent energy. Or at least enough to drag his apathetic form from the bed, and slither down the stairs.

Trudging into the kitchen, he found his mother rinsing off a few of last night's dirty dinner dishes, carefully avoiding an erratic spray from a faucet badly in need of a washer.

"Now see what you've made me do," he announced in his best whiny Toby. "Expend all this energy. I'll never get it back. Once it's gone, it's gone."

"Do my eyes deceive me, glory hallelujah, Lazarus has arisen. And what about replacing this old washer, Laz?" Mom inquired.

"How many miracles do you expect in one day?" Toby replied. "I must be going now. I'm off to spread happiness and joy, wherever I may tread."

"Try treading over to the hardware store to pick up some paint for that back porch." Mom ducked another errant squirt. "And a washer might be nice."

"Why? I think the porch has that very sought after weathered look. A peeled gray patina is very "*in*" these days...and can I help it if you're *faucet challenged*."

"Don't be a wise guy, *Buckaroo*," Mom said.

Toby winced at the sound of his old nickname, but pretended not to notice.

"See ya later, Mom."

"Bye *Toby*, try not to have too much fun."

"You can count on it," he said as he trudged off the peeling porch, squinting his eyes against the overbearing sunshine.

Down at the corner, he found his buddies playing ball.

WHACK!

"Home Run!" Billy Bartles proclaimed, watching the wiffle ball sail over the hedges into Mrs. Schulman's rhododendrons.

Billy was the resident jock and *"do-no-wrong, whatever he did"* kind of guy. Only problem was - Billy knew it, and always wanted to make sure everybody else knew it too.

Unlike Toby, who was decidedly average, if not a bit below, in height and build, Billy was lean, despite his propensity for food - any kind...any time - and athletically muscular. He was waiting on, as he made a point of telling anyone who would listen, the next growth spurt that would catapult him into the six footers club. He was also Toby's best friend; the *"Yin"* to his *"Yang"*.

"Foul ball!" Peter Plantier aka *"Peter Planet Eater"*, for obvious round and pudgy reasons- deliverer of the *"Gofer"* ball - cried. "That ball was *outside* the telephone pole."

"You're nuts, yodel breath, that ball was fair by two feet," Billy responded, then flipped the bat in his best *"Home Run King"* routine.

"Foul ball," Herbie Johnson shouted. Both arms motioned wildly toward foul territory in *his* best *"third base umpire"* routine. The fact that he was as nearsighted as Mr. Magoo and wore thick glasses, seemed to make him a natural.

"Foul ball!" he repeated.

"Oh sure, like I'm supposed to believe you? You're on his side, Magoo," Billy whined.

"It was foul by ten feet, Bartles," Toby said as he approached the squabble. "I could see it from half way up the street."

Actually, Toby had no idea where the ball had gone but he just loved sticking it to Billy whenever an opportunity presented itself.

"Who asked you, you're not even playing. What ya do, just roll out of bed or something? You look as wrinkled as my old grandmother," Billy cracked. When it came to wit, Billy's was mostly dim.

"No, actually I'm trying to market a new fashion line called *`Forever Wrinkled'*," Toby said. "You've heard of permanent press, now comes permanent wrinkled. Just think of it, everyone who's anyone will come from all around to bring their clothes to my special facility where - for a standard fee - my secretly patented wrinkling process will *`Forever Wrinkle'* their clothes. If you're not wrinkled, you're not anywhere."

"Huh, where anywhere? What are you talking about, Pierce?" Billy was oblivious to a wit master when he saw one.

"Never mind," Toby sighed. "Besides, what do you have to cheat for? You'll probably hit the next four fair for home runs, anyway".

"That's easy for you to say," Billy said.

"What's the score?" Toby asked.

"I think it's sixty seven to three, mine."

"What inning?"

"Top of the second."

"How'd you give up three runs?"

"Pitching lefty."

"I dunno Billy, pretty careless. You'll ruin your reputation if you're not careful."

"You might be right," Billy said. "Okay, foul ball...new game. Slates clean. Me and the Tubman against you two."

"No way," Planet Eater shouted. "We can come back. It's only the second inning. Besides, we don't stand a chance against you and Toby."

"They don't stand a chance against *Hobbits*," Billy muttered, referring to the tiny fictional characters in the JR Tolkien book they had just finished in school. Actually, Billy hadn't gotten past more than the first few chapters - he planned on catching the flicks on demand...*one of these days* - so naturally, he didn't know that Bilbo Baggins and cousin Frodo were pretty resourceful little fellows, when pressed.

"Nah, that's okay, I don't feel much like playing. I'll just sit here and soak in all the excitement," Toby said.

"Ah come on, Tobe. We can really kick some butt here," Billy said. "You used to love to play. Now you hardly ever want to do anything fun, anymore."

"Jeez, what is it with all you people, can't a guy just lie around and vegetate? Why do I have to entertain everybody?"

Annoyed, Toby found a comfortable piece of curb and stretched out by the third base telephone pole. His mind flashed a picture of him and his dad sitting under a blanket of summer stars, watching baseball on a very old, very small, battery powered, black & white TV. Toby would have preferred the crisp, green grass of HD, but his dad always proclaimed that the games were better back in the day when you could only watch them on a black and white TV. Toby chuckled, as he always had, and knew he really wasn't there for the game, anyway. Then, he turned the picture into fuzz and chased it away.

Lori McSwain stepped from her front door and immediately spotted Toby sprawled out by the pole. Without hesitation, she bounded down the stairs of her very own *"unfashionable"*, freshly painted porch and prodded Toby with her toe.

"Hi Tobe, what are you up to...or down to, I should say."

"Hi Lor, not much. Please, don't *you* start with me, too."

"Jeez," Lori said. "Somebody's touchy today. Isn't it a great day? Don't you love it? Summer's finally on its way."

"Don't get too excited, Suzy Sunshine. It's only the last week of March. We might get fifteen inches of white stuff tomorrow."

"You're such a positive thinker, Toby Pierce. I think that's what I've always found so fascinating about you."

"Thanks, I always thought it was my *He-Man like* physique," Toby pulled back the sleeve of his T-shirt and bounced an under developed bicep.

"Wow, neat trick," Lori said, as she pushed a long strand of shiny, chestnut hair back around her ear and feigned admiration.

WHACK!

"No doubt about that one!" Billy shouted. "That ball is outta here! Kiss that baby good-bye!"

"Alright, alright," Planet Eater said. "Hurry up Herbie, get it before it goes in the sewer...and stop circling your finger in the air, Bonehead!"

"What's he doing that for?" Lori asked.

"I don't know," Toby sighed. "Some secret umpire code for a home run, I suppose."

"Oh."

"It fell down the sewer!" Herbie shouted.

"Ah, not again. " Billy said. "Where's the fish hook? This is all your fault, Planet Eater."

"My fault? How is this my fault?" Peter said. His face turned a bright crimson as they ran toward the sewer.

"If you'd ever learn to pitch, I wouldn't hit so many home runs," Billy answered with his typical convoluted reasoning that seemed to make sense only to him.

Toby and Lori took it all in and watched the pair run off toward their fishing expedition.

"Want to go check it out?" Lori asked.

"Nah, we'd only end up listening to old wiffle ball stories about the big ones that got away. Besides, I think the spaldeens are biting over on Sherwood. Now that's a ball worth fishing for. What do you think?"

"I think your brain's a spaldeen, that's what I think. Come on, let's go for a walk, down to *The Lake*."

"What and give up this perfectly good telephone pole? Besides, I'm watching a ball game, here."

"No you're not, the game's been called on account of sewer. Now, you're just a derelict teenager loitering against a telephone pole. Better hope the sloth police don't come and lock you up," Lori, again, kicked and prodded him until, finally, he struggled to his feet.

"Oh, if only they would...and throw away the key...please," Toby pleaded.

"Farewell, *mien pole*. You've always been supportive and upstanding in my hour of need. And now...let us not say good-by...but *averiderci*, as the French like to say."

"Auvoir," Lori corrected.

"What's that, my dear?" Toby asked.

"Auvoir is French. Averiderci is Italian."

"Right, but the French like to say it. It has so much more of a ring to it, don't you think? And what the heck is the sloth police?"

Lori couldn't prevent a smile, followed by a giggle, from escaping, "You are truly one of a kind, Toby Pierce."

Toby suddenly noticed that *look* in Lori's eye, and, as always, felt -as he called it - a little "*flustrated*". You know, *"the look"* that made him think that she thought he was kind of...*special*.

As with Billy, Toby and Lori went *way back*...all the way to kindergarten...and they had instantly became automatic, reluctant best buddies. Reluctant, since little boys weren't supposed to be best buddies with little girls, and vice-versa. An unspoken code or something passed down from pre-school.

It hadn't been long - only this past year, he thought - since he'd begun to notice *"the look"*. Right about the same time, in fact, that he'd begun to think that *"the look"* was looking good; not that he would ever let his *"old buddy"* know, of course. How could he, when he didn't even know himself?

Besides, it might all be twisted in his tangled head, confused with all the other junkyard clutter. *Nothing's simple up there*, he thought. But he did know that Lori was always there and, more importantly, he could always talk to her without feeling stupid; unlike Billy or Peter, who were as deep as a puddle, or Herbie, who found it difficult to deviate from whatever delusion he was currently riding.

Toby returned his thoughts to the present and discovered they'd already begun strolling, downhill toward *The Lake*.

"What's the matter, Toby? You seem distracted. And you've been keeping yourself scarce these days," Lori said.

"Ah, I don't know, Lor. Just haven't felt like seeing much of anybody...doing anything."

"It has been pretty cold."

"In more ways than one," he replied.

"What's that mean?"

"Nothing...just kidding."

"Ah, the old `*just kidding'* disclaimer."

"Right...just kidding."

"So, are you all set for the midterms, next week?" Lori thought she'd better change the subject.

"What's to get set?" Toby replied. "Either I'm ready or I'm not. Does it really even matter?"

"If you want to go to a good college it does...of course it matters. Then again, I suppose you'll be fine. You're one of those people who'll be great at whatever it is you do."

"Yeah, I'll make a terrific *space takerupper*. A burden to society."

"Oh, stop making a joke of everything, Toby. Now's the time when we really have to get serious about, you know, our futures and stuff. You must have some idea of what you want to be."

"Look," Toby continued. "I don't really want to get into it...okay? I guess I'm just not like everyone else. I know it sounds dumb, but I feel like I don't fit in, here. Like the rest of the world is all settled, enjoying the show...except for me. It's like...I know I have to do something...maybe even something great...but I'm terrified that I won't...that I can't."

"Toby, I think you're getting a little ahead of yourself, here."

"Forget it. I probably shouldn't have even mentioned it."

Lori usually had a lot of patience when it came to Toby's moods, but today, for some reason, maybe because of the promising weather, she had zero tolerance for his chronic gloom.

"You are such a negative pain in the butt, Toby. Do you know what the *key* to your problem is?"

"The key *is* the problem."

"What?"

"It's always the key...."

"Yes the key...the answer."

"Prey, enlighten me, Herr Freud," Toby said with a sneer.

"Your problem is you have to read everything inside and out. Analyze and criticize. You look at everything *way* too deep, and you just plain *think* too much."

Toby stopped, looked at Lori with his piercing eyes and said flatly, "Tell me about it." And with that, they walked the rest of the way to *The Lake,* silently...several steps apart.

Chapter 2

They called it *"The Lake"*, but it was more of a deep puddle-pond, really, hidden in the woods on the old Walden estate. Back when you were eight years old, it just seemed like a lake, and you hoped it always would.

Not too long ago, Toby and the gang would ride their bikes down to these swampy old woods two or three times a day. *The Lake* could take them anywhere they wanted to go. To the past, to fight dinosaurs...the future, to fight space monsters...or to the present, just to hang out and be friends.

The only thing they didn't do - or want to do - at *The Lake* was swim in it. They might have been kids, but they weren't stupid. There were times - in fact, most of the time - when the surface of *The Lake* was the color and consistency of pea soup with a suspect sort of vegetation breaking through the surface.

"Hey, look Tobe. Come on up here. Can you believe it? I haven't thought about this in years."

Lori had a specific plan in mind when she suggested this particular trip to *The Lake*. Upon arrival, she immediately climbed up a huge Weeping Beech, known as the *"Elephant Tree"*, and found, among hundreds of others, the initials she and Toby had once carved into its thick twisted trunk.

With its large spindly limbs that snaked toward the sky, then abruptly plunged down to its bulging root system, the ancient *Elephant Tree* had been named for its *pachydermian* resemblance.

"Ha, too cool," Toby said, straining to climb up past the knot of branches.

"Can you believe it...after all these years?"

"Yeah, it's like perfectly preserved. We're almost immoral," Toby teased.

"Immortal," Lori corrected.

"Yeah, that too."

"How many others besides ours do you think are up here?" Lori wondered.

In his head, Toby heard a familiar voice, *"People come and people go, but magic places seem to live forever, Buckaroo."*

"Do you remember the day we did this? It was so much fun," Lori said.

Amazingly enough, Toby did remember, in vivid detail.

It was a crisp autumn day, the kind of day you could actually *smell* the color in the leaves. Like today, Toby and Lori were the only ones down at *The Lake* and they were terribly busy trying to save the universe from total destruction. Some evil fiend had placed an equally evil, toxic, orb on top of the *Elephant Tree* and it was due to explode at any moment, destroying the world as they knew it. Toby - *a.k.a. Tubman* - and Lori - *a.k.a. Queen of The*

Lake - had to climb to the top of the tree while defeating the evil villain and his horrible brigade, and - at the same time - defuse the dreaded "*Whatchamacallit Device*".

Luckily, they were victorious and were rewarded with a ticker-tape parade given by the always grateful citizens of the world.

Later, as they sat resting between the twisted branches, savoring their victory over evil, exhausted by the parade, Lori suggested they should do something special to commemorate the event. Toby thought that a great idea, and proceeded to carve their initials into the thick old bark, using the little pocketknife his grandfather had given him as a birthday gift, much to his mother's dismay.

At the time, there was no thought, at least not in Toby's mind, of making some kind of mushy heart to connect the brave warriors. Uh, uh, this was serious stuff; so instead, he cut a fierce lightning bolt and joined the two Super Heroes together, forever:

T.P.

L . M.

And the world was a safer place for all *mankind*...and *womankind*, as Lori had reminded.

Now, hoping to unlock the past, Lori ran her fingers across the jagged edges of the primitive lightning bolt and released a flood of happy memories.

"Give me your hand...here...can you feel it?" Dates and details, long since stored away came rushing back to her.

"Do you remember that Halloween, in third grade...?"

It wasn't that Toby didn't want to share in Lori's memories, mix them in with the precious few he did recall, but, when he went into retrieval mode he found they just weren't there.

"Nah...get out...you're kidding...I don't...I don't remember any of it...really."

It would take some major mining to unearth those gems. In fact, he thought, *it might as well have been somebody else's past.*

Yet, in spite of himself, Toby was actually enjoying this retreat from his solitary confinement. He wrapped himself in the warm spring air and happily listened to Lori recount their grammar school adventures, politely nodding his head and voicing agreement in all the appropriate places.

Still- as always - in the end, his restlessness finally won out and he hinted they should probably start heading home.

"Man, this old tree is doing a number on me. I can't feel my butt anymore."

"I wish we could stay here, forever," Lori sighed. "Isn't it great reliving the past?"

"Yeah, especially if you only remember the good stuff."

"What'ya mean, Tobe?"

"Nothing—"

"I know," Lori finished. "Just kidding."

"Yeah, right. No really, we'd better get going. It'll be dark soon, and I think there's a storm moving in."

Lori looked up and saw patches of blue between newly sprouted leaves, "What are you talking about, silly. There's not a cloud in the sky."

"Well, you know how weird the weather can be this time of year. It just feels stormy to me."

Lori smirked and shook her head in frustration.

"Really, it does. Come on we'd better get back before we get stranded down here."

"Ooooh, wouldn't that be horrible." Recognizing a lost cause when she saw one, Lori reluctantly followed Toby out of the tree.

"Lead on barometer breath, I'm right behind you."

Toby walked most of the way back in silence, carefully inspecting the sidewalks for cracks. Lori continued making idle chatter, hoping to stumble on something that might spark an actual conversation. Eventually, they arrived at the third base telephone pole and said their farewells.

"*Maybe* we could watch a movie or something later," Lori suggested.

"Sure...I'll be around...you know...*maybe*. I'll give you a call." Toby said.

"Great, then I'll see ya later, alligator...you know... *maybe*," Lori sang, as she skipped up her front steps and disappeared through the door.

Toby watched the door close behind her and found himself smiling. Then he continued his short walk home...more confused than ever.

A gust of wind whistled by and attached a sharp chill down the length of his spine as he shuffled off for home. The deceptive warmth of early spring was beginning to retreat with March's setting sun. Toby shook off the chill, hopped over the small wooden gate that led into his back yard and surveyed the modest, postage stamp of land he considered home. He saw a lot of runaway bushes and way too many weeds.

Welcome to reality, Buckaroo, he thought, then plodded up the *"very chic"*, peeling gray steps.

The back door was closed but, as always, unlocked, so Toby pushed it open and stumbled across the same familiar threshold he had left behind only a few hours before.

"Hi everyone...I've returned from spreading goodness and light throughout the land," he announced to the silence of an empty house.

A note was magnetically stuck to the refrigerator door, attached to some sort of crochet porcupine thing:

Toby,

There are hot dogs and beans in the fridge.

Some potato salad, too, if you want.

The pots are on the stove and the rolls are

in the bread box. Please don't make a mess

and don't leave any dirty dishes.

You can reach me at work if you have any problems.

I should be home around midnight.

Me.

P.S.

If you want sauerkraut you have to open

a can from the pantry....

"Jeez, open my own can.... What sort of nonsense is this?"

He plucked the pot off the stove, walked to the sink, turned on the faucet and was immediately spritzed by its welcoming spray. Ducking, he gave the handle a firm shot on its side and the spray stopped.

"The magic touch," he sighed, then put the pot back on the stove and waited for the water to boil.

Three hotdogs, minus sauerkraut *and* one Tubman super special ice-cream sundae for dessert, later, Toby called Lori and said he wasn't feeling all that well and would have to take a pass on the movie.

Soon after, he went to bed...and the dream began.

Chapter 3

At first, sleep was slow in coming. No matter how many tosses and turns he performed, he just couldn't get comfortable. Toby figured it might have been a lot of things: the ton of ice cream sundae he'd devoured, for one; the pound of mystery hot dog meat for another. But, most of all, there were the many mind-twisting events of the day. A lot of grist for the mill, as it were.

Too many thoughts...not enough energy to sort it out.

Toby finally began to give in to the drowsy music of a light spring rain. Semiconscious, he turned toward the *"Door to Nowhere"* and wondered, *did I really see...the light, the door...that night.*

"The key...always the key..." he mumbled, then slowly...drifted...off....

....Toby dreamed he was in a small, sparsely furnished room; not his own, yet, all the same, vaguely familiar. The room

contained a bed, a dresser and a chair. He was dressed in pajamas, which he thought was strange, since he hadn't slept in anything but shorts for the last couple of years. He wanted to change...but he couldn't. There was nothing to change into.

He felt uneasy. The meager room was unsettling and he wanted to leave. He saw a doorway and immediately walked toward it. He opened the door and found, to his surprise and frustration that it opened only onto a wall. A wall of bricks.

What do I do now, he thought? I'm stuck here. I can't get out.

Sliding to the floor he was overcome with despair, not by the seemingly hopeless situation, but by the frustration of not being able to change out of his pajamas.

Sitting back against the dresser he looked up toward the bed. Maybe I should just crawl back in and wake up, he thought. Wait...what's that...under the bed...a glint, a sparkle of light...a key? Always the key....

He scrambled to his feet and ran toward the bed. It seemed so close, yet it took him forever to get there...as if he were swimming in Jell-O.

Finally, summoning every ounce of strength he could command he flung himself onto the bed and was swallowed by a mountain of suffocating old, woolen blankets. Choking, he threw the blankets aside and a blizzard of dust instantly filled the room. He hacked and fought through the dust and then, effortlessly, pushed the bed out of the way.

No...not a key...it wasn't a key at all, but a shining brass handle that he saw. The handle to some sort of door...a trap door, in the floor. Where could this lead? He didn't know...he

34

didn't care...he had to get out of this room. It was choking him with dust.

He grabbed the sparkling handle and was surprised by its comforting warmth. The door opened, easily...as if it were hollow.

The opened door revealed a ladder. It went down into a dark endless shaft. Without hesitation he dropped into the opening. Maybe I can get out of these pajamas, *he thought.*

The ladder took him into a dimly lit hallway. It seemed to stretch for a mile. In fact he couldn't see where it ended. It was sort of twisted, like a fun house maze, without the fun. The hallway was lined with doors...a thousand doors...so many doors. Still, like the room, somewhere above - above what *- it seemed uncomfortably familiar.*

*Without thinking he entered the first door he encountered on his right. He heard the sound of a ballgame coming from a television or something. There was a man, a frighteningly frail man, sitting in a chair, watching the game. There was a woman sitting on a couch...knitting or sewing something...he wasn't quite sure...*damn these pajamas.

"Hi Toby, come on in...we're just watching the game...naturally," the woman said.

He was puzzled, as now he recognized the woman. It was his mother. How could I not've recognized my own mother, *he thought. Again, frustration tugged at him...*

"Mom, have you seen my clothes...I need to get dressed...I can't find my clothes...."

"No Toby, I haven't...sorry. Maybe your father has...."

"What..?" Toby said, clearly confused.

"Hon, have you seen Toby's clothes," Dream Mom said to the fragile looking man in the chair.

He knew the man. It was his father, yet...some ghastly different version. Illuminated by the dull, flickering light of the old TV, it appeared as if the man were made of papier mache' and stuffed with feathers. He looked...almost breakable.

Toby knew he should be shocked...stunned by all of this...but he wasn't. His father had come back. It was all a mistake, after all.

"Hey, there, Buckaroo." Dream Dad said. "I've been waiting for you. Come on in and watch the game with me. I can't believe this lousy team."

"Don't get excited...don't get excited..." Dream Mom said to Dream Dad.

"I can't, Dad...I need to change...I can't seem to change...I don't know where my clothes are," Toby said.

"I think I saw them in the hall closet," Dream Dad said.

"Yeah, but there must be a million doors. Which door, Dad?"

"Oh, one of them...I suppose...not really sure...you'll have to find out. Hey, what do you say we go out and have ourselves a catch, Buckaroo?"

"Now don't get excited...don't get excited...." Dream Mom said, over and over again in a dull monotonous chant.

Toby closed his eyes and covered his ears, then slowly backed out of the room. He needed to get away from this bizarre tableau. He felt the room squeezing him; felt its walls closing in. He was going to suffocate in here...had to get out.

He found himself back in the hallway, again, overwhelmed by the vast number of doors. I'll never find the right one...but, I have to...I have to find my clothes...I have to change...have to get ready.... But, get ready for what...?

A panic suddenly gripped him and he began running down the endless hall, throwing open door after countless door. He found no clothes, only more empty rooms.

"Where are my clothes? I need my clothes...not these pajamas," *he shouted. His frustration grew.*

Leaning helplessly against the crooked wall, he looked up to see another door, one he hadn't noticed before. Then, proceeding with caution, he opened it and was overwhelmed by an incredible sight...stars...nothing but stars.

Stepping through the door he found himself in a field, in the dead of night. It was a magnificent night capped with a canopy of brilliant, swirling stars and the brightest moon he could ever dream.

He was on a hill; a small village sparkled like a hidden jewel in the valley below. In the foreground, twin cathedral spires of cypress reached upward, as if longing to touch the tantalizing stars.

Above him, crouched further up on the dusty hill, was the solitary figure of an odd looking man. The man was hunched over an easel, scratching furiously at a canvas. Toby approached the man cautiously.

"Excuse me sir," *he said to the man. The man didn't notice, or simply ignored him.*

"Excuse me sir," he said again, this time with a little more urgency. *"I can't find my clothes and I have to get out of these pajamas. I have to change."*

Again, the man continued to work, oblivious to Toby's despair.

Just what kind of weirdo is this guy, he wondered? *The man's face was cracked, weathered by the sun and the wind. His hair resembled stalks, like a burnt field of dry corn, and he, let alone his clothes, looked as if soap had been unavailable for a year.*

"I don't suppose you care about my clothes?" he said resignedly.

Toby turned away and walked toward yet another door, inexplicably standing in the middle of the field. This door opened into some sort of wooded area. It was a place he knew. It was comforting. It was The Lake.

Strangely enough - but what could get stranger - Billy Bartles was standing on a rock in the middle of The Lake. *He was laughing that annoying, self-assured cackle of his, holding a small bundle of clothes in his hands.*

"My clothes! Hey Bartles, give me back my clothes!"

"Hey Tubman, nice lookin PJs," Dream Billy shouted.

"Don't drop my clothes in The Lake!*"* he screamed, feeling utterly helpless.

"Come on out and get em, Tobe...the water's fine...cept for the green stuff, of course. I wouldn't want to get that gunk on my clothes."

"Come on Billy...I need to change!" he was red faced with anger.

"You'll never change..." Billy mocked. *"You know that."*

"Ha-Ha...very witty Billy...like nit wit," he shot back.

Suddenly, Billy started walking toward him, carelessly dangling his beloved clothes inches above the slime. The strange thing was...he was walking on top of the green, murky water.

"Be careful Billy...even you can't walk on water. You'll fall in and ruin my clothes."

"More like dissolve them, from the looks of this stuff...cheech," Billy pinched his nose. "Don't worry, buddy boy, I know where all of the solid parts are."

"Oh," Toby said, as if this made perfect sense.

From somewhere beyond his perception another familiar voice said, "Don't worry, Toby. You know Billy...always showing off."

It was Lori, he was sure. "Lor, where are you? I can't find you. I hear...but I can't see you."

"I know," Dream Lori answered sweetly. "You always did have a convenient blind spot when you wanted to."

He completely forgot about Billy and his clothes. "What? What are you taking about, Lor? Doesn't anything make sense?"

"Besides, I think you look cute in those little P.Js," Lori teased.

"My pajamas...these stupid pajamas...." he said, totally flustered and embarrassed.

"Billy, give me my clothes...now!" he shouted, turning back toward The Lake.

Billy had made it across, but now, he was, somehow, on the other side of The Lake, which was no longer a little pond, but now, really the size of...well...a lake.

He was furious with Billy. "My clothes...bring back my clothes, Bartles."

Even though Billy seemed to be miles away, Toby had little trouble seeing his goofy grinning face, making out every detail as if he had some sort of super vision.

"Who are those tiny little people, talking to Billy?" Lori asked. "Aren't they the strangest things you ever saw?"

"Huh, what little people...where are you, Lori...stop hiding."

"I will if you will," Dream Lori teased. "Up here, in the Elephant Tree. Where else would I be?"

"Oh right," Toby said, again, as if this too also made perfect sense.

Then he turned back to The Lake and grimaced in horror. Billy was handing the bundle of clothes to the two very odd, very small, men. Was that a nose...were those ears?

"Hey give me my clothes...I need to change," he shouted, but suddenly realized that he was no longer miles away. The strange little men stood no more than five feet from his side.

The little men ignored Toby. Instead, they simply took the bundle of clothes and walked into the woods. From the point where they entered, Toby perceived an eerie, green glow, coming from something, in the darkness. The small men walked toward its source.

"Hey, where are you going...my clothes...I need my clothes...I need to change..." Toby squeaked, wanting to cry.

The tiny men continued walking, deeper, into the empty unknown. Then, one of them stopped and turned. He spoke in a peculiar voice, unlike anything Toby had ever heard before.

"You have the key...use the key to change," *was all the little man said.*

"Hear that, Tubman...you got the key..." *Billy laughed.*

"Yes Toby...you have the key...use it or lose it..." *Lori chided.*

"The key...always the key..." *Toby said dreamily...and then...*

Toby bolted upright in his bed...."THE KEY!"

He dripped with sweat as his eyes danced around the room, trying desperately to regain his bearings. His heart pounded.

Absently, Toby rubbed his palm against his chest and discovered his T-shirt clinging to him like a rag, but most of all, he was relieved to find that he was not wearing pajamas. He took a deep breath, closed his eyes, and quietly lay back on his mountain of pillows.

"A dream...a crazy, screwy dream," he whispered. "Where do I come up with this stuff? Chocolate fudge caramel dreams...."

It was just about then that he turned and faced the *"Door to Nowhere"*.

There wasn't much he could do...much he could say...even if words would come. All he *could* do was lay there...lay there and stare...stare numbly, as two tiny sets of muddy, green footprints, walked back toward the door. Then, a fading band of dusty green light, receded through the small crack running through its center.

"With a Cherry on top..." Toby mumbled, then, closed his eyes and returned to sleep.

Chapter 4

Despite the somber tinge of gray that had arrived with the morning, Toby stirred awake earlier than usual and immediately noted something peculiar. He was surprised—astonished, actually—to feel refreshed and rested for a change.

His stomach growled and demanded breakfast.

Maybe I can get Mom to whip up some pancakes, he thought, and instead of lulling in bed - a frequent occurrence - Toby tossed aside the covers and jumped to his feet.

Hoping to increase his pancake leverage he quickly made his bed and neatly stacked his mountain of pillows.

"What a guy!" Then he dug through his closet and pulled out a pair of well-worn jeans, his favorite old sweatshirt and his always reliable sneakers.

Never before had a boy been so happy to put on clothes...but he wasn't quite sure why.

He dressed quickly, then laced up his sneaks and bounced into the bathroom. Besides the usual morning bladder blast, he was filled with a hefty dose of anticipation and excitement. He wasn't sure *about what*, but he knew it was *something*. Then, he noticed one of Mom's famous notes taped to the mirror.

Toby,

Sorry, but I have to do a double today. I didn't have time to fix you anything for supper (or breakfast for that matter), but I'm sure you will be your usual resourceful self. Try not to spend all day in bed, even though it is supposed to rain forever.

Me

Toby peeked through his Mom's favorite "sunny yellow" bathroom curtains and saw she was right; this was *not* going to be a bright, "sunny yellow" day. He pulled the note off the mirror, shrugged his shoulders in a *"what can you do"* sort of gesture, and tossed a perfect jumper into the toilet.

"Yessss...so much for pancakes," he said with sarcastic enthusiasm. It was going to take a lot to spoil *this* day.

He grabbed a wash cloth and zipped it across his face then slapped some toothpaste on to his toothbrush and poked it into his mouth. Just then, a blinding flash of light exploded in his mind.

Toby froze.

The light receded but was immediately replaced with images of last night's dreamfest popping on and off behind his eyes. *Pop...Pop...Pop...*appearing and disappearing, in no apparent order...confused...jumbled.

Nothing seemed to fit...not in a way that made any sense...yet somehow he knew...it all made sense.

He saw something about that pain in the butt Billy ...and his clothes. Being frustrated about pajamas ...something about Lori...and wasn't there something strange...about...his Dad....

No, something strange, about the key...always the key...and a light...the crack in the door....

Finally, he pulled the frozen toothbrush out of his mouth.

He had to go back to his room. He thought the answer was there. He knew the answer was there. He knew the key was there.

The key...always the key....

Toby entered his bedroom and approached the *"Door to Nowhere"*. He looked down and inspected the surrounding carpet.

Nothing there, nothing at all, he was relieved.

Suddenly, a hollow blast exploded in the room. Toby spun around in a haphazard swirl of arms and legs, prepared for the worst...prepared for...

...Curtains...flapping...and roaring, having a great laugh at his expense as a mischievous gust of wind rushed through a small opening in the window.

"You suckers." he exhaled.

Again, the roar erupted; the morning showers appeared to be developing into a full-fledged Nor'easter.

Toby sucked some wind and felt like a nut case for being so jumpy. *Can't let the spooks, spook ya, Tubman.*

He shook his arms, trying to shoo away the *jeebees*, and cautiously turned back to the *"Door to Nowhere"*.

The first thing he noticed was that the multi layered, coat of paint that had, in effect, sealed the door closed for so many years, now had a large, uneven edge running all the way around its perimeter...as if someone had recently...opened the door.

CRASH...BABOOM!

Lightning exploded somewhere, very close by and again, Toby nearly jumped out of his socks.

Instinctively, he crouched toward the ground and swallowed another generous helping of air. He gathered himself, regained his composure, then continued his inspection of the cracked seal, conveniently concentrating on its lower regions.

I know what it is, he thought. *That butthead Billy cracked the door when we were wrestling, the other day. He bounced off it, trying to launch a sneak attack; lucky he didn't fall right through it – but through it to where?*

The curtains flapped again and this time a strange clump of dust settled onto his sneaker. The dust was covered, or coated, with something...*a peculiar, fine, greenish powder*. In fact, the closer he looked, Toby discovered a thin layer of this...*powder*...on almost everything surrounding the door. It was tough to see in the murky light...but there was no mistaking...*it was there*.

Hoping to convince himself this wasn't a dream - *or maybe that it was* - Toby swiped a sample of the curious substance onto his forefinger and rubbed it against his thumb.

KABOOOOOM!

"Ahhhhhhhhhhh!"

Toby collapsed flat onto his rear end.

"SHUT...UP!" he shouted toward the taunting curtains...but, as if in defiance, the skies, instead, opened up and a torrent of rain ripped across the glass and splashed into the room. Toby scrambled to his feet and slammed the window shut.

"Who needs air?" he muttered, then stepped back toward the *Door*.

He studied the small crack in its center panel. There were very fine bits of the strange emerald powder heavily concentrated around its edges. Toby blew on it and the fine dust floated away.

"This is getting a little *too* weird."

He followed a trail by tracing his finger along the crack and out across the broken seal of paint. There, he found himself staring directly into a museum poster...the one of his all-time favorite painting.

The picture had hung on the wall, right next to the *"Door to Nowhere"*, ever since his sixth grade field trip to the big art museum. He recalled being mesmerized by this artist's work and by this painting, in particular...a painting of stars. He could still see the rich, thick textures of paint...and the maddening passion of those relentless, yellow swirls against the dark blue sky. He wanted to reach out and touch the ridges, feel the stars...but he knew...he really didn't have to. He could feel the colors...the brilliant colors of night. He could feel the textures, in his soul...in the *artist's soul*.

Now, the poster was hanging terribly askew. Again, *probably knocked silly by that big clumsy goofball, Billy Bartles.*

Not to his surprise he found more green dust, speckled over the surface of the plastic frame.

"Hmmmm-hmmm." Toby straightened the picture and backed away until the edge of his bed nudged the back of his knees and he plopped onto the mattress.

Another deafening blast assaulted the house. Windows rattled, walls creaked, and a large crash resounded from the yard.

But Toby didn't budge. Instead, his eyes were fixed on the top ledge of the *"Door to Nowhere"*.

At first, he thought he'd imagined it - this had happened once before...that night...the wind...that cold night- but with each new flash of lightning, and every ear-splitting roar, Toby saw...he definitely saw...a glint...a sparkle from the door. And he knew *exactly* what it was.

"You have the key...use it...use the key to change..." said a strange, yet familiar voice, from a place where dreams are neatly stored.

"The key...always the key..." Toby said flatly.

He rose to his feet, grabbed the small wooden chair that usually collected his dirty laundry and slowly walked toward the door. He placed the chair directly in front of it, stepped up, and stood eye level with the ledge. Nestled there, obscured by a ton of *real* dust - *whew, I guess Mom really doesn't clean up here* – was the protruding tip of an old fashion skeleton key. Badly corroded and covered with dust, he couldn't imagine how it had *possibly* reflected the light he'd just seen.

Toby's hand trembled, his fingertips floating above the key.

KABOOOM!

Another crash of thunder bellowed through the room.

Toby's stomach twisted into a knot and he jerked his hand away, almost tumbling from the chair as a result.

He paused, forced himself to breathe and said resolutely, "This is nuts. I watch too many crazy movies." And with that, he quickly reached out, snatched the key and jumped off the chair.

As the tension left his body, he retreated to his bed and took a casual peek out the window.

"April showers bring...muuuud," he muttered. "And lots of it."

He returned his attention to the funny looking key and mentally kicked himself for getting into such a dither over something so stupid. Completely encased in a thick, green crust of corrosion, *the key would just break in two if anyone* actually did *try to use it,* he thought.

Then, suddenly, a peculiar warmth began to fill his hand. It was coming from the key.

"Uh, oh..." Toby said. "I was *afraid* of something like this."

Amazingly, before his disbelieving eyes, the tarnished coat of corrosion slowly began to transform into a brilliant emerald sheen.

"This could just be another product of my over active imagination, you know. Too much TV...bad for the soul and all...nothing that a few decades of head shrinkers won't be able to fix."

Looking up, he was *not* surprised to see that a green, phosphorous light, teeming with fine particles of floating - *magical* - dust, streamed from the broken seal surrounding the door and the crack in its center. Then, a singular focused beam shot from the keyhole and nested in his open hand. The hand with the key....

The wondrous light filled the room and wrapped around Toby like a comforting friend.

"I guess a little *dithering was* in order, after all," he said without a hint of fear.

He was transfixed, amazed by how quickly the light seeped into every nook and cranny.

"Mom is gonna freak when she sees this funky, green dust over everything. *Who ya gonna call...Dust Busters...*" he sang, actually starting to feel, somehow, at ease.

He looked back into the palm of his hand and discovered that the crumbling artifact was gone...now replaced by a solid, gleaming key.

"You have the key...use it...use the key to change..." Toby whispered, as if repeating some ancient mystic chant.

"The key...always the key," said that peculiarly pitched voice.

"Maybe I *have* lost my mind...finally."

Toby rose to his feet and knew exactly what he was supposed to do. What he *had* to do.

Steadily, and with purpose, the focused light emanating from the keyhole drew him forward like some sort of supernatural tractor beam.

Carefully, he ran his fingers over the glowing edge of the *"Door to Nowhere"*. The sparkling light was warm, tingling within every fiber of his being. It was inviting him. Inviting him to open the door.

Looking at the brilliant key, he knew exactly what he had to do. What he was *supposed* to do.

"Use it or lose it, said the lady," he repeated from the dream.

Deliberately, he slid the key into the radiating keyhole.

Then suddenly...he stopped.

"Use it or lose it, said...Lori...Lori. I have to get Lori...and Billy...the dream; they were part of the dream...the dream...*The Lake*...the dream...the key...always the key."

Toby pulled the burning key away from the door and shoved it deep into the pocket of his jeans.

"Gotta call Lori...call Billy...*The Lake*...meet down at *The Lake*." He hurried down the stairs to find the phone...

The wondrous, emerald light swirled, then returned from where it had emerged....

Chapter 5

"What'da ya mean I gotta meet you down at *The Lake* in fifteen minutes? I think you've really gone over the deep end this time, Tubman. What happened, Lori Lovestruck too hot to handle for ya? Some sort of a post-pubescent anxiety attack?"

Toby sliced through Billy's obnoxious, but expected, comments and pleaded with his best friend. "Billy, please, this is really important. Just meet me down at *The Lake*."

"Uh, maybe you haven't had a chance to look outside your tomb yet, Tobe ol' buddy - you know, *outside*, where the rest of the world is - but there happens to be one heck of a storm going on out there. And I don't think that old mud hole is the best place to be right now."

"I know," Toby answered with a spate of confused logic. "I think the storm...is part of it...somehow."

"Part of what? Tubman, you're not making much sense...ya know."

"I know, Billy. I can't make much sense of it, myself. Please, just be there. Fifteen minutes...*please*...it could change everything."

Something about the desperate tone of Toby's plea shouted to Billy: "*Hey Bonehead...your friend really needs you!*"

"Okay, I'll be there. Fifteen minutes. Besides, it don't look like we're gonna get a game in today, anyway."

"Thanks Billy, you don't know—"

"I know, Tobe. Fifteen minutes."

Toby closed out the call and exhaled. *That was the easy part. Getting Lori out of the house in this storm—now that's gonna be tricky.* He brought up her number and pressed send.

"Hi, Lor, guess who?" *Clever opener.*

"Hi Toby, what's up? Can you believe this storm? My Dad thinks we're gonna lose power soon; the way the lights keep flickering on and off."

"Yeah, so much for that early summer you were all excited about, huh. Hope you've got plenty of candles."

"Yeah, wouldn't that be neat. I love blackouts. It's amazing how yesterday could be like the most perfect day of the year, and now this. Too bad it's so terrible out; you could come over and play Monopoly by candle light."

"Ooooo...spooky," Toby said. He was trying desperately *not* to sound like a nut case.

"Well, I thought it would be more like...you know, romantic or something," Lori said slyly.

"Yeah, well, I never did like Monopoly much. You know, too much pressure keeping track of all that money. And those annoying hotel guests you have to put up with...room service and all, not to mention the jail time...bummer. Besides, your Dad always cheats. He'd get away with murder in the dark."

"My Dad doesn't cheat...that much, anyway," Lori giggled. "Besides, who said anything about my Dad playing?"

"Listen Lori, uh...the storm is kinda what I called you about in the first place."

Another blast of lightning struck nearby and crackled through the phone.

"Wow, did you feel that one?" Lori said. "It sounded close. It's really nasty isn't it?"

"Yeah, well I think it's pretty much past us now...don't you think. In fact, it seems to be letting up a little. Just a squall or something. Besides, a little moisture never hurt anybody."

Toby, the radio says it's supposed to be like this all day. In fact, I don't think the worst of it's supposed get here for a while."

Toby took a deep breath...exhaled, and blurted out in one quick burst of energy, "Lori something strange is happening and it has to do with me, you and Billy down at *The Lake*. I don't know what it is exactly, but I need you to come to *The Lake* with me right away. I think...I think...it could change everything."

"Toby, what on earth are you talking about? What could change everything? My parents aren't going to let me out of the house in this weather. You know that. And besides, yesterday you couldn't wait to get away from *The Lake*. Did finding those old initials on the *Elephant Tree* mess with you or something?"

Toby winced at the thought of that decrepit old tree and said, "I could meet you around back, you know, by the big pine tree, near

53

your bedroom window. Say you're gonna go read `War and Peace' or something, and you don't wanna be disturbed...until there's peace."

"Toby, I—"

"You could climb out the window, onto the roof, like we used to do when we were little, and then just scurry on down the tree. Remember? Nobody ever did figure out how we could go upstairs one minute and then end up coming back in through the front door the next. Remember how much fun it was?"

"Toby, I haven't been out on that roof - or in that tree - for years. I could break my neck or something."

Toby tried to swallow his irritation.

Why is it, he thought, *that kids never worry about breaking their necks? It's only when you get older that this becomes such a threat to your existence. What is it, some sort of grown-up disease? Does your neck suddenly become more brittle or something?*

"Lori, please...you know I wouldn't ask if it wasn't important. It would mean a lot to me...it would mean everything to me. I promise, you won't break your neck."

Lori was silent for a moment and Toby started to lose hope.

"Alright Toby, if it means that much to you. Sure, I'll do it."

"What? You will? Great! Lori I lo—" Toby quickly made an oral adjustment. "I think you're really great."

"Thanks...*pal*," Lori said.

"I'll meet you outside your window, right away."

"Right away? Can't you give me a few more minutes?"

"I told Billy to meet me in fifteen minutes...ten minutes ago. What'da you need the time for?"

"To dig up a copy of `*War and Peace,*' you knucklehead."

Toby absently fingered the key in his pocket. "Oh yeah, right...."

Chapter 6

Staring up at Lori's bedroom window, Toby discovered a little
moisture actually *could* hurt somebody, as a barrage of raindrops
needled his face. The storm *was* getting worse. The wind blew
with a hungry howl, threatening hurricane status, and the
branches of the large pine swayed violently back and forth.

Maybe this is just a little bit dangerous....

Toby decided it might be a good idea if he climbed up the tree
and gave Lori a little hand. Funny, he never recalled being terribly
worried about Lori's welfare before. *I guess there is something to
this "adult disease" thing.*

He shook away the thought then sloshed toward the tree and
plunged into its slapping limbs. Despite the mass of wet sticky
needles, the climb was pretty easy and he approached the roofline
just as Lori was gingerly backing out of the open window. He
couldn't help thinking just how cute she looked in her sensible,
powder blue rain slicker, the hood securely fastened around her
chin.

Good ol' Lori...the right outfit for every occasion.

"Pssst, Lori...over here," he whisper/shouted, although it was doubtful that anyone but Lori could hear him over the driving rain.

Lori shrieked, startled by the sound of Toby's voice. "Eeeeeek...who's that! Toby, is that you...where are you?" She reached back and grabbed hold of the window frame to steady herself.

"Over here, in the tree. I thought you could use a hand...or something."

"Great, we can break our necks together! Toby, *I am* going to get blown off of this roof!" Her voice quavered a full octave higher than usual.

"No you're not," Toby said, though he wasn't entirely sure. "Come on, you've done this a hundred times."

"Maybe a thousand lifetimes ago...and never in a hurricane."

"Just a little shower. I don't think the heavy stuff's gotten here yet. Just stay low to the roof and you'll be fine."

Lori inched around, then shimmied on her rear end toward the angry tree. Finally, after a few seconds, that might have been years, she made it to the edge and lifted her feet to avoid the torrent of water raging through the gutter.

"Here," Toby said, full of false bravado. "Grab hold of my hand and step onto that branch."

Lori's face dripped with fear.

"Which one?"

"The one on the end of my arm."

"No, you dope head," She couldn't stop a small giggle from escaping. "Which branch?"

"That one, there; the one that looks like it's gonna snap off any minute."

"Ooooh, Toby, I think *I'm* gonna break *your* neck, when and *if*, we ever get down from here," she shouted, then reluctantly stepped onto the dancing limb.

"You can't. It's still too immature."

"What?"

"Nothing. Just kidding. Come on now, just follow me. Step where I step...go where I go."

"Slowly I turned..." Lori giggled, mimicking some long ago movie they had once seen together.

"Step by step..." Toby joined.

"Inch by inch..." they shouted, trying to ignore the whipping pine...until, at last, their feet squished into an inch of welcome mud.

"Terra muda," Toby proclaimed. "I told you, all you had to do was follow me."

Lori turned to Toby and squinted through the downpour. Wet strands of chestnut hair slipped from beneath her hood and plastered against her face.

"Toby, you know I would follow you anywhere...anywhere at all. You know that, don't you?"

Then, to Toby's total amazement, Lori wrapped her arms around him and hugged tightly. Even more amazing, Toby found himself hugging back.

A first time for everything, he thought

A moment later - which also might have been a year - Toby pulled away, a bit red in the face, and said, "Come on, Billy's waiting."

Down at *"The Lake"* they discovered Billy stomping around and skimming rocks along its slime green surface. He was soaking wet, despite the huge army poncho draped around him like a tent.

"You know Pierce, I have an uncle who's a head shrinker. You might be interested in paying him a little visit someday."

"That might not be such a bad idea," Toby answered distractedly. His eye was fixed more on the angry sky than Billy. "I'm sure you can tell me all about him."

"What're you doing out here, Lori? I thought I was the only sucker in the neighborhood. Nice little slicker...you look like a Muppet."

"Nice to see you too, Billy. Do you always talk just to hear yourself talk?" As usual, Lori had passed her limit of Billy Tolerance very quickly.

"Basically," Billy said. "What kept you guys? I've been waiting out here for hours."

"Come on Billy, it's only been a half hour since I called you."

Billy shook the rain from his poncho like a big wet dog. "Well, it feels like hours."

"Come on," Lori shouted. "We'll be drier under the *Elephant Tree*."

"Why didn't I think of that?" Billy said.

"Cause you never do," Toby shot back.

"Do what?" Billy asked

"Think," Toby said, then dashed after Lori toward the sprawling limbs of the ancient tree.

Billy followed close behind and, without missing a beat, crashed through the curtain of branches, spewing, "So Tobe, are you gonna tell us what this big deal is that could change everything, or what?"

A curl of thunder rolled overhead and Toby wondered just how wise it *actually was* to stand under such a *big* lightning rod.

Lori placed her arm protectively around Toby's shoulder. "Don't be in such a hurry, Billy. Toby will tell us soon enough."

Billy threw Lori a suspicious look, "Oh yeah...*righhhhhhht.*"

"It's about this," Toby said. He stepped away from Lori and pulled the corroded key from his pocket.

"What!" Billy spewed. "An old key. It's about an old green key...great. I *am* calling my uncle."

"Stop it Billy...give him a chance," Lori reproached. "What about this key, Toby?"

"It's not just a key..." Toby said. "It's, uh...the key to the door."

"What door?" Lori asked.

"Oh no...don't tell me," Billy said in disbelief. "This is the key to—"

"—The *Door to Nowhere*," Toby completed.

"What do you mean the *Door to Nowhere*?" Lori asked, even more confused.

Billy started to answer, "You know, the *Door to—*"

"—*Nowhere*...now I remember," Lori said. "The door to the *Kingdom of Keys.* That story your Dad used to tell."

Toby shifted a little uncomfortably, knowing just how crazy it all sounded.

"Come on Tobe, that was just an old fairy tale that your Dad made up," Billy said. "You don't really believe— How do you know that that's even the key?"

"I saw something sparkle...like from a light...or something, I don't know, on the ledge over the door. One night, last winter...just before Christmas," Toby answered...hesitantly.

"Oh, like a Christmas present from the *loyal subjects of Keys*," Billy said.

"Something like that...I don't know." Toby started to wonder if this *was* such a good idea, after all.

"Leave him alone, Billy," Lori scolded. "Can't you see that he's really serious about this?"

"Yeah...I guess he is." Even *Billy* could see the confusion on his best friend's face. "Go on Tobe, I'm sorry. Tell your story."

Toby pressed on. "After I first saw it, I tried to ignore it. I tried not to look up in that corner. I thought that maybe it'd always been there...I just never noticed...or I couldn't see that high, before."

"Why were you afraid of this key, Toby? What's it mean?" Lori asked.

"That's just it," Toby answered. "It shouldn't *mean* anything. Just a long overlooked key left to rot in a corner. But, somehow, I knew it meant something...to me. That it could change everything."

61

"Whadaya mean change everything?" Billy snapped. "How can a stupid key change everything? What's everything? Whose everything?"

"I don't know..." Toby answered softly. "I guess mine."

As Toby spoke the wind steadily increased. The Elephant Tree's gangly branches stretched and moaned, allowing trickles of rain to sneak through its patchy cover. Beneath their feet the ground rumbled but the three young friends remained oblivious to it all.

"Anyway," Toby said. "Even though I pretended that I never saw it, I knew that it was there...and it haunted me. It just about made me nuts trying *not* to think about it. I just didn't want to know...*anything.*"

"Is that why you've been so out of it lately?" Lori asked. "You poor guy."

Toby smiled and said, "Yeah, I guess...part of it, along with...the rest of it. I didn't know it was so noticeable."

"Yeah right," Billy said. "About as unnoticeable as the daily eruptions on the Planet Eaters chin."

"Billy!" Lori reprimanded.

"Sorry." Billy said.

"So when did you decide to confront...you know...the key...?" Lori asked.

"Last night—" Toby stared into a puddle of mud and proceeded to tell of last night's unsettling dream, along with this morning's discovery, not to mention...the strange emerald light....

"...So then I realized I couldn't do it on my own. I needed you guys, too...and that's when I called you."

Billy and Lori didn't move. In fact they hadn't moved throughout most of Toby's story; just stood slack jawed in the rain. On one level, they knew his story was too incredible to believe...yet, on another, *they* did *believe*...like only a kid could believe.

"But Tubman, why did we have to meet down at *The Lake*...in this storm, no less?" Billy said.

"Yeah Toby, why *The Lake*? Lori asked.

"Don't you see? Weren't you listening? *The Lake* was a big part of the dream I just told you about," Toby answered. "Along with you and Billy. I don't know what it all means, but I think we'll find out. Just like the storm. I think the storm...the storm is also a part—"

KABOOOOOOOOOOOOOOOOOOOOOOM!

A violent explosion swallowed the rest of Toby's words. Something electric streaked overhead and when they looked up through the tangle of limbs, a brilliant light tore from the sky and curled into a funnel.

"Ahhhhhh...I can't see!" Billy screamed.

Toby saw a cloud of dust attacking Billy's eyes.

"Billy!"

Lori shouted something but her words were lost within an intense rush of pressure that suddenly swamped their heads. A strange popping filled Toby's ears and the roar of the hungry gale now diminished to a low, distant buzz.

Toby clawed at his ears and shook his head, trying to release the pounding pressure. He saw Lori doing the same.

63

Down below, another swirl of dust had quietly gathered around their ankles, slowly circling, weaving in and out between their legs, like a snake in search of prey. Then, without warning, a blast of damp musty air rushed from the ground and staggered them.

Directly above, hovering ferociously in place, a cone shaped mass descended from the clouds. It inhaled all that stood - or tried to stand – in its path, into its powerful vortex. The eerie gale released a deafening howl and in seconds engulfed the entire length of the time worn *Elephant Tree.*

At first, the majestic tree resisted the powerful wind. Large knotted limbs creaking and groaning, roaring with centuries of defiance...standing it's ground...refusing to yield. A literal shower of sticks and stones rained from above.

Toby herded his friends around the base of the tree's thick hoary trunk, hoping to avoid the heaviest of the fallout. It was there that something whispered to him: *"Up...look up...!"* And when he did, what he saw was more than enough to render a mere *earthly* tempest powerless to his senses.

A dazzling blossom of green phosphorous light shot from the peak of the old twisted tree, rose through the storm like a rocket, and pierced the churning clouds. Then, slowly, the light dripped from the sky, slithered around the tree's spiraling trunk, and enveloped it in a soft emerald cocoon.

Toby's eye's widened in mind numbing wonder. It was all too incredible, but *did it make sense?* He thought that it did...*perfect sense, the only sense....*

Now, humming with purpose, the light whirled around the tree's entire circumference.

Toby stepped forward, wanting to embrace the light, but his arms hung passively at his side. Lori reached for his hand, but it fell limply away.

The light continued to hum, continued to circle, until a slow, yet steady, concentration emerged from the tree's center and expanded into multiple streaks of intense fire.

Billy cleared the dust from his eyes, then wished that he hadn't. A swell of fear tightened his stomach, but still, he couldn't look away.

Along the length of the tree's ragged bark, hundreds of initials, carved with a diligence, spanning decades of youth, suddenly ignited, and began to burn. An intense emerald sheen emerged from the fire and filled the recess where they stood.

Lori gasped, yet Toby knew...somehow he knew...the carvings were reaching out to him, speaking to him.

Then, blazing brighter, surpassing the rest, he saw it...and Lori saw it, too...*T.P & L.M*...their initials, connected by a jagged bolt of carved lightning, searing a hole, straight through the heart of the tree...hanging, impossibly, in mid-air.

"Toby, what—" Lori whispered.

"I don't know, Lor...I don't know," but he thought, maybe he did.

They approached the blazing epigraph, hands outstretched, reaching to feel its incredible warmth.

The heat wrapped around their fingers and they accepted its inviting warmth, lost forever in the moment...until the moment was swallowed by a sharp obliterating crack. It punctured the storm, shattered their wonder, and split the top of the struggling tree in two.

The blast echoed with startling power and knocked the three friends instantly onto their backs. Toby skidded through a puddle and felt an unnatural howl rumble through the earth. He tried scrambling to his feet, but crashed back onto his rump when a boulder exploded and the tree's powerful roots suddenly smashed through the hard packed soil. Lori was thrown aside like a weightless doll.

Billy screamed, "Watch out...I think the whole thing is going over!"

"That's impossible! How could that be!" Lori shouted. She fought to remove a tangle of root that had wrapped around her leg.

"I guess anything's possible now," Toby said with an unnatural calm. He felt the placating warmth of the key, resting in his hand...*always the key.*

The majestic old beech roared once again - it's proud, final act of rebellion - and the last of its clinging roots tore through the earth like giant tentacles fighting for life.

Billy sprang to his feet and literally dragged Toby and Lori up and away to safety.

Again, the mighty tree bellowed, flinging large clumps of mud and rock as they ran, chastising them for desertion.

They reached the relative safety of a clearing and crumpled to the ground. One by one they turned back and, through the maelstrom, they were unable to believe, yet forced to believe what they saw.

The immovable *Elephant Tree*, swirled madly, rose high on the wind, and finally...mercifully...and gracefully, surrendered to its fate and toppled onto its side.

As suddenly as it had arrived, the threatening wind and hellish lightning disappeared.

Without thinking, Toby held the key out in the palm of his hand.

Billy and Lori gasped. A phosphorescent beam shot from the key and encircled the tree's freshly exposed root system. And they gasped again...for the effect of this weird, glowing light gave the impression - *for an impression was all it could be* - that a pair of...creatures...tortured and soulless creatures, writhing in pain...a terrible unknown pain, were tangled amongst the roots; or even, somehow, they *were* the roots, themselves.

"Ugh..." Billy said. "Are you seeing what I'm seeing?"

"No...I don't want to see it!" Lori answered. She buried her head deep into Toby's shoulder. "It's awful. What is it Toby? Make it stop!"

"I don't know," Toby replied. The light from the key intensified and burned a hole directly through the center of the beast's heaving belly.

Suddenly, something moved, something that looked like a long, slithery arm, extending from the wretchedness. Pointed hands, fingers writhing, probing its own searing wound.

They *watched* the grotesque arm burrow deep, then deeper still, into the steaming lesion.

They *heard* a wet, sucking sound, follow it into the hole.

They *saw*, when the arm began to withdraw an assortment of mud, slime and rot plop onto the ground in a sickening pile. And they also *saw* embedded within the steaming mass, something that appeared to be...a sack...a small muddy sack.

"What the heck is that," Billy cried out.

"Like I'm supposed to know," Toby shot back.

"This is your fantasy, not mine," Billy said.

"It's more like a nightmare," Lori said, wishing she could, but unable to divert her eyes.

"No." Toby said. He pulled away from Lori's grasp and walked toward the sack, allowing the green light to guide him. "Not a nightmare at all. I think it's something...special."

"Toby!" Lori screamed. "Toby, what are you doing. Don't go near it. Billy, stop him."

"I don't think I could if I wanted to, Lor," Billy replied.

Toby walked without fear toward the strange alien figures. He saw their horrible, sinewy arms open wide in submission...*or welcome*...then, reach into the muck and nobly hold aloft the small craggy sack.

By now the rain had rinsed away most of the mud, and he saw that it was made of a yellowish, canvas like material. The sack appeared to be filled with...*objects*...small, but a lot of them. He thought he knew what they were.

"Here within, lay the keys to your future," both creatures said in a single voice that only resembled human. They spoke from a pain, so deep that no human could possibly endure it.

"Use them not...until it is time."

Without hesitation, Toby reached out and took the sack; it flared, then glowed a magnificent emerald green.

"You have the key...use it...or not...the choice is yours."

Toby was about to speak. Thought it important that he reply.

"Is the choice really—" but his words were again severed by a streak of lightning ripping from above.

The root creatures raised what might have been heads to the sky and embraced the strike in a blinding flash.

The explosive force of the flash swept Toby off of his feet and deposited his limp form nearly ten feet away from the fallen Elephant Tree.

"Toby!" shouted Lori, terrified that the strike had been fatal.

She and Billy immediately rushed to their friend's side and found, to their relief, a dazed but unharmed Toby, his hair somewhat spiked and smoking. In his hand he still grasped the small sack of keys.

"Believe me, now," he croaked as he pulled himself up to his elbows.

"I don't believe we're ever gonna get your hair to lay flat again," cracked Billy.

"Stop it Billy," said a shaken Lori as she tried in vain to flatten Toby's slightly scorched "new doo."

"We'd better get going," Toby said, aware that the storm was intensifying once again.

"Going where?" Lori asked, hesitantly.

Toby felt a strange tingling sensation course through his blood. He glanced up at Billy.

"To the Kingdom of Keys," said Billy, matter of factly, and pulled Toby to his feet.

Chapter 7

Outside, the storm continued to rage. Tree limbs swayed and thunder cracked. Inside, a small, irregular rivulet ran from a stack of rain soaked coats and pooled into a puddle.

Standing in the puddle, the storm was the last thing on the three friend's minds as they silently stared at the *"Door to Nowhere."* Staring at it as if they saw all the answers to all their questions, even the ones they didn't *want* to know.

Billy, as usual, was the first to break the silence.

"So when does the big show start, Tubman. Where's all the green stuff you were telling us about."

Toby slicked his wet, slightly singed, hair, back with his muddy hands. "Uh, I guess, maybe, I should take out the key...huh?"

"That might be a start, I would guess," Billy answered. "Uh, of course it's probably not too late to change our minds and forget anything ever happened...I guess."

"No, I think it's a little too late for that," Toby said quietly.

"Toby, are you sure about all this?" Lori asked, hesitantly. "I mean, I know what I saw before and everything...but I mean, what if we're misinterpreting this? What if this isn't something good...what if it's something...evil?"

"Yeah...good point Lor," Billy said. "What if this is one of those exorcist type things...and somebody's head starts doing three sixties or something."

Toby gave Billy a whack on the chest.

"Nobody's going to get their head twisted around, bone brain, but in your case it might not be a bad idea."

Lori continued staring at the door.

"Seriously, Toby...sometimes evil can be disguised as good. What if we're not able to tell the difference?"

"Lori, believe me...somehow I know. In my heart, I know...this is good...this is right."

Lori looked back at Toby, at the little beads of water that rolled down and collected at the tip of his nose. She looked into his startling blue eyes and knew...he was right...that he believed, he was right...and right now, that was all that mattered.

"Then I believe too, Toby. I believe it too."

Lori reached out, took Toby's hand in hers and squeezed it gently. Toby felt her warmth and smiled.

Suddenly, from within Toby's pocket - the pocket containing the key - the emerald glow began to seep silently into the room. It spread like a mist into an ever-expanding cone until it enveloped the *"Door to Nowhere"*.

Lori and Billy gasped, eyes open wide, while Toby again smiled. He had seen this act before.

He reached into his pocket and removed the glowing key. Immediately, a sharp, focused beam zeroed in on the waiting keyhole.

"*Crumb...Buns*," Billy said. "I've never seen anything like this before...even at Disney World."

"Look," Lori giggled and ran her trembling hands across her sweater. "It's even dried our clothes."

Toby followed the pull of the emerald light. He knew it wasn't forcing him, merely guiding him. It was still his choice. He could end this now - all of it-by merely turning away...and that would be that. But, he also knew the unknown restlessness stirring in his soul would not allow him to turn away. He *knew* he would see this through.

Toby approached the door and a sharper, more defined, brilliance slithered from its cracks. It was as if whatever was on the other side was overflowing and about to burst. Toby looked toward Lori...then toward Billy...and then, followed the light into the keyhole. Finally...he turned the key.

Without warning, the door exploded open. Toby was blown to the farthest corner of the room where he skidded on the floor and bounced his head off the wooden nightstand next to his bed.

Lori felt her feet fly out from under her and was swept viciously to the side of the corner dresser. Billy, feeling as if he were sucker punched in the stomach, doubled over then was thrown back and pinned hard against the wall closest to the *"Door."*

A thick mass of green, phosphorescent light stirred ferociously at the portal like a thousand angry snakes. To Toby, sitting in a daze, it looked mean and hungry.

Maybe I have done the wrong thing, after all. Maybe I have opened the door...to something horrible.

"Toby, what's happening?" Lori screamed, from somewhere across the room.

"Not sure, Lor," Toby's speech was slow and slurred, still numb from the blow he took to his head. "Guess I really opened up a can of worms here...huh."

Just then, another blast of green, a deeper, darker green, consumed the room. It was as if the storm, raging outside, had somehow found its way inside, through the *"Door to Nowhere."*

A small army of green, twister like clouds broke from the mass and began to swirl every which way. They gathered up everything in their path, furniture, knick-knacks, clothes, and spun them into tight little circles that bounced around the room.

"Holy poltergeist, Tubman...help me out here!" Billy cried. A small brown chair flew past his head and a green funnel slipped around his ankles. *"Toby please...help...I think it's got me...it's wrapping me up!"*

Toby muttered something foggy and watched his best friend in the world consumed by a weird, green, twisting cloud. Then...Billy vanished through the *"Door"*. "Go with the flow...bro...just go with the flow. Hey get it...*the flow, like in...whatever."*

He turned toward the place where he sort of remembered Lori landing.

"Quite a show, huh Lor...just like the movies."

"Toby...help—" Lori's voice...weak and distant....

Toby lifted his head and strained to see through the haze that had wrapped around his brain.

There, in the corner...Lori...he saw her.

She too, was wrapped in the same kind of ominous, twisting cloud that had engulfed Billy.

She too, was spinning wildly in place.

She too, was swept through the portal and into the angry green vortex.

"Bye, Lor...*see ya later, alligator*...I hope...."

And then, Toby saw the unrelenting green cloud coming for him.

"Whoa, here we go. Tighten your seat belts, everybody."

He sensed being lifted from the floor...the peculiar moisture of the cloud clearing his head. Suddenly, he knew...he knew exactly what was happening.

He wasn't afraid...not really, he thought. No...instead he was...*ready.*

An object swirled by his head. Toby reached out and snatched it. It was the sack of keys. The keys to his future...to his life. With these...he could change everything.

"Okay...let's go," he said boldly...but with confidence, uncertain. And with that, he twirled wildly in his vaporous cocoon of green and shot through the door.

Somewhere behind he heard it close.

Chapter 8

Toby soared through streaks and rushes of fabulous colors and magical light. Wondrous bands of sparkling dust pervaded the alien atmosphere, swirling madly around him as he fell - *or was it more like flying.*

Unrecognizable objects swooped by with amazing speed. Faces, vaguely familiar, yet unknown, called out to him – *again, a welcome...or a warning?*

A complete timeless sense of peace filled his mind; tranquility so deep he believed he could easily stay - *where?* - forever.

Was he dead...had he died? Was this the answer to the fabulous mystery of life? *The end of the road, the big super highway in the sky? So, what's all the fuss about?*

Faster and faster, deeper and deeper, he soared, weightless and carefree, riding brilliant streams of light.

It was all so silly. So much time...wasted...so much energy...spent...so much...so little....so much...time....

Toby's eyes drifted closed. He absorbed all that was around him...all that was in him. When he opened them...it was all gone....

"Toby...Toby...are you all right...Toby?"

A sweet familiar voice penetrated the murky haze surrounding his brain.

"Hey Tubman, are you alive or what...?"

That irritating tone he knew, for sure.

It had all been a dream, he thought with disappointment. *A stupid dream. But then again, why is the sky green...and the clouds...blue*?

"Billy...Lori...where are we, what happened?" Toby asked, groggily.

"Toby, it's incredible," Lori said. "Look...look it...is this it...is this—"

"I don't think were in Kansas anymore, buddy boy," Billy said.

"It's as if we've fallen through the looking glass or something," Lori marveled.

Toby sat up slowly and surveyed the strange terrain. It was weird, that was certain, but not entirely unfamiliar. He had seen *The Lake* a hundred times before...but never quite like this.

Stretched out - *for what seemed like miles* - was a huge, glistening body of crystal, green water. It *was The Lake*, he was sure of that, but as it had been...*ages* ago.

Everywhere he turned, the landscape burst with a kind of rainbow foliage. The woods overflowed with incredible wildlife creatures, some familiar, some not. In many ways, they reminded him of a million cartoon animals he had seen as a kid. Maybe it was the unnatural way in which they moved, almost gliding, effortlessly, from place to place.

Or maybe, most of all, it was the uneasy sense that these creatures seemed to be performing...for them.

Toby looked at the sky and was dazzled, yet perplexed, by its rich green intensity. Lofty blue clouds, with an almost neon quality, floated by a blazing sun; a sun of a color he had never seen. He related it to some shade of purple, but he knew that was *not* what he would call it.

"Way to go Pierce," Billy said in a manner that suggested *he* was not quite appreciating the *wonder* of it all. "You have a dream, drag me out into a hurricane, with some creepy mud things, pull out a haunted old skeleton key, and open the door to the *Twilight Zone*. And then, after flying through some cosmic nightmare, I end up back at the stupid old *Lake*. And, to top it all off...I'm now completely color blind!"

"Not quite in the spirit of things, are ya Bill?" Toby replied.

"Oh don't mind him, Toby, he's been complaining for days. I guess we're both a little scared."

Toby looked blankly at Lori. "Did you say days, Lor?"

"Well yeah...I was terrified something had happened to you. What took you so long to follow? Why'd you wait?"

"Yeah, Toby, I've been here even longer than Lori. I figured you both crapped out on me and decided to go watch 'Be Mine Valentine,' or something."

"Billy, I told you I went through the door right after you. I couldn't have stayed behind, even if I'd wanted too," Lori shot back, hotly.

"Wait, wait, wait a minute. You mean it's been days since you two got here?"

"Two or three at least," Lori said.

"Yeah it's a little hard to tell, though. All I know is that weird purple sun has come and gone quite a few times," Billy said.

"But I saw you two go through the door...it was no more than a minute before me...and I felt as if I were gone only a few minutes, at most."

"Obviously you got the *Le Tour Deluxe*," Billy said snidely.

"Weird...really weird," Toby said. "What've you been doing then, all this time? How did you eat? Where've you been staying?"

"Right here, mostly," Lori said. "We were afraid to go too far off on our own...and we were waiting for you. I knew you wouldn't have just left us here."

"Yeah...wherever *here* is," Toby said, still marveling at the wonder of it all.

"Yeah, well if you really want to see weird, wait until you see these crazy cartoon animals bring us our food...all wrapped up in little napkins and everything," Billy was obviously finding wonder in this particular feature. "It's like they know what we're thinking or something. All you gotta do is think of what you want. Wait, watch this...I'll show you."

"He loves this part," Lori giggled.

"Let's see...I'm thinking cheese burgers...a big platter full."

"Don't forget the fries," Lori said, playfully.

"Right, fries...maybe those curly kind, this time," Billy said.

"And pickles...those big fat deli ones...not the icky kind that come in a jar," Lori said.

"But of course, madam. I would not dream of ze icky," Billy replied.

Toby heard, then glanced, toward a strange rustling sound coming from deep inside the woods; there was some sort of busy activity taking place.

Then, in seconds, from the treetops, he could see a small flock, of what he might call strange, - *but then again, the strange was beginning to appear normal* - blue birds, with large puffy feathers and most unusual beaks.

Their beaks curved upward, like hooks of some sort, and as they flew in a carefree, yet precise formation, Toby noticed that these unusual birds were carrying something hooked over those beaks. He was reminded of that old cartoon of the stork, delivering a new born baby...or *pickles*.

Toby glanced toward Lori, who watched the flock with genuine *appreciation*...and then, toward Billy, who licked his lips in genuine *anticipation*.

"Someone want to fill me in on what's happening here?" Toby asked, hesitantly.

"Suppertime, Tubman...supper like you never had before," Billy answered.

The brilliant birds drew closer and swooped toward the plush, blue green grass that surrounded the area. Two of the birds dropped a large white blanket, and it floated gently to the ground. Three other birds fluttered majestically in the air, then slowly lowered trays of steaming food onto the blanket.

"Alright!" Billy shouted. "Let's eat, I'm starving."

"Try to eat like a human, Billy," Lori chided. "He's been attacking piles of food for days. Come on Tobe, dig in."

Toby was speechless.

"Yeah, come on Tobe, you never tasted burgers like these before. I think it's the cheese or something," Billy proceeded to devour two at a time.

Toby hesitated, then jumped onto the blanket, "Hey pass me those pickles," and grabbed up a burger, and a handful of fries. "What, no ketchup? And liquid refreshment...we must have liquid refreshment, my dear lady and sir."

"But of course, noble squire," Lori replied. "Your wish is our command."

Toby looked toward the bright green sky, expecting another flock of the peculiar birds. Instead, he heard a stirring from the bushes and saw some sort of orange, blurring, rolling figure, heading his way.

"Uh...is this something I should be concerned about?" he asked flatly.

"Nah," Billy replied. "That's just our weird cocktail waitress."

Rolling to an instantaneous stop just short of the blanket, its short stubby arms filled with soft drinks, was, indeed, a very odd looking creature.

Toby surmised it to be something of a cross between a groundhog, raccoon...and porcupine. The creature eagerly passed out bottles of cherry cola, root beer and orange soda to the group, all the while chattering something unintelligible.

"How did it know I wanted a root beer...I didn't say?" Toby asked.

"Told ya, all you gotta do is think about it, and it's yours," Billy answered. "Is this great, or what?"

"This is Emily. She's very industrious; always one step ahead," Lori said.

"You know its name," Toby said.

"Not *its*, Toby...*her* name. *It's* a *she*."

"How can you tell?" Toby asked. Emily poked her snout up against Toby's nose and stood defiantly with paws on hips.

"Because we women have a sense about these things," Lori answered. She grabbed Emily from behind and scratched her soft underbelly. "Don't we Emily...don't we."

Emily waggled her hind legs wildly and actually seemed to be making *laughing* sounds.

"Hey watch out for those needles, Lor, they look sharp."

"They look it, but she's as soft and cuddly as a stuffed animal...feel."

Lori took Toby's hand and gently guided it over the velvet texture of Emily's prickled back. Emily purred with contentment.

"Far out...but how did she tell you her name?"

"Oh, she didn't...she just reminded me of an old Aunt of my Dad's. Very fastidious and all."

Emily rubbed against Lori's leg, and if Toby didn't know better, he was sure she was warbling, *"Emiiiileee."*

"Hey where's that ketchup," Billy demanded. "The fries are getting cold."

"Hold your horses, Doc, hold your horses...ya know Rome wasn't built in a day," said a new voice...a disturbingly familiar voice.

Toby turned again and was *truly* surprised - if there was any surprise left in him - by the sight of another peculiar creature, pulling himself out of, what appeared to be, some sort of rabbit hole, carrying a huge bottle of ketchup.

"That's not who I think it is...is it?" Toby was now genuinely shocked.

"Nah...just some sort of wannabe, I suppose. Too much of the Toon channel, I'm guessing," Billy answered. He reached over and snatched the bottle out of the hands of the *all too* familiar, long eared, buck toothed creature as it casually checked out its manicure.

"Dat's gratitude for ya," the wannabe said - *"And don't forget to put the cap on tight when you're finished this time, buster...cheeesh!"* - then vanished into its hole.

Billy waved a dismissive hand toward the spot where the creature disappeared. "I never thought I would sympathize with that ol' Fuddy guy."

Lori glanced at Toby and giggled at his astonished reaction. "Come on Toby, dig in before Billy eats it all."

Toby bit into his burger and thought...*but what happens now?*

Chapter 9

Billy and Lori seemed more at ease since Toby's arrival. It was as if they were whole again; where they were supposed to be.

They had wolfed down every last morsel of their enchanted lunchtime feast, so now, the three friends decided they'd just sit back and savor the magical flavor of this most unusual place.

"So fearless leader, what's our next move?" Billy's arms were folded over his newly expanded belly.

"I was kind of wondering the same thing," Toby replied.

Lori was playing fetch with Emily; throwing sticks and watching the strange creature run off to retrieve them. Emily found it a little puzzling as to why Lori continued to throw the stick away, time after time, after she went to all the trouble of bringing it back. At one point Emily decided that, maybe, the best course of action would be to just leave the stick out where the girl had thrown it. But this tactic didn't seem to work either, since she was then coaxed and urged to *"gofetchit"*. Whereupon, when she did *"gofetchit"*, the girl just threw it away again.

"I guess maybe we should go take a look around...see what's out there," Toby said.

"Toby, do you really think we should go off wandering? We have no idea what could be out there," Lori said.

Toby smiled, "Well, It doesn't look too scary; so far, anyway. Maybe a little off color, but other than that, I don't see anything to be afraid of."

"Yeah, but what if we get out there and things start to change?" Billy said. "What if these little food guys only work this area? I mean we could starve or something. I vote we stay put until somebody or *something* comes and *fetches* us."

Emily's little ears pricked up and wiggled at the sound of the dreaded word. *Oh no*, she thought, *here we go again.*

Toby looked at Billy, the same way he'd looked at him a hundred times before: part amusement, part disbelief...and part *honest admiration*, for his never ending devotion to using the smallest fraction of brain matter necessary to sustain life.

"Ya know, Bill, if the rest of the world had your sense of adventure, there might never've been any streaming TV."

"What!" Billy exclaimed. "No all night, *"Breaking Bad"* marathons?"

"Not even the *"Brady Bunch."*

"No way!" Billy said. "But...I still think we ought to stay put for a while. I'm starting to get a little hungry again."

Lori just sighed and shook her head, then saw Emily drop the stick she was "*gofetchin*" and scamper up to Billy. The unusual little creature began to nudge him. "*Goooooo...gooooo nooooow,*" she muttered. Her soft needle like coat bristled and pointed at *"Target Billy"*.

"Hey," Billy shouted. A hint of concern crept into his voice. "Call your little *pit thing* off me."

Emily stood up on her badly bowed, prickly, hind legs, and made a little furry fist with one of her paws. She put her snout right up against Billy's nose and said, what appeared to be, *"Why I oughta."* Then, she happily rolled backwards into a little ball and began to *laugh* hysterically.

Toby broke into a big smile and Lori started laughing, too.

"That thing gives me the creeps," Billy whined.

Lori, still giggling, said, "I think she knows a problem child when she sees one."

Toby scratched Emily's belly, "I think *we've* been *fetched.*"

Emily wiggled her fuzzy little ears and murmured, *"No fetch...goooooo...."*

Chapter 10

Emily waggled down a thick-forested path and confidently led the reluctant entourage further into the multicolored woods. The warm rays from the odd purplish sun felt good on their backs, but, with every cautious step, the group was struck by the uneasy calm that pervaded their surroundings. From time to time they heard, and sometimes saw, a slight rustle of leaves, as if they were being watched, by something, all along the way.

Off in the distance they saw more of the peculiar woods creatures. Variations on deer, raccoons, chipmunks...even some kind of funny, hippopotamus type things. Cartoonish, yet, also very real.

"Toby...look at all these wonderful animals," Lori said. "It's as if we're imagining it all."

"I know, Lor. It's like we're a part of some sort of weird special effect. Like we're in some sort of movie, and we don't even know it."

"I wonder what it's rated," Billy muttered.

Up ahead, Emily continued to wiggle and waggle at the point, easily skirting under brush and pointing out various hazards.

Suddenly, she halted, and stood erect. Her soft needles bristled and pointed toward some unknown prey.

"Toby, look at Emily," Lori said anxiously. "Something's the matter with her."

Emily's coat changed colors, right before their eyes; her entire demeanor transformed into something dark, fierce, and wildly dangerous.

Sharp and deadly, her needles took aim.

"Geeez," Billy said. "I don't think I'd want to piss her off, again."

"Lori...what's she doing...what does she see?" Toby whispered.

"I'm not sure," Lori answered. "But I think she senses something out there...something—"

"Baaaad...oootttheeere," Emily snarled in her strange, guttural voice. She rolled into a small protective ball. *"Daaaangerooottheeere...."*

Suddenly, her sharpened needles bunched together, taking on the form of a large arrowhead.

Phoooooooosh!

The arrowhead launched from Emily's arched and pointed back, flying into the woods like some sort of heat seeking missile. Twigs and leaves rustled and snapped; the weapon relentlessly approached its unseen target.

Billy shouted, "Look at that...I don't bel—"

Suddenly, the large arrowhead scattered into groups of smaller, sharper clones of itself, veering off at extreme angles; it spread out into the foliage like a shot gun blast.

Finally, with deadly accuracy, and sickening thuds, they heard the needles find their marks.

Thunk...thunk...thunk...thunk...thunk...thunk...!

Muffled screams and cries for help howled from deep inside the woods. They were awful...*real* sounds of pain.

The pounding of heavy footsteps followed close behind, then faded in the distance; whoever, or whatever was out there, had apparently made a hasty retreat.

Behind Emily, three colorless faces stood on the path and gaped into the forest. Lori had grabbed hold of Toby's arm and refused to let go. Billy somehow crept behind the two of them and peered through the space that remained.

"What the heck was that all about?" he whispered.

"Toby, what do you think was out there?"

"I don't know, Lor...maybe we should ask your little buddy ball over there."

Everyone turned toward Emily, who was slowly rolling out of her protective ball. She was trembling, coated with a wet, sticky form of perspiration.

"Oh no!" Lori cried. "I think she's hurt!"

"I think she needs a bath. Get a whiff of that stuff, will ya," Billy said.

Emily glanced toward Billy and cocked her version of an eyebrow.

"I mean...boy is that a great smell or what, huh Tobe?" Billy said, frantically recalling the deadly accuracy of those needles. "What is that, some sort of a musk? Boy, I'd like to bottle that and sell it. Probably make millions...maybe billions. Say, that was great shootin there, Emily, old pal. Right guys?"

Emily rolled her eyes and sighed, *"Goofetchit...."*

"What's that you say, Emmy?" Billy asked.

"I think she wants you to take a hike," Lori said, stroking Emily's tattered hide; already, signs of new needles were appearing, replacing the old ones she had jettisoned.

"Uh, I think I'll go sit over here, on this rock for a while, and mind my own business. Okay?"

"Good idea, Bill," Toby answered. "How is she Lor? She's gonna be okay, right?"

"I think so," Lori said. "I think this is some sort of normal protective behavior for her. Look. She's replacing the lost needles already, and they're as soft as could be."

"What was it Emily?" Toby asked. "What was out there that spooked you?"

Emily peered at her new friends and made a strange sound from deep within her throat.

"Tic tic...tic tic...tic tic...tic tic...."

Toby looked at Lori and shrugged.

Meanwhile, their curiosity was shoved aside by the shriek of another frightened creature: one Billy Bartles.

"Ahhh...what's happening now...! I hate this place! Somebody get me off of this thing!"

90

With a steadily diminishing dose of amazement, but with more than a growing bit of amusement, they discovered that the *rock*, Billy had chosen to sit on, had decided it was time to move on and mosey about.

Perched ten feet atop something that resembled a turtle...and an elephant, Billy was once again in his, more recent, customary state: being in the wrong place at the wrong time.

"If you ever wake up from this nightmare, Pierce, I'm gonna kick your butt for making me a part of it!"

"Ah, come on, Bartles," Toby answered. "I wouldn't dream of having a nightmare without you...at least just for laughs."

The *Turtlephant* thing meandered toward an overhanging tree branch and Billy frantically grabbed a handhold, allowing the creature to peacefully walk off into the woods.

"Come on Billy, cut the monkey business and let's get moving," Toby shouted.

Lori swallowed a chuckle while Emily rolled on her back, made a strange gurgling sound and pointed her funny little paws at Billy, swinging from the tree.

....*tic,tic,tic,tic,tic,tic*....

"Well," said the figure, shrouded in the shadow of time. "Tell me...is it true? Has he come?"

"Yes," replied a second figure, huddled in terror. "I'm afraid it has come to pass...just as they said it would."

"You are sure...it was...*him*?"

"Yes, yes." the messenger trembled. "I am fairly certain."

"Fairly certain!" the figure within the shadow roared.

"Fairly certain does not mean certainty! I must know...*for certain.*"

"Please, my Lord. We were kept at a distance, by the Guardian. It sensed we were near. We did nothing to alert it; I swear by the tock, it is true."

"Spare me your feeble oaths of fidelity. If you were truly loyal, you would have brought him to me. Instead, I find a tattered rabble of foot soldiers, shaken in defeat. I need certainty...confirmation...*I must have it!*"

"Yes, my Lord. I would stake my time on it. Yes...yes...it was him. He has come. We were, indeed, close enough to see...*his eyes.*"

The brooding figure considered this new information, while the soldier standing before him trembled with each timeless moment of silence.

"The key?" the figure asked.

"Yes...I could see it; also in his eyes."

The dark figure turned and receded further into the weight of the shadows. *"The key...always the key...."*

....tic,tic,tic,tic,tic,tic....

Toby and Lori stuck close to Emily while she continued squirming and wiggling down the winding, forest trail. Billy lagged behind, hands in pockets, distraught by the entire state of affairs; and besides, he was hungry.

"Come on Bartles...quit your moping," Toby teased. "You're depressing all these happy little...*things*."

"Leave me alone," Billy replied. "You know all about that, don't ya Toby? Being alone; shutting out the world?"

Toby stopped and eyed his friend.

"Billy, quit being so rotten," Lori said, angrily. "We're all scared. We're all lost...and we're all in this together."

"That's okay, Lor," Toby started.

"No Toby, it's not okay. I'm sick of Billy, constantly whining and complaining. Pointing fingers...looking to blame someone...anyone...for all of this...to blame you. It's nobody's fault that we're here, Billy. Not Toby's...not mine...not yours...nobody's."

Billy stood stone still in his tracks, stung by the intensity of Lori's angry remarks.

"We're here," Lori continued, "because we wanted to be here...with Toby...with each other...we chose it."

Billy dropped his head.

"Come on Bill," Toby wrapped his arm around his friend's shoulder. "This isn't just about me. I think it's about all of us."

"I don't know Tobe. I'm just not used to this. I feel a little lost, that's all. Well...maybe a lot lost."

"Believe me, pal, I know the feeling."

Just then, they heard Emily, up ahead, on the ridge of a hill, jumping and flipping, yammering away in some sort of communication. *"Cooooome....cooooome noooow."*

Toby put his other arm around Lori. "Hey, I think we've just been found."

"Or maybe...we found *it*," Billy said.

"Yeah...maybe...whatever *it* is," Lori agreed.

Chapter 11

"Looks like a pretty wild party to me," Billy said. They stood on the crest of a hill, looking down into a narrow valley. What they saw both confused and delighted them.

It was some sort of a celebration, and the *celebra-tors* were unlike *any* they had ever seen *before*. Small and, well...funny looking, would be the best way to describe them, these *people* - but not *really people*, at all - also possessed that odd, cartoonish quality that Toby had observed earlier. Yet still, he knew they *were* very real.

Emily continued to flip and yip, while her three charges, to her chagrin, stood in silence. *What's wrong with them, now*? she thought. *We're missing all the fun*!

"What is it, Emily? What're you trying to tell us?" Lori asked.

"Fuuuun..." Emily responded. *"Miiiiisssit."*

"Phoonmsit...? Nice enunciation. Have you ever thought of some speech therapy, pointy?" Billy cracked.

Emily turned toward Billy and arched her brow again.

"Just a joke! What's the matter, you got no sense of humor or nothin?"

Toby was transfixed by the scene below but still managed to smirk. "Talk about speech classes...I'm not sure who's worse."

"Toby, I think she wants us to follow her," Lori said.

"Where, Lor...down there?"

"I think so. You think it's dangerous?"

Billy spoke up, full of optimism for once. "Why would it be dangerous? Nothing's hurt us so far. Besides, the little mutt *was* pretty sharp, watching out for us before...if you know what I mean."

"Well, well, aren't we getting brave," Toby said. "What's this, the old, confident Billy returns at last?"

"Shoot, look at those guys, Tobe. They're about all of three feet tall...and they're nothin but cartilage."

Billy was correct on that point. Undoubtedly, these strange people *were* no more than a few feet tall, and they did, indeed, possess unusually, large noses and ears.

"Man," Billy continued. "If one of those little munchkins tried to start something, I bet even little Lori here could kick their butts all by her lonesome."

"I don't suppose you read or saw `Gulliver's Travels', did you Billy?" Lori asked.

"What? You mean that show about the skinny sailor guy and fat captain, marooned on an island or something, with those babes and a millionaire."

"—And his wife," Toby completed.

"That's Gilligan...not Gulliver," Lori said, clearly exasperated.

"Yeah, right...Gilligan. So what's that got to do with this."

"Nothing," Lori just shook her head. "Nothing at all."

"I swear Lori, sometimes you think of the darndest things."

"Come on," Toby said. "Let's get closer."

Cautiously, they crept further down the hill and began to hear the sounds of music and dancing. Scattered about the area, they saw tables, overflowing with large platters of food.

"Hey, look at that," Lori said.

The little people had gathered around a larger person, and then excitedly, a small group of them began to lead him toward some sort of...opening...in the fabric of the field itself.

"Do you notice anything strange about that guy in the middle?" Billy asked, studying the proceedings.

"Yeah," Toby said. "You mean that he looks *normal*?"

"You got it. He looks...you know...like us...human."

"*Hooooomoan....*" Emily repeated.

"Well, most of us, anyway...." Billy said.

"Where are they taking him?" Lori asked. "What are they singing?"

"*Hoooologoadbooooy....Hoooologoadbooooy,*"   Emily murmured.

"It looks like it's some sort of door or something," Toby answered.

"Right, just your average door, hanging in the middle of nowhere...going no place," Billy said sarcastically.

"Sounds vaguely familiar to me," Lori said.

Down below, the merry celebrants formed a circle around a young man and began escorting him toward a seemingly innocent doorway.

"*Hello-goodbye...Hello-goodbye,*" they sang, over and over again.

When the throng reached the open door, the young man turned and waved. In response, they too, as one, raised their tiny hands and enthusiastically waved and sang.

"*Hello -goodbye... Hello -goodbye... Hello -goodbye.*"

With that, the young man confidently stepped through the open portal and closed it behind. Again, as one, the crowd gave a large cheer and threw their peculiar hands high into the air.

"*Hello -goodbye... Hello -goodbye... Hello -gooodbye.*"

"Whoa...did you see that!" Billy Bartles said. "That guy just vanished...into thin air!"

"Yeah," Toby replied. "One minute he was there...and then the next...he's gone."

"*Hoooologoadbooooy...Hoooologoadbooooy,*" Emily sang.

Lori said, "Haven't you geniuses figured out this *just might* be some sort of magical place...where *anything* is possible...even things that you might never have considered before,".

"*Geeenoooousays....*" Emily repeated.

"*Hello, Toby...we've been waiting.*"

Billy spun around, "Huh...who said that?"

"*Relax Mr. Bartles. There is nothing to fear.*"

"Whose been waiting for me?" Toby swallowed.

"*Pssst. I don't think they can see us,*" said another voice. "*We've forgotten to materialize again.*"

"*Oooops...sorry.*"

Toby, Lori and Billy looked at each other. Then, just as Billy was about to offer another pearl of his singular wisdom, something miraculous began to occur. The atmosphere around them tingled, suddenly charged with life. A narrow slice of unoccupied space rippled and bowed, rippled and bowed, and then rippled and bowed some more.

"*This way, Malok. You're going the wrong way again.*"

"*No, no, Musso. I'm quite certain it's this way.*"

"*Malok, why must you be so stubborn? The last time I listened to you, I materialized into a cauldron of milisk fat.*"

"*Yes...and tasty it was, Musso...tasty it was*"

Suddenly, the empty space transformed into a shower of incredible sparkles and two little men stepped through the wavering seam.

"See, I told you I knew how to do it," a small, chubby man said.

The men were clothed in the same bright colored garb as those they had seen dancing in the field below. While one was portly, the other was slim, but both were *graced* with the same large encumbrances...namely, huge ears and enormous noses.

"Geeez, ya don't want to offer one of these guys your hankie," Billy whispered.

Toby nudged him with his elbow.

Pinpoint sparkles of light shed from their diminutive forms and the men busily brushed the magical remnants of their appearance away. One of the men sniffed and—

"*Ahhhhhchooooo!*"

"Look out!" Billy shouted.

"Oh my. It appears to be my allergies, acting up again," the rounder of the pair said.

"Bless you," Lori said, quietly.

"Ah, bless *you*," repeated the man. "How very kind of you, Lori. Thank you. Say young man, you wouldn't have a handkerchief handy would you?"

"Oh great, now *these* guys can hear everything I *say*, too," Billy said.

"Well now," the other small man said. "It would be a waste of good ear material if we didn't put them to proper use, now wouldn't it?"

Toby looked down and studied the two little men.

"Sorry for the confusion," the first little man said. "We're actually a bit new at this sort of thing."

"Yes," the slimmer man said. "I told you we weren't ready for *transference*."

"Well, as they say, `nothing ventured, nothing gained'. Correct, Toby?" the fatter man said.

"What do you mean...you've been waiting for me?" Toby asked, ignoring the man's question.

"Why waiting for you to arrive...to open the door...to use the key, of course."

"To use the key...*use it or lose it*," Toby whispered. "The key...always the key."

"Yes, indeed...*the key*," the slimmer man said.

"Keeeeeey," Emily purred.

"Where are we...exactly?" Toby asked.

"Come, come now, Toby, I think you know the answer to that, better than anybody."

"Yes...I do."

"Tobe, can this get *any* weirder or what?" Billy said.

"Well, Billy, that's entirely up to you. Things will only get as, *weird*, as you say, as you will allow them," the fatter man said.

"Huh?" Billy's face scrunched into one big question mark.

"Never mind," the man said in his strange little voice. "You'll catch on as we go along."

"Go along...where?" Lori asked.

"Why Lori, further into the Kingdom of Keys of course," the other man said.

"Who are you?" Toby asked. "Why should we trust you."

"Trust?" the first man said with a hint of surprise. "This has nothing to do with trusting *us*. Come now...you'll see. You will all see. It's all about you...and you...and especially you, Toby."

"Toby, let's go with them," Lori said.

"What are you nuts, Lori," Billy said. "Didn't your parents teach you about stranger danger?"

"These aren't strangers. I think they're our friends. Right Toby?"

Toby started to answer. "I think—"

But the fat one interrupted. "No, we're not friends...nor are we enemies for that matter. We just *are*. That's all."

"Just are what?" Billy asked.

"Hmmmmm?" the skinny one said.

"Just are...*what*?" Billy repeated.

"Just *are*...that's all," the fat one said again.

"Who's on first?" Billy said to Toby.

"I don't know," Toby answered.

"Third base," the fat one said, then shot a wink to his thinner partner. "Always one of my favorites."

Billy glanced at Toby. His mouth hung in disbelief.

"Shall we join the party," the skinny one said. "The others are waiting."

Toby shrugged, "I guess we can't keep them waiting any longer. I guess I've kept you *all* waiting long enough."

"And no more *transference* nonsense," the skinny man said to the fat one. "I knew we'd get stuck!"

"I've always preferred a good walk, myself," the fat little man said and led the group on their way.

They soon reached the open field and the party was once again in full swing. Everywhere, the unusual people, jammed into tables, stuffing themselves with unlimited amounts of peculiar food and drink. A band manipulated bizarre looking instruments and played odd sounding tunes that were surprisingly pleasing.

Billy turned to ask something but found that the two little men had disappeared into the group to fill their bellies.

"Hey where'd the Cookie Elves go?"

"I don't know," Toby said. But here's all that food you've been belly aching about."

"Yeah, look at these munchkins go after it. You think I've got an appetite...look at that guy."

Billy was pointing in the direction of an earnest young man who was in the process of emptying the contents of a large flask of bluish liquid directly into his wide open mouth. As the contents poured out, his already ample belly swelled in direct proportion to the incoming flow.

"Man," Billy said. "Do these guys know how to party or what?"

Suddenly, Emily jumped up and started tugging on Lori's sleeve. "*Offfheeerrrr*," she warbled.

"Come on you guys, Emily wants us to follow her," Lori said.

The needle laden creature led them over to a large table in the middle of the celebration. "*Siiiittttere*"

"She wants us to sit down."

"Yes, please sit. There is much to be done. Much to celebrate. Much to discuss. Much, much, much."

The three looked up to see a woman, a normal looking woman...in fact, a beautiful, normal looking woman, standing beside their table.

"Whoa...what a babe," Billy whispered. "Now we're getting somewhere. She must've had *quite* a nose job."

Toby ignored Billy's comments and introduced himself to the woman. "Hello, I'm Toby. These are my friends, Lori and Billy."

"Hey...what happened to Billy and Lori?"

Lori nudged her hip into Billy's thigh.

"Yes, Toby, we *all* know who you are. We've been waiting for you. But, I guess I'm getting a bit ahead of myself. You're probably a little confused and—" the woman glanced toward Billy, "—a little dazed by all that you have been through."

"Well, maybe just a—" Billy started.

"I am Samira, *Queen of Keys*. The *King of Keys* has sent me to welcome you and regrets that he will not be able to join us in this realm."

"Thank you, Samira," Toby was awed by the sight of the Queen. He suddenly understood what was meant when it was said that a person had a *majestic* presence. It was more than just physical; there was something about her that made her seem...*uncommon.*

"Where is the old King," Billy said unceremoniously. "Off fighting dragons or something?"

"Or something." the Queen said. She smiled sweetly, yet conveyed an underlying sadness. "But you will know more of that later. As for now, my friends, please enjoy the celebration and make yourselves at home. Emily will assist you, and I believe you have already met Malok and Musso."

"If you mean Bud and Lou, yeah we had a small meeting, if you catch my drift," Billy was clearly pleased with his cleverness.

"Please don't mind him Samira," Lori said. You know how *immature* little boys can be."

"Yes, Lori, I know, indeed"

Billy's eyebrow arched with suspicion. "Hey, how'd you know that we named her Emily?"

"What else would she be called?" Samira replied cryptically. "Now if you will all—"

Samira's words were suddenly shattered by a large blast that shook the hills surrounding the quiet valley. Another blast, and another, froze everyone in place. All eyes turned toward a distant hilltop where several large plumes of thick, black smoke rose toward the emerald sky.

"What was that?" Billy shouted.

"Samira...it starts again," Musso said, dodging his slender form through the crowd.

Samira peered in the distance toward the dissipating clouds of smoke. "Yes Musso, my conscientious Guidesman. *He* starts again."

The Queen turned to Toby and his friends. "But perhaps this time...*we* will end it...once and for all."

Billy whispered to Toby, "I don't think I like the looks of this."

"Nope," Toby said. "I don't think *all's well* in the *Kingdom of Keys*."

"Man...this is quite a closet you've got, Tobe."

From off in the distance, only the residents of Keys, being blessed - or cursed - with round, prodigious ears, could hear the sound....

....*tic,tic,tic,tic,tic,tic,tic,tic,tic,tic,tic,tic*....

Chapter 12

"Report" spoke the foreboding figure, from deep within the shadows.

"I am happy to report, my Lord, that the current operation has ended in a rousing success. We have met their numbers and have advanced as planned."

"The *Temporalus Contagion*?" the shadow man queried.

"It is spreading, my Lord. By this hour and a week we shall have infiltrated all remaining barriers."

"The King?"

"Contained, my Lord. I am pleased to say that the effects are progressing at a rate that we could only imagine. It was only—"

"*The boy?*"

"Ahemmm...yes my Lord, the boy. The boy has taken part in the welcoming ceremony, this is certain. However, I can assure, my Lord, that our victory has had a very disruptive influence on the celebra—"

"*THE BOY!*" the shadow figure roared. "*WHAT IS BEING DONE ABOUT THE BOY?*"

"Well, my Lord, at present we have had our difficulty getting close to him. He seems to be particularly well guarded at the present time, you see. We hope to—"

"Hope to! I will not tolerate, *hope to*...I will only accept action."

"Yes, my Lord."

"This...*boy*...must not be allowed to use the keys. To open the doors. To obtain the knowledge of the keys."

"Yes, my Lord."

"His knowledge will finish us forever...so it has been *foretold*."

"Yes my Lord."

"Tell me, soldier...do you believe in the *Foretelling*?"

The soldier trembled, "Yes, my Lord." He had seen these tests before.

"*Yes?*" the shadow man said.

"No, I mean no, my Lord. I—"

"*No?*"

"I mean, my Lord...I don't know...what to say. How to please you, my Lord."

"Ah...so you wish only to please me. But at what cost would you please?"

"At any cost, my Lord," the frightened soldier said.

"At the cost of your own...knowledge...you mindless fool."

"I suppose, my Lord."

The man stepped out from within his darkened shroud. A wide, sinister smile spread like venom across his long, narrow face. Strewn with hollows, where hollows shouldn't be, his countenance was mottled with fetid puddles of evil, concealing his most telling features.

"Rise up, soldier. You are harmless enough. You have nothing to fear. Yes, indeed...you have *pleased* me."

The soldier rose and allowed a smile to cross his face. *All would be fine now. He had pleased his master. He had given the right answers.* "Thank you, my Lord."

"Please, my loyal soldier...do not thank me. I should thank *you*, for giving me such pleasure."

The soldier grew even brighter, Lord Tkler walking with him side by side. *How easy it was to please this powerful man. Perhaps this would mean a promotion. Maybe even an advisorship.*

"Yes, you do not profess to have knowledge or an opinion; merely to please your Lord. Therefore, you are neither offensive nor inoffensive."

"Yes, that is so, my Lord."

"Therefore, you do not *be* at all."

"My Lord?"

"You do not *be*...and your time has been wasted. So, it is wasted no more."

"My Lord?"

The shadow man slowly, yet purposefully, raised his arm and pointed a sinister finger directly at the befuddled soldier. Without warning, a violent flash of angry light streaked from the lethal digit and the soldier disappeared ...disappeared from time.

"Yes, my friend. That pleases me immensely."

The shadow man walked toward an irregular opening cut into the stone tower that encircled him. He considered the dark landscape spreading before him as far as his telling eye could see.

Could he possibly lose all of this?

Was it doubt that filled the hollow space inside?

"The boy...the key...he must not use the key....*always the key*...."

Chapter 13

"Come Malok, its time we got on with it."

"Don't be so impatient, Musso...the party has just begun." The little, fat man was busy filling his belly with plate after plate of delicious *Keysian* cuisine. The other little man looked at his partner and impatiently scratched his chin.

"Really, Malok, we've been given the most momentous assignment in all of *Keys*, and you can only think of personal gratification."

"Oh, don't fool yourself, Musso. You know, as well as I, that we've only been selected because all of the favored ones are busy with the defense."

"My Poor Malok. Has it never occurred to you that we may have been pre-ordained to fulfill this promise?"

Malok considered this statement. "You truly humble me, my friend. I suppose I should permit us a tad more credit. After all...he *is* among us."

"Yes, and if we don't get busy with our work, it could all be for naught."

Malok dropped his fork, wiped his spotted chin, and blew his very large nose. *HOOOONK!*

"These allergies surely test me, Musso. I tell you the air around here has not been the same since the *disturbances* began."

Musso studied his partner closely. The sneezing and sniffling *had* begun suddenly enough, that was certain. And he supposed he *could* attribute it to the changing atmosphere.

Still, he'd better remain alert for any of the *other* changes that were said to occur. They had come too far.

Meanwhile, Toby and company continued to enjoy the celebration.

"Man, these little guys sure know how to do it up right. Have you tasted this stuff? It's outta this world...wherever *that* is," Billy was doing what came naturally...eating.

"Nah...I'm not really hungry, right now, Bill," Toby was cautiously scoping out the surrounding territory. "But you feel free to eat enough for all of us."

"Thanks, man, I will."

Lori sat in the chair besides Toby and Emily sort of squatted on the chair next to that.

"Look, Toby," Lori said. "Here come those two little men, again."

"Yep," Toby said. "I guess it's time to get down to business."

Lori glanced at Toby and noticed he was starting to get that troubled expression again.

"What sort of business?" she asked.

"I guess the reason why we're here in the first place, Lor. You didn't think it was gonna be one big party did you?"

"Why so anxious, Tobe? Hasn't everything been great so far?"

"Well, everything except for that little fireworks show earlier," he answered.

Lori sat back and crossed her arms in a solitary hug. She suddenly felt cold and uncertain.

"Greetings, guests of honor," Malok said. "How are you enjoying our humble celebration? Is everything to your liking?"

"Pretty good so far," Billy answered. "Say, what do you call this stuff over here? I've had about a ton of it."

Malok looked toward Musso and gave a knowing wink. "That my dear boy is referred to as *Garlgo*. Not too many of us are able to acquire a taste for it. However, it appears to be perfectly suited to *your* unique palate, Billy."

Musso leaned into Malok's large ear and whispered, "You can't let him eat the table decorations, Malok. He may get sick."

"Nonsense, Musso. If he hasn't gotten sick by now, he never will. I believe this boy is one after my own soul. If it smells good...taste it. If it tastes good...eat it."

Toby shifted uncomfortably. "Uh...mind if I ask what the big celebration is all about?"

"Why Toby," Musso replied. "I must say I'm a bit surprised that you don't know. You have a reputation as being quite the intuitive one."

"Well I—" Toby started.

"Come, come, Musso," Malok interrupted. "You can see these young folks have been through quite a disorienting experience. They cannot be expected to be completely up to snuff."

"Well I—" Toby continued.

"I suppose you're right, Malok. I keep forgetting that these adventures *can* be a bit trying. Do you suppose we'll ever get the hang of this business?"

"Most certainly, Musso...most certainly."

"You see, my friends and I—" Toby tried to break in.

"That's what I admire most about you, Malok. Your unflagging confidence that—"

"May I please ask a question?" Toby shouted, interrupting the mindless chatter of the two little men from *Keys*.

Malok and Musso jumped back, startled by Toby's sudden outburst, then bowed to him in unison.

Now, Toby was embarrassed.

"I'm sorry. I didn't mean to shout. I'm just a little confused as to how you all knew that I was coming. I mean...I didn't even know I was coming...until—"

"Well, you see Toby, we've had our eye on you for as long as most of us can remember," Musso said.

"What do you mean? You've been watching me...how?" Toby glanced toward Lori.

"I think what my good friend Musso is trying to say, is that we have been *aware* of you. Not literally, as in watching your every move, but an *awareness* that you were in need of our services." Malok eyed the unfinished portion of Toby's meal. "Are you going to finish that corboil?"

Toby released a sigh of frustration, and perhaps relief. "What services? You mean giving me the keys to the doors? Help me find what's behind them? But that's just an old fairy tale that...my Dad...made up."

Malok considered Toby's uneven expression. "But aren't fairy tales products of imagination, Toby?"

"Yeah...I suppose so."

"And isn't anything imagined a mere leap of faith away from reality?"

Toby replied in a voice barely louder than a whisper, "I don't know."

"Ah yes," Malok said. "Therein lies our task."

Just then, Billy let loose a tremendous belch. Everyone turned and saw him holding his stomach, looking a bit on the peaked side.

Toby was happy for the distraction. "I thought you couldn't fill up on this food, Bill?"

"I guess a person's only got room for so much...even this stuff," Billy said weakly.

"I told you, we shouldn't have let him eat the decorations, Malok," Musso admonished.

Malok absently wiped his nose and directed his gaze to the dust rising over the mountains. "Oh don't worry, Musso. The boy will be fine." His large ears twitched at the incessant ticking.

"Perhaps we should retreat to a more secluded area, my friends, where we won't be distracted by all of this revelry," Musso said. "I think you will want to hear every word of what we are about to tell you."

"Ohhhhh...you guys wouldn't have any of that fizzy stuff handy, would you?" Billy moaned. "I'm feeling a little green."

"Don't be concerned, Billy," Musso replied. "In the Kingdom, green is very desirable."

Toby and Lori laughed then followed Musso and Billy back into the woods.

Malok lagged behind and snatched up Toby's leftover corboil. He popped the Keysian delicacy in his mouth and eyed the mountains with concern.

Chapter 14

In a small, wooded clearing, far removed from the ongoing celebration, Toby and Lori sat down on an old petrified tree stump. Billy, having been surprised once already by seemingly inanimate objects, sat on a soft pile of pine needles and rested his back against a firmly rooted tree trunk...he hoped.

"Now, this is a little more peaceful," Musso said. "Don't you think? I always enjoy a little solitude in the wood, now and again. Good for the soul. Good for the mind."

"*Ahchooo!*" Malok sneezed. "Yes Musso, good for your mindful soul...*Ahchooo*! But terrible for my...*Ahh...Ahh* ...allergies....*Ahchooo!*"

As Malok sneezed, the wind stirred across the treetops and small balls of dust danced randomly along the ground.

"Geez," Billy said. "Maybe you should put a muzzle over that thing."

Toby smothered a chuckle when Emily scampered over to Billy and snarled, "*Muuuuzlegoooodideee.*"

"Hey, keep this little pointy mutt away from me, huh. What's she got against me anyhow?" Billy complained.

Lori walked over to pacify Emily. "Good girl Emily, good girl. Yes, you're right. We've been looking for a way to put a muzzle on Billy for years."

Malok grinned and wiped his prodigious proboscis. "Emily is only following her natural protective instincts, Billy. You see, she takes her job quite seriously, and she is aware that there is much important business to attend to. A sense of humor, unfortunately, is not one of her strongest attributes. Unless...something truly remarkable strikes her, in which case, she will laugh like a—"

"Yeah...tell me about it," Billy said.

"What's with the strange breezes...and all the dust swirling around?" Toby asked. "I mean, I don't think all of that was from Malok's sneeze."

"No indeed, Toby," Musso replied. "We are experiencing some...*atmospheric events*...brought about by—"

"Oh there will be plenty of time to discuss our little domestic situation," Malok interrupted. "I think our young visitors may have more immediate questions they would like answered."

"Yes, of course," Musso agreed. "Where shall we begin?"

"Is this really the *Kingdom of Keys*?" Lori asked.

"Yes, Lori," Musso responded. *"The Kingdom of Keys*, where anything is possible, and the choice is always yours."

"Why do all these animal things look like something from a cartoon...and why are the colors all screwy?" Billy asked.

"Everything in *Keys* is as *you* perceive it to be. As you would imagine it to be," Malok said. "The three of you have shaped all that you see around you. We *Keysians* are very flexible and always willing to accommodate our guests. Am I making myself clear?"

"Huh?" Billy said.

"Do you mean that we're imagining...all of this?" Toby asked.

"Oh no...not at all," Musso said. "This is *all very real*. Very tangible indeed. However, much of our world is comprised of fantasy...of things imagined. Therefore, many external elements, such as landscapes, shapes and colors, are formed by the imagination of our visitors. Our substance is *very real*...but the rest is just window dressing, to accommodate *you*."

Lori was clearly awestruck. "You mean, all that we're seeing is how we imagined it to be?"

"Collectively, yes," Musso said. "Though, I must admit that many from your world do see things very similarly. I think we can thank young Walter for that."

"Who's Walter?" Billy asked.

"Oh, just one of our past guests from the *"Other"*, Malok said.

"From the *other* what?" Billy asked.

"Why the *other* than here, of course," answered Musso.

"Yeah...okay, whatever." Billy decided he better get back to the basics. "You mean, if we wanted to fix the weird colors, we could adjust it...like a TV?"

"Just like a TV, my dear boy."

"Cool...let's try it."

Billy closed his eyes and scrunched his face into all kinds of contortions. Slowly, the sky changed from emerald green to the richest blue imagined. Trees turned green...then purple...then back to green...and the world seemed a lot more comfortable.

"Nice job, Billy," Toby said. You may have a future in computer graphics someday."

"Are you kidding, Tobe. With a power like this I can open my very own theme park."

"Yes, the future," Malok said. "The future is what we are here to discuss."

"Specifically, your future, Toby," Musso said.

"Why just mine?" Toby asked hesitantly. Why not Lori...and Billy?"

"Because *you* are the *one* that has been crying out to us, Toby. *You* are the *one* that had the ability to reach us."

"I...I never reached out to...you....did I?"

"Yes, Toby. I think you know that you did...for quite a while now. In too many ways to say," Malok answered.

Toby looked at his friends. He didn't want them to hear any of this...to feel sorry for him.

"I don't know what you're talking about," he said harshly. "I don't make it a habit of crying out for help...to anybody."

"No...not in your world," Malok continued. "But, when there is nowhere for those cries to go...then they come to us...and then—"

"—We wait," Musso finished.

"Wait for what?" Lori asked. She walked over to Toby and reached down to take his hand.

"We wait for those, such as Toby, to make the choice...to come to us."

Toby impatiently shook Lori away. "I had no choice. There were the dreams, the light shows, the...*key*. There was the key!"

"Well, I must admit that we do nudge events along occasionally," Musso said. "Only if necessary, of course. But, Toby, *you* had to use the key...*you* had to open the door. The choice was always yours to make...or not."

Billy walked over to his friend and stared at him dumbly. "Man Tobe, I always knew you were a little strange."

"What do you mean this is about my future?" Toby asked, pushing Billy aside. The woods seemed to be closing in on him and his patience was growing thin.

"Well," Malok said, picking up the conversation. "We don't really acknowledge the future in *Keys*. After all, what is the future other than today, disguised as tomorrow?"

"Huh?" Billy replied.

Lori merely looked at him.

"You see, Toby," Malok said, continuing. "It is really more about abilities. About natural gifts, and learning to use them...not waste them. About purpose."

"Who was that other person we saw, when we first came to the party?" Lori asked.

"Yeah," Billy piped in. "The guy who disappeared behind door number two."

"Oh that was just another *lost boy* who had come to us for purpose, and left with it secured," Musso said. "He may not have discovered it fully...but then, his purpose may be to find his purpose...and until then....."

"Huh...?" Billy said...again.

"*Lost Boys*...like in `Peter Pan`," Lori said.

"You might say that, my dear, and lost girls," Musso answered. "Sir James was also one of our guests. Delightful lad he was, too. Confused at first, but he left here with the *knowing*."

"Knowing what?" Lori asked.

"That it was all possible...if he let it be so."

"Let what be so?" Toby was becoming more confused by the second.

"I'm afraid we're making this all a bit too perplexing, Musso," Malok interrupted. "Perhaps it would be a little clearer if we were to show you."

"Show us what?" Toby asked.

"Come this way," Malok said.

The little man led them through a thick stand of trees and stepped onto a craggy ridge.

"Behold...."

And what they beheld took their breath away.

Beneath them, spread out for an impossible distance, was a field; an amazing *Field...of Doors*, glistening in the afternoon sun

"You see, it is all really very simple. In the *Kingdom of Keys* we are taught that we each have our own singular purpose. The reason why we exist, so to speak. No *one* is the same. We are given the keys and then any or all of the doors are *ours* to open. Each door leads to another door, and so on, and so on. We are all given the keys...but it is left to each of us to decide which ones to use...and how to use them...if we use them at all....."

"How do you know which key opens which door?" Toby asked.

"You just do. It's as natural as the current flowing in a stream," Musso answered.

"Whoa," Billy said. "How can anyone have enough time to check out all those doors? I mean, like what if you want to check'em all just to make sure you're not missing anything. By the time you finish, you could be fifty or something, and then you might as well just cash it in."

"Yes, Billy...time," Malok said. "Time, time, time."

"Time is a concept that does not exist in the *Kingdom of Keys*," Musso said. "The King forever banished *time itself* from the Kingdom. He recognized it for the distraction that it was and felt that we would all better serve our purpose without the curse of time."

"How can you banish time? What do your clocks say, half past nothing?" Billy asked.

"No clocks, no time. Just purpose and passion and then...."

"And then what?" Toby asked.

"And then," Malok continued. "When our purpose is fulfilled, we happily fade away, moving on to find our next."

"Fade away to where?" Lori asked.

"Nobody really knows for sure," Musso answered. "But, everyone is content to go."

"Sounds an awful lot like croaking to me," Billy said.

"No, Billy, not at all. Without time, there can be no end...nor, for that matter, can there be a beginning. Once you have found purpose, you have found life. Once you have fulfilled life, it can never be taken away."

"Unless of course...." Malok started.

"Unless what?" Toby asked.

Musso looked toward Malok and said, "Really Malok, I'm not sure this is the right place to get into all of this."

"They may as well hear it all, Musso. After all, without them, there may not be anything left to tell."

Musso considered this. "Very well. I suppose it must be done."

Toby glanced at Lori, then Billy, sensing they were both developing a major attack of the goosebumps; he didn't blame them.

"You see, my friends," Musso began. "While the King had the power, and was, indeed, able to banish time from the *Kingdom of Keys*, he was not able to eliminate it, entirely. His power, you see, is only absolute within our own borders."

"You mean there are other places...like this...out there?" Billy asked.

"Oh yes, indeed. As many as a mind can imagine," Malok said.

Musso continued. "There are some who are jealous of our freedom. They are not as content, or at ease, with their true purpose. They struggle and toil in order to live up to what they perceive as purpose...but, in reality, they are only fighting time."

"They would have us *all* consumed by the same evil that consumes them," Malok said. "In fact, he has already dealt us a severe blow."

"Who's he?" Toby asked.

"Tkler," Malok said gravely. "There is no greater threat to the *Kingdom of Keys* than the *Evil Lord Tkler...Keeper of Time*."

"What do you mean, the *Keeper of Time*?" Lori asked.

The gentle voice of Queen Samira suddenly spoke to them from behind.

"When the King banished time from the Kingdom, it was immediately absorbed by Tkler. Lord Tkler is a tyrant and rules through fear, doubt and destruction. He uses time as a snake uses venom; he would destroy *Keys* to solidify his power."

Toby turned to face the Queen. "But how will destroying *Keys* strengthen Tkler?"

"Whenever a soul is able find *true* purpose, beyond the constraints of time, Tkler is diminished. That is *our* purpose: to help those who are lost find their special gifts. To give them the keys to unlock the doors."

Toby nodded.

"But not all, I'm afraid, succeed," Samira continued. "Not all are willing to help themselves. All are given the keys, but only those with the courage...to seek the doors...to use the keys, fulfill their promise."

Toby looked out and studied the massive Field of Doors.

So many to choose from. Where would he ever start?

"Why are some of the doors opened?" he asked.

"Many have passed this way, Toby. You are not alone...not the only lost soul. Those are the doors that others have left open, refusing to shut them, always hoping to return...to what cannot be. When they return, they will have found that nothing has changed. Not even time."

"How will I know which door to choose?"

"You will know," Samira answered."

"And if I choose not to open the door?"

"The choice will always be *yours* to make, Toby."

Toby suddenly began to experience a warm sensation emanating from the pocket of his jeans. It was the sack of keys. He'd crammed it in there; it seemed so long ago.

"Whoa, Tobe," Billy said. "It looks like something's burning a hole in your pocket...and *I know* it ain't money."

Toby reached in and pulled out the sack. Its comforting glow immediately encircled his hand. Samira looked at the sack of keys and smiled.

"The King believes that you will choose wisely."
Toby looked up from the sack and met Samira's gaze.

"Can I ask, why haven't we met the King?"

A shadow of sadness fell across Samira's face as she considered Toby's question. Malok and Musso shifted uncomfortably.

"Everything will be made clear, dear boy," Musso fussed. "You will soon know all you need to know."

Samira smiled at Musso. "I believe Toby is entitled to know." She turned to Toby. "I am afraid the King is in a much weakened state. Like many of our *true ones*, he has been infected."

"Infected by what?" Lori asked.

"*Tkler's Curse*, the *Temporalus Contagion*."

"Sounds ticklish to me," Billy piped in. Toby and Lori shot him a disapproving glare.

"Sorry...couldn't help it."

Samira smiled and said, "I know, Billy. Humor is your sword. We are, all, well served by it. And you...*we*...will need its power."

Billy smiled back at Samira and gulped, "Thanks...*I think.*"

Samira continued, "The *Temporalus* is a virus created by Lord Tkler. It contains the toxic seeds of time. The atmospheric disturbances began slowly, without much notice. However, soon after, some of our people began to notice changes."

"What sort of changes?" Lori asked.

"Aging, primarily, and the sense of urgency and regret that accompanies it. You see, in a timeless world we, each of us, grow and age timelessly, until we discover our true purpose. Some find it soon, others later. That is why you see what appears to be some more advanced than others. Then, once purpose is discovered, aging stops and the only measure we live by is fulfillment. And fulfillment will always take as long as is needed."

Toby's head was about to explode with questions, but he couldn't put a single one into words.

"I know this is all very abstract and difficult for you to understand, Toby, given circumstances from which you come," Samira said. "However, I am sure you will all see that it is really very simple."

"What's the King's problem, exactly, or even abstractly for that matter?" Billy asked.

"Once the virus was detected and it became obvious what Tkler was up to, the battle to defend *Keys* began in earnest. All of those who had *discovered* true purpose were enlisted by the King to defend the Kingdom. It was thought that they would be immune to

Tkler's poison. But all too soon it became apparent that *discovering* purpose and obtaining fulfillment were not one and the same.

"And Tkler was prepared. He had his forces at the ready, and soon, many of *Key's* finest and truest were gone. The King was also breached, and now he lies in the castle, fading rapidly, cursed with regret and hopelessness; clinging only to a thread of his purpose."

"What *is* the King's purpose?" Toby asked.

"What it has always been and what it will always be," Samira answered. "To preserve the *Kingdom of Keys* for all that will choose to come."

"But how did—"

Toby stopped in mid question as a strange, high pitched whistling suddenly vibrated in his ears. The ground shook with a loud, jarring vibration.

Musso gasped, "Oh no...."

From up above, a bolt of light streaked from the sky and crashed inches from Toby's feet. Then, one after another, long red bolts of fire blasted holes across the entire clearing.

Malok and Musso ran frantically around in circles, avoiding flash after flash of the searing flame. It struck trees and shattered rock; large plumes of acrid smoke rose toward the sky and blackened the sun.

Billy and Lori crouched low to the ground, not knowing what to do, or even where to go to do it, if they did.

But Toby and Queen Samira stood calm amid the chaos, looking deep into each other's eyes - "What's with those two?"

Billy screamed - until finally, the strength of the moment was shattered by an explosion of bark and leaves high over Toby's head.

"Toby!" Lori shouted. "Watch out!"

Toby looked up just in time to see a fiery branch separate from the tree with a deafening crack and plummet toward his head. Instinct took over and without thinking he dove out of the way and into a soft pile of leaves.

"Samira!" Musso cried. "The final advance has begun!"

"No, dear Musso," Samira answered. "This is merely Tkler's way of letting us know he is aware of the boy. He needs him as much as we do."

Lori and Billy plucked Toby out of the mush of leaves. Emily nudged his face and brushed him with her stiffened needles, ready for attack.

"Toby, are you alright?" Lori was shaking.

Toby answered with an unnatural calm "Yeah, Lor, never been better," and held the glowing sack of keys up to his face.

"Ya know, Tobe," Billy said with some urgency. "I don't think it would be such a bad idea to find out which one of those doors leads back into your bedroom, and get the heck out of here...now!"

"We can't leave now, Billy," Toby said. "I think we're needed here."

"No...*we're* not. Maybe you are, but not me. None of this stuff has to do with me!"

"No Bill, you're wrong...it has to do with all of us," Toby said.

Another jagged bolt of crimson struck the ground, inches from Toby, and knocked Lori and Billy to their knees.

Toby ignored the blast and calmly walked toward Samira.

"What do I do now? What does all of this have to do with me?"

"The King believes in you, Toby," Samira replied. "He believes that you can help us...once you *discover*."

"Purpose." Toby said.

"Yes."

"Why me?"

Samira, again, looked deep into Toby's penetrating eyes.

"Because it has always been you, Toby...you know that."

Toby stared back, without emotion.

"I understand...."

Flash after flash, the lethal light continued its assault from above, pounding the small perimeter in which they stood. The wind twisted large piles of powdery dust and fallen leaves into threatening funnels. The treetops shook and swayed, as if their very boughs might actually bend and sweep the ground.

Malok and Musso grabbed Tobys by his arms and hastily spun him toward the *Field of Doors*.

"Run Toby...run to the *Doors*...this is your only chance!" Musso cried.

"But what about Lori and Billy? I can't go without them!"

Malok sneezed, over and over again. His large red nose appeared as if it might explode. "They will be fine as long as they are with us. You must go!"

Toby bristled at the thought of leaving his friends behind.

"But I can't leave them...I brought them here...I got them into this...."

Samira turned to Toby. "You must go alone now, Toby. *This* is for *you*."

Toby felt something welling up inside of him. He turned back to the *Field of Doors* and closed his eyes.

Suddenly, he screamed and with a primordial strength he ran wildly toward the *Doors*.

Chapter 15

Emerging from the dark, weighted shadow of time, Lord Tkler strode purposefully toward the viewing screen. Up until now there had been no reason to monitor the events with the naked eye. Up until now there had been no progress.

Now they had him. The boy would soon be his.

As the huge, three-dimensional vision took form within the chamber the totality of Tkler's pleasure became more and more apparent. Throwing back the sleeves of his long dark robe, Tkler rubbed his hands together with sinister glee.

"Excellent, excellent work, Engineer. He won't escape us, now."

"Yes, my Lord," Engineer answered. "We have zeroed in on his parameters and have calculated all of his variables...although, he appears to be most predictable."

"Still, Engineer, take care not to underestimate him. I almost envy the power he stores within."

"Stores, yes, my Lord...but uncontrolled."

"Yes, and so it must remain."

The wavering image filled the chamber and showed a scene of destruction and chaos. A boy and a girl lay huddled in terror. All around them bolts of hyper-beams crashed to the surface.

Tkler chuckled while the two insipid *Keysians* ran round and round in small-frightened circles. Only the boy and the Queen stood their ground. *No...do not underestimate this boy.*

"Bring him to his knees," Tkler ordered. "Let's see what mettle our young friend possesses."

"Yes my Lord," Engineer was eager to please and applied a small amount of pressure to a large rectangular device on a panel set before him. Engineer glanced back at the viewing area just as a large explosion shattered a tree above the boy's head.

Tkler watched the boy nimbly dive to the side.

"That should shake his confidence a bit," Engineer said smugly.

Lord Tkler remained silent but studied the vision before his eyes. He was disturbed to see the boy's primary response: turning to the sack of keys...at *this* moment. It also irritated him to see the boy's banal little friends fussing over him so.

With a swift, lashing hand, he pressed the rectangular button himself and watched with satisfaction as another bolt of lightning knocked the two *friends* on to their respective knees.

"Peek a boo, I see you," he said with disdain.

Suddenly, the boy ran to the Queen.

What are they saying? What is she telling him? Tkler did not like this at all.

"Quickly...intensify the attack," he commanded.

"Yes, my Lord," Engineer replied. He twisted several knobs and pushed countless buttons.

Flash after flash of menacing light struck like hale, yet still, the boy remained unfazed.

Tkler studied the vision with grave concern. The boy...was turning to face the *Field of Doors.*

"Not to worry, my Lord," Engineer said bravely. He will not attempt the *Doors*...not yet."

Still, without surprise, Lord Tkler observed the boy dash from the hill and run toward the *Field of Doors.*

No...I will not underestimate this one...

"Your perceptiveness is outstanding, Engineer. Perhaps you would like to perceive my displeasure with this turn of events," An evil sneer stretched across Tkler's face.

"My Lord...I don't understand...I—"

"Precisely, Engineer...precisely."

"I will stop him, my Lord," Engineer frantically pushed and turned countless switches and buttons, unleashing a furious attack that followed the boy down the hill and into the field.

"No...he's gone." Tkler said with resignation. "Now, we must prepare for his return. Take the friends...and the Queen."

"The Queen, my Lord?" Engineer asked.

"My good Engineer, perhaps it is time for an adjustment. Your senses seem to be slowing a tad. Do you think?"

"Yes, my Lord...I mean no, my Lord...I mean yes, my Lord...the Queen."

With that, Engineer quickly returned to the control panel, made the proper calculations, accessed the appropriate switches, and entered the codes.

Now, it had truly begun.

Chapter 16

Toby's heart hammered from the inside out.

THUMP! THUMP! THUMP!

After every frantic stride a bolt of deadly laser light crashed at his feet. Up ahead he could see the *Doors. The Doors, I gotta make it to the Doors...it's my only shot.*

BOOM! BOOM! BOOM!

Toby burst through the first set of half opened doors. One after another they banged aside.

He gained strength from the abandoned doors and ran even faster; the further he ran, the keys in his pocket intensified into a raw, searing heat.

He knew he was getting closer - *Closer to what* - and an unnatural calm rose above his panic.

Suddenly, a light, more brilliant than any he had ever seen, shot through his head —*KABOOOM!* — and Toby found that all of his previous thoughts had suddenly disappeared.

He also found that he was *suddenly* stretched out flat on his back.

Toby peered through blurry eyes and saw a very large, very solid, wooden door. It appeared to be, *the what*, he was looking for.

"Knock knock...anybody home," he mumbled weakly.

Slowly, his vision cleared..."Man, if I keep whacking my head...." and struggled to his feet.

Balancing himself on wobbly legs, he saw the door was actually nothing special, no larger than any average door. The only difference was this door seemed to be free standing, in the middle of a field.

Suddenly, the sack of keys shot out of his pocket and up into his open hand.

"*Owwww!*" Toby dropped the burning sack to the ground. He inspected his hand and saw that a small welt had raised on his palm. "I guess it doesn't get any hotter than this," then he placed his throbbing hand against the door.

A bad feeling rippled through him and instinct told him to spin back toward the hill. He focused on the small pinpoint of rock at the precipice of the hill, from which he had just come. Suddenly, he saw an overpowering flash burst from the ground and his stomach sank with doom. He gasped at the incredible brilliance of the light; trying to see beyond the endless rows of doors...trying to see what had happened.

But there was nothing to see, only blackness.

"Lori...Billy...!" Toby screamed.

From somewhere, deep within, he heard...no, he felt...a diabolical chuckle. Somewhere, someone...was very pleased with his anguish.

Toby remembered Samira's words. *"You must go alone Toby. You must go alone."*

Toby looked into the void and wiped tears from his eyes. Somehow he knew if he went through with this thing, whatever it was, his friends would be all right.

I can't let them down.

He picked up the brightly glowing sack and opened it. He selected a key. He knew it would be the right one.

Toby placed the key in the lock and turned it. The door opened. It was surprisingly easy....

....tic,tic,tic,tic,tic,tic....

Lori stood on the edge of the hill, straining to see Toby, far in the distance, running like a madman toward the *Doors.*

"I believe in you Toby." Tears rolled down her cheeks. "I'll always believe in you."

All around her the wind blew like a hurricane.

"Come on Lor," Billy said. "It's not safe near the edge of this hill. Not with all this stuff flying around."

The attack of laser light had intensified tenfold ever since Toby had raced down the hill.

"Samira," Musso cried. "We must take cover. It's not safe out here."

Malok sneezed again and again. In between sneezes he agreed with his partner. "Yes Samira, there is a burrow over here. Perhaps we could all squeeze in."

The Queen looked about as the turbulent conditions worsened. "I am afraid, Malok, that our size prohibits us from taking advantage of your shelter. But there is room enough for the two of you."

"We cannot leave our Queen...and the children. We are responsible for the children," Musso shouted over the gale.

Samira looked toward Billy and Lori. "I don't think we can call them children anymore. Please, go. We will be fine, as long as Toby succeeds."

"But Samira," Musso pleaded.

"Come, Musso," Malok said. "The Queen is right, Tkler needs them. I'm afraid the same cannot be said for the two of us."

A tremendous roar suddenly buckled their knees and a huge crater was blown out of the surrounding surface. Malok grabbed Musso by the elbow and pulled him into the burrow. "May the *Keys* be kind to us."

Samira approached Billy and Lori and gently placed her arms around them. She whispered something into each ones ear, then, quietly, they sat crossed legged on the ground. Emily purred and bristled.

A harsh, swirling light abruptly encompassed them, followed by a deafening roar. The rumbling ground on which they sat, trees, rocks and all, creaked, ripped and then...all of it, in a single blinding flash...tore away. The shaking behinds of two tiny

Keysians were all that remained, no longer concealed deep beneath the surface.

Musso gasped, "Incredible."

Malok sneezed, "*AHCHOOOOO!*" Then peered into the black hole of time.

Chapter 17

Toby stepped through the door and entered what appeared to be a big empty *nothing*. Looking back toward the door, he considered propping it open so he could find his way out...if he needed to. Then, he thought of all the unclosed doors he had passed through.

"Gotta go for it," he whispered, then cautiously closed the door and was swallowed by the darkness.

"Great, what do I do now, grope around in here, forever?"

As if to punctuate his words, Toby tripped over something...something sort of long and stringy. Then, his foot stumbled into something wet and foul. Unable to find a handhold in the dark, he lost his balance and crashed to the ground, then gasped when the wet stringy thing wrapped itself tightly around his head.

"What the—" He was under attack from some sort of unworldly monster.

He tried scrambling to his feet, but in his panic leaned against what he thought was a wall and immediately spilled out into a dimly lit room.

It was a kitchen of some sort, dark and dingy, and it seemed he had fallen out of a closet. The diabolical attack was mounted by none other than a fearsome bucket and a relentless mop.

Toby scrambled to his feet, peeled the clinging mop off of his head and tossed it back in the bucket.

"Who knew," he muttered. "It could happen."

Feeling a bit foolish, he turned back to face the room and saw that the kitchen was illuminated by a solitary candle, which someone had carelessly left burning.

"Hmmmm, power failure of some sort, I guess."

Upon closer inspection, Toby determined this was, indeed, a very *old* kitchen; no microwaves or ice making refrigerators here. In fact, all Toby saw was a small, iron stove and a table, surrounded by some rickety wooden chairs. A few stale pieces of bread and moldy hunks of cheese served as a nifty bacterial centerpiece.

"You're gonna get ants, buddy, if you're not careful," Toby said, for lack of anything better.

The rest of the rooms were dark and Toby decided he wasn't in much of an exploring mood. Instead, he moved cautiously toward what appeared to be the entranceway.

Another door, he thought, and reached down for the sack of keys; but this time the keys were silent - "Well, what do you know...a door that's just a door" —so he merely turned the knob and stepped out of a small yellow house.

He found himself in the center of a small village. A simple, outdoor cafe stood silent and dark, just down the street.

"Man, is it hot or what," he was swamped by a stifling heat, particularly for what appeared to be the middle of the night. Little beads of perspiration began forming on his forehead.

Looking around, he saw the streets were deserted and surmised that there would be no remarkable revelations waiting for him here...not in this burg, anyway.

Toby shrugged and wiped a small puddle of sweat away from his upper lip. He was about to re-enter the little house, figuring whatever he was looking for was waiting for him inside - *probably in one of those dark spooky rooms, no less* - when the sound of a man, singing drunkenly to himself, sliced his ear.

The man strolled unevenly up the street and Toby approached him. "Excuse me sir, I was wondering if you could tell me where—"

Toby stopped in mid sentence, suddenly realizing he was speaking *fluently*...in French. He didn't speak French. He couldn't even eat French Toast.

The man stopped singing and inspected this strangely dressed young man, blocking his passage.

"Could tell you where, what?" the man said, in a slurred French tongue. Somehow, Toby comprehended every word.

Toby smiled, clearly pleased with his new found talent.

"I'm sorry, don't mind me, monsieur. I'm afraid I've been...*closeted* for a while."

The man stared back with a confused expression. "Eh?"

"I was wondering," Toby continued. "If you might tell me where I could find the occupant of this house?"

"Oh, of course...the painter," the man spoke with an edge of disdain. "I should have known. You will find him up on the hill, overlooking the village. I believe his brain has been fried by the afternoon sun. Now he seeks the shelter of the stars."

Toby looked in the direction the man had pointed. Off in the distance he could make out the flicker of candlelight.

"Thanks, I appreciate it. Catch ya later," Toby said, then eagerly started off up the hill.

"Catch my what?" the Frenchman asked, clearly puzzled by the strange boy receding into the night. "Bahh...more of the *artistes*!"

Strolling purposefully up the road, Toby kept an eye on the glow of the distant candle. He wondered *how* he even knew who he was looking for.

He gazed up into the deepest, blackest sky he had ever seen and was struck by the multitude of stars. Entire constellations, piercing the veil of night, reached out to him. There was something breathtakingly familiar about these stars.

He followed the path to the top of the brushy hill, then left the road and continued in the direction of the flickering candlelight.

As he drew nearer, Toby found a solitary figure, hunched over a simple wooden easel. On closer inspection, he noticed that the light came from not one, but several candles fastened together.

Not wanting to disturb the man's feverish work, Toby quietly stood back and observed. He was fascinated by the ease with which the man transferred reality to art. *No...that wasn't right*, thought Toby. *It was more like his* impression *of reality.*

Toby could tell the artist knew instinctively what colors to choose and how to mix them. He didn't think...he acted.

Toby recognized the painting immediately, and he knew this man...this badly worn out man.

"Hello, boy," the man said, without turning from his work. "So you've come to see the painter...to find what makes him tick."

"No sir," Toby answered. "I've come to find out what makes me tick...I guess."

Now, the painter did turn toward Toby and held the oily brush up to his weathered face.

"Tick tick, tick tick, tick tick," he dabbed the brush on the end of his nose with each successive tick.

Toby couldn't help but giggle at the sight of this strange fellow with a big gob of yellow paint on his nose.

"What's the matter, never saw a man with a nose for painting before?" the painter said. "Oh, I see you've found your clothes."

Toby grinned at the man and looked down, surveying his jeans. "What do you mean?"

"Nothing," the painter answered. He wiped the pigment off his nose then turned back to his canvas. "I guess it was a dream."

Toby just shrugged and stepped closer to the canvas.

"This has always been my favorite painting." He reached out and touched one of the brilliant swirls, surprised to see it smear under his finger.

"Oh, that *is* a nice touch," the man gave Toby a sideways glance. "This is *no* finger painting, boy. What's wrong with you?" He placed his brush to the smear and produced another brilliant swirl.

Toby looked to the night, at the real stars above, and saw them twinkle with approval.

"I'm sorry, I've just always wanted to touch it. They won't let you touch it in the museum."

"What are you talking about boy, what museum?" the man said with increasing annoyance. "Don't tell me someone else has done this canvas. How could that be...I was so certain...it was so right."

"No...no, sir. No one else could ever paint this scene...not the way you did...do...are...it's worth millions."

The man chuckled a throaty growl. "Millions, eh. I'm sure my brother would be interested in knowing that."

"Yes...he would," Toby said quietly.

"He's been trying to sell my work for years and hasn't seen more than a single note. Still...he believes...as I believe."

"Believes in what?" Toby asked.

"In the work...in the artist...in the soul."

"The artist's soul," Toby whispered.

"And the soul of the work...the soul of the work, boy. I think you know what I mean. I think you have it too...inside."

"You mean I'm a painter, too?"

"Oh, I don't know what you are, exactly...but, whatever you are...you are, indeed, one who has it."

"I don't understand...has what?" Toby asked.

The man ran paint stained fingers through the remnants of his parched, red hair. Then, he thoughtfully stroked the stubble on his chin, and carefully chose his words.

"I'll try to make it clear for you, though I admit, I paint much better than I speak."

"Yes, they do."

"Do...do what?"

"Your paintings...they speak...forever."

The man nodded silently and considered the dusty ground at his feet.

"You see, boy, each of us carry a seed inside...a seed that want's to grow. It needs to be nurtured...it wants to flower.

"Most of us are unaware of this seed, yet, still, we feel it as it begins to grow, as if it has a will of its own. If we ignore the seed, it can cause us much discomfort. If we recognize it and greet it with light...it can make all the difference."

"Make all the difference..." Toby nodded.

"But, sadly, there are many who lack the courage to acknowledge this seed. They distract themselves with other pursuits and are enticed by that which is easily within reach."

"But, your paintings...your art, has produced billions of dollars," Toby said."

"So you say...but what good does that money do me, now? Does that money inspire me, now. No...I paint because I'm a painter. If I worked for material reward, I would have quit...given in, long ago."

"But people need to work...to provide for families...to eat."

"Yes boy, this is very true. Once, I buried the seed and sought out a life that *others* saw as *respectful* and *proper*. In fact, I tried many things, but never found my soul in any of them.

"Then, I found my sketches...and the seed stirred. It started to grow, and I found the oils...and then...I found my soul.

"Now, the flower blooms. It bursts from my heart and I *will* paint...I will paint everything that I feel...and then...I will be done...and in the end, I will have graced every second that I was given...with the passion that it deserved...nothing less."

"But, you don't look like a man who's enjoying his life," Toby said cautiously. "You look like a man who's lived a very *hard* life. You look like life took a club and beat you silly with it."

The painter smiled and looked down at his tattered clothes and badly beaten body. "Quite the sight, am I?"

"Well, I don't think you'd make the cover of GQ."

The man raised a brow but ignored the unknown reference.

"True, I have been unkind to this body and sacrificed its health in many ways. Oh yes, of course...it would be nice to be a rich man...to indulge in the luxuries that wealth provides. But, if the price of luxury is even a spec of the soul that drives my work...that would be the greatest sacrifice of all."

"But, if you don't take care of yourself...you'll die."

"This vessel will die...when it's time, it will die...that's true enough. But my soul...my passion...my art ...will live on forever."

"How do you know...for sure?"

"Because...it's true."

Toby stared deeply into the bloodshot eyes of this peculiar man and thought he could actually see the passion and the soul of which the man had spoken.

Despite his ragged appearance, Toby had no pity for this man. No, instead, he only hoped *he* could live, just one day of life...*his* life, with the passion of this artist; he too wanted to feel the colors.

Far off on the horizon, the sound of thunder rolled and angry red flashes cracked the sky.

The artist steadied his easel against the wind and put his brush back to the canvas.

Toby sat on the hillside and watched the artist create.

Chapter 18

Malok and Musso stood helpless and watched as an island of trouble consumed the sun. Rock and soil rained from the sky in clumps.

"Ahchoo...ahchooo...ahchoooo...ahchoooo!"

Musso turned a concerned eye toward Malok, whose sneezing and sniffling was definitely getting worse.

"Sit down, Malok; you must take care of yourself."

"Oh, I'm fine, Musso. Who wouldn't sneeze with all of *this* flying around."

In truth, the violent winds had now subsided and except for the blackness that surrounded the pair it might even be considered peaceful.

"I do think I will sit for a while, however. My old bones are feeling a bit sore. It seems that everything is getting so complicated. Things just aren't like they were, back in the good old days, Musso. Why, if I were twenty years younger, just think of all that I could accomplish."

Musso's eyes widened in horror. His jumbo ears wilted. Malok was showing more signs. It had advanced. His friend *was doomed*, like all the rest.

Musso turned toward the *Field of Doors*.

"We must return and report to the King, Malok. We must tell him about the Queen...and the others."

"Yes Musso, and the boy...we must tell him about the boy. If the King can still understand, that is."

"Yes, we will tell him about the boy...and he *will* understand...he will understand, Malok."

Malok silently nodded his head, and together, the two small men climbed out of the massive crater and walked down the wooded trail.

Their ears twitched with the ever present sound that poisoned the air.

....*tic,tic,tic,tic,tic,tic,tic,tic,tic,tic,tic,tic*....

The cold, hollow click of Lord Tkler's heels echoed threateningly down the long winding corridor of Castle Endlum's tower. The way was cleared. No one dared to interrupt his purposeful stride.

Bursting into the chamber, he was greeted by stone faced guards, poised at the ready with deadly weapons.

Tkler looked about at the splendid scene before him and was pleased.

Centurion, high commandeer of all of Tkler's forces, followed his master into the chamber, gasping to reclaim his breath; Tkler allowed a sinister smile to cross his lips.

"Ah, my good Centurion, come see what we have here before us."

"Yes, my Lord...if...you would...allow me...just a minute...to...." Centurion doubled over and clutched his cramping sides.

"A minute Centurion...just a minute...why yes, indeed, take all the time you need. I would say that, now, we certainly have *time* on our side."

Centurion managed to straighten and scanned the massive chamber; he too smiled.

"Yes my Lord. I would say that we certainly have advanced the clock of doom for the *Kingdom of Keys*."

Spread before them was a large slab of once fertile wilderness; grass, rocks, plants, even trees stretching in vain toward the missing heavens.

Huddled in the center of this island of desolation stood Queen Samira and Emily, both perfectly relaxed and at ease. Behind them, Lori and Billy sat crossed legged on the ground, oblivious to all that was taking place. They appeared to be in some sort of a trance.

"Greetings Samira," Tkler said smugly. "It *is* such a pleasure to see you again, after so much...*time*...has passed between us."

"Well Tkler," Samira said. "You will forgive me if I do not return your courtesy. I find your very presence ...chilling to the marrow."

Tkler smiled and approached the Queen.

"You are looking well, Samira - haven't aged a bit I see. No, none of those telltale lines and wrinkles - not on that majestic face of yours. And tell me...how *is* the King, these days?" he sneered.

Samira didn't answer. Instead, she stared deep into the shadows that concealed the eyes of her enemy. It disturbed Tkler more than the sharpest reply ever could.

A long, endless moment followed and Tkler broke from Samira's icy stare. "Ah, I see you've brought us guests. Wee ones from the *Other*."

Tkler approached Lori and Billy who still remained silent on the displaced soil. He circled them, like an animal examining his prey, slowly taking in every detail.

"What's wrong with them...*Hypospacial Shock*?"

"I taught them to escape into the tranquility of their minds. They are protected by the serenity of thought."

"You can do that?" Tkler was clearly perplexed. "So quickly?"

"The mind is a simple conquest, Tkler. If you allow it to be." Samira answered.

"My mind is impenetrable," Tkler said with pride.

"Yes," Samira said coldly.

Tkler reached down and lifted a handful of Lori's long, chestnut hair.

"A pretty little thing, isn't she, Samira. The innocence practically oozes from her. Disgusting, really."

Tkler dropped the strands of Lori's hair and rubbed his fingers with disdain. "Nothing that a bit of *Hypertemprocity* won't cure."

Tkler approached Billy and prodded him with the toe of his boot. Billy teetered, a little like a wobble toy, then fell onto his side, legs crossed and all.

"Now, this one has some merit. He understands the angles. He knows what he wants. He is capable of doing what is necessary. Yes, he has some worth to me, this one."

"Leave them alone, Tkler," Samira said. "They are worthless to you. I am all that you need. Send them back."

"No! You are wrong, Samira. They are important to *the boy*. As long as they are mine...the boy will come."

"And, are you sure you want the boy to come, Tkler? Are you sure?" Samira said with a placid smile.

Now, it was Tkler who stared into Samira's taunting eyes, cursing the serenity that remained within. "Yes Samira...I am sure...I want the boy...*he will be mine.*"

And with that, Tkler spun on his heels and retreated from the chamber.

"I want those two coherent when I return," he barked to Centurion.

"As you command, my Lord."

Emily purred and shot a single needle toward the door.

"*Ouch...!*" came a solitary cry from somewhere down the corridor.

Chapter 19

The tattered painter struggled with a gusting wind, unresponsive oils, and his fickle inner eye. Nonetheless, Toby was amazed by the cumulative effect of his efforts. Not only had the painter completed the first canvas, now he had begun work on a second, relentlessly racing the approaching dawn spilling over the horizon.

"Away these winds," the painter squinted and wiped grit from his nose. "How is a man to work in these winds."

A tube of paint blew from his palette and the painter was torn between securing his canvas and losing the valuable tool.

Without thinking, Toby jumped up and chased the flying pigment down a grassy hill, racing toward the edge of the woods. "I'll get it," he cried into the wind.

He seemed to be doing a lot of that lately. *What's with the wind?*

Patches of lightning lit his way, and just ahead he caught a glimpse of the wayward tube. He slid to his knees and scooped it up.

"Gotcha...*Ahhhhch!*" A searing pain shot into his right knee.

"Ahhhshoot," He looked at the tiny hole that appeared in the knee of his jeans. "Not one of those stinkin knee things again...I hate these things."

He plopped onto his butt and gingerly pulled back his pant leg to inspect a small, strawberry shaped wound.

"Hmmm, not too bad, I guess." He rolled his pant leg down and slowly rose to his feet. Looking at the tube in his hand, he noted that it was blue. "I hope you appreciate the sacrifices I've made for you, Ol' Blue."

He wasn't sure, - *not that he was sure of much, any more* - but he thought he felt some sort of vibration coming from within the tube, as if it were responding.

"Nah...I think I'm letting my head get away from me, here," he said.

Still, somewhere, in a corner of that head, he remembered someone saying: *"It can be whatever you imagine it to be."*

Toby shrugged and stuck the tube of paint into his back pocket.

"I better give this back before I start hearing more voices in my twisted bean brain."

He turned and took a painful step back up the brush strewn hill. "Man, that hurts a—" Then he stopped.

Somehow, he was no longer on the edge of the woods; instead, he found himself right smack in the middle of them. And, from where he stood, seeing nothing but a wall of trees, surrounded by a thick undergrowth of bramble and weeds, this didn't seem to be the place he most wanted to be, just now.

"Oh great...now this is just great. How do I get myself into these things? I'll never find my way out of here."

He could hear Billy Bartles laughing from wherever he was.

I wonder how those guys are. I hope Lori's okay...wherever wherever is.

Collecting himself, Toby reached into his pocket and pulled out the small sack of keys. He hoped they would give him a sign; point him in the right direction.

Zippo...the keys remained quiet, *silent as a tomb*, he thought. *Don't say tomb, Bonehead. I've got enough trouble here.*

He wanted desperately to find a way back to the painter. He liked it there; it seemed safe there. *I can learn so much from that man. How can I get back?*

But somehow, he didn't think he could go back. He doubted if the painter was even there anymore; if he *was* even real, at all.

Toby reached back to his pocket and felt for the tube of paint, expecting it to be gone. Surprisingly, it was not, and this reassured him.

He knew what he had to do: he had to move on, to see what lay ahead. So he gathered his courage and began to walk...further into the woods.

Just then, the quiet darkness was broken by an unearthly howl.

"Aoooooooooooooooooooooooooooooooooooh...!"

Toby's stomach froze in an icy swell of fear, and instinctively, he dropped into his favorite crouch position.

"Beware the full moon," he heard from somewhere in the recent past. *"It carries the sign of the wolf...it can mean...only death...."*

"Ha, the full moon," he said loudly, mocking the voice...mocking the woods. "There is no full moon...in fact, it's almost dawn...right?"

Cautiously, he peered up through a mix of dancing pine and churning clouds. What he found was a pitch-black sky...and a brilliant, *full moon*.

"Man...I knew it."

"It can be whatever you imagine it to be...." he heard that voice again.

"I'm gonna cream whoever said that to me."

"Ahoooooooooooooooooooooooooooooh...!"

Toby spun in small erratic circles. *Which direction should I go? It all looks the same.*

"Ahoooooooooooooooooooooooooooooh!"

"I think I'll just go in the opposite direction from wherever that thing is coming from. I know it's just a bad figment of my imagination...but—"

He suddenly heard the sound of heavy brush, thrashing...the ugly snapping of twigs and branches.

"—I have an excellent imagination!" he sprang like a frightened rabbit, deeper into the shrouded woods.

Something...something out there, low to the ground, is hauling butt through the forest and heading in my direction.

He ran until he thought he had enough stitches in his sides to hold the *Frankenstein* monster together...*don't say Frankenstein!*

But still, the thing came. He felt it's hot, musty breath on the back of his neck.

"Have to stop...have to hide," he panted.

Off to his right he saw a thick stand of bushes. *Probably some sort of poison ivy. But, better to itch to death than be eaten alive by some monster.*

He made a beeline for the bushes and quickly dove behind, cursing his screaming knee.

Now, the woods were completely hushed. Even the wind had ceased, leaving only the sound of his pounding heart. He thought it threatened to wake the dead. *Don't say dead, idiot!*

He squatted, and tried willing his heart to stop; *although*, he thought, *the way things were going, I may not have to worry about that much longer.*

SNAP...!

Something *was* out there. Something smart was sneaking up on him. Smelling him out.

"Rroooowwwl"

A low guttural snarl vibrated through the pit of Toby's stomach. Was it him or..."*it*"?

"Grooooowwwl"

He concluded it was "*it*".

He decided to be brave - *or stupid* - and peeked out around the bush.

"Oh man, I was afraid of something like this...why me?" he whispered.

Crouched directly in front of him, but looking away - looking *for...dinner* - was some sort of...hairy thing...some sort of hairy, *Wolfman* thing, with your basic *Wolfman* fangs.

But, he thought, *there's something wrong with this* thing...*something not quite right.*

"Holy Lugosi," Toby whispered, still eyeing the *Wolfman*. "This is great, just great...now I've got the *Wolfman* after me. How weird is this?"

"It's as weird as you want it to be," said that annoying voice again.

"Right," Toby answered, looking up toward the trees. When he looked back, the *Wolfman* was gone.

"Hey...where's *Wolfie*?" All was quiet...too quiet, he thought...deadly quiet.

"I don't like this...at all."

Then, suddenly, the *Wolfman* pounced.

"*Ahhhhhhhh!*" Toby screamed...the thing was suddenly on him...everywhere, slobbering over everything.

"Oh man, is this gross or what," he desperately tried to push the beast away.

Wolfman sprang to his feet, yanked Toby off the ground and shook him like a rag doll. Toby thought he was toying with him, waiting for the kill. *Probably gonna bite my head off or something.* His senses numbed with fear.

Wolfman pushed his dripping snout directly into Toby's face and let loose a tremendous roar.

"Ahooooooooooooooooooooooooooooooh!"

"Oh man, talk about bad breath. Do you ever brush...I mean at all...."

The Wolfman answered with another tremendous howl....

"Ahoooooooooooooooooooooooooooooh!"

"Just...kidding...."

...and savagely flung Toby up and over the bushes.

Toby fell hard to the ground and lay motionless, curled in a ball. The Wolfman scampered over, poking and sniffing his prey.

Nothing...Toby was lifeless as a stone.

The Wolfman howled- *"Aowwwwwwwwwwww!"* - stretched upward, preparing to go in for a feeding frenzy.

Suddenly, Toby lashed out with an old, petrified tree branch and landed a solid shot to Wolfman's mid-section.

"Ahoooohumph...!" the beast spat out, then doubled over, and fell onto the ground, gasping.

"Ha...!" Toby shouted triumphantly. "Fell for the old decoy move."

The Wolfman struggled for air and rasped, to Toby's utter amazement, *"Decoy move...banned...long ago...."*

Toby glared at the beast. "Huh...?" Then decided he better just run, before this thing gets its wind back.

And run he did, deeper and deeper, into the forest. Behind him, the footsteps had returned...coming faster ...faster. He guessed Wolfie's break was over.

Toby tore around another stand of trees and turned down a more heavily wooded trail, hoping to conceal himself in the tangle of vegetation. He looked over his shoulder, happy to discover that his Wolf friend was out of sight.

"I need a door...any door will do...door number one, two, or three...please just show me a door!"

Have to keep running, he said to his brain. *Have no choice...it's still coming...hear it coming.*

Suddenly, his foot hooked onto of an errant root and Toby went sprawling over an assortment of fallen branches and miscellaneous rocks. Finally, he crashed to a stop against an old toppled tree.

"That's it...enough...I give up...come and get it furry," he muttered weakly. He just didn't care anymore. He couldn't move and he was paralyzed with fear.

He saw the Wolfman coming, slowly moving up to the salad bar, smacking its lips. It was in no rush...no rush at all. It knew he was done. The running was over.

It was then, that Toby suddenly *knew* what it was...what was *wrong* with the Wolfman. He didn't see it before, but now, he knew...*he knew*: the Wolfman is in *black and white*. Black and white...*like an old movie. He even has film scratches...running all over him.*

Suddenly, he remembered his Mom...how she put the kibosh on his precious remote control.

"You're not real," he said loudly. "You're just a bad flick that I saw on TV. And all I have to do...is pull the plug."

And with that, the Wolfman transformed into fuzzy, white video noise...and disappeared.

"I watch *too much* TV," Toby said....

Then, closed his eyes.

Chapter 20

"You know, Musso, I could have done so much more. I could have gone right to the top, if I had the right opportunities. Why, I see these young whippersnappers today kissing everyone's butt. It's a wonder they—"

"Malok, please. Try not to expend your energy on such useless prattle," Musso said. He was doing his best to get the pair back to *Castle Keys*.

It was not a particularly strenuous journey, but Musso could see that his friend, Malok, was having his difficulties. "You must save your strength for the King."

"Ha...the King...that old wind bag. Just look at all the trouble we're in because of him."

Malok began to mock the King.

"Time, time, time...who needs time. I banish time from the Kingdom of Keys. It shall therefore now be a timeless realm. You all have only to live your lives and fulfill your purpose. Time no longer matters...blah... blah...blah...blah...

Musso was alarmed by Malok's condition. "Malok, please...you don't know what you're—"

"Oh sure...easy for him to say...he's the friggin King...I should be the King, you know. Then you'd see this mess get turned around...I coulda...I shoulda...I woulda...if I only—"

"Malok, please! Listen to yourself...!" Musso shouted. He grabbed Malok by the collar and shook him violently. "Please listen to yourself!"

Malok lost his balance and fell backwards. He landed squarely in the middle of the road where a cloud of dust rose around him and he began to sneeze.

"Ahchoooooo...ahchooooo....ahchoooo...."

Musso pulled a cloth from his pocket and stuffed it against Malok's nose. Malok took the cloth and buried his face in it.

"Regret, Musso," he said quietly. "I have the *regrets*. *Icouldashouldaswouldas*. My mind feels heavy; it weighs on my thoughts."

"Well, perhaps it's just the dust," Musso replied, a false cheerfulness coated his words. "We *have* been through quite a bit."

"No Musso, it's not dust, or confusion. We both have known all along...deep down, we knew. It's Tkler. It's time. I've been infected."

Musso protested. "It's not fair Malok, why has this happened to you?"

"Me? Why not me, Musso? It's *happened* to so many, why not me. Is there one of us, who has not thought of *everyone else* as the `other one'. It's always a bit of a surprise to find out that we are, *all*, just the `other one', too."

"But Malok, if only we—"

"Careful, my good friend. You are beginning to sound regretful."

"Oh my," Musso raised his hand to his lips, trying to restrain the words.

"Come Musso...we have a King to see. All is not lost, not yet. There is still the boy. I have a good feeling about this boy."

"The *Foretelling*," Musso said quietly.

"Yes," Malok answered. "The *Foretelling*...."

....*tic,tic,tic,tic,tic,tic,tic,tic,tic,tic,tic*....

Chapter 21

Toby's mind stirred then slowly surfaced from a deep, dreamless sleep. He flipped over onto his back, made a strange smacking noise with his lips, then slowly opened his piercing blue eyes.

"Man, I think I was out like a light."

Yawning, he turned his head and rubbed his nose directly into an unpleasant pillow of moss and mold.

"Ugh...what the...."

Suddenly, a series of bizarre images flashed through his brain. His body tensed, every muscle ready to spring.

"Wolfman!"

Then, just as suddenly, another image overtook the former and pushed it aside. The Wolfman...slowly dissolving...into television fuzz. His body relaxed and a huge grin spread across his face.

Energized by a jolt of confidence, Toby scrambled to his feet and swallowed a huge breath of pine soaked air; his spirit soared.

"Come on...give me some more...I can take anything you've got here...but, uh...maybe first I should figure out...*where's here*."

Walking a bit further into the clearing he found himself standing in the middle of a crossroads; three distinct paths converged, then went their separate ways.

Undaunted, he checked out his choices - *this way or that...or maybe there* - then arbitrarily picked a direction, and marched ahead.

"All paths lead to Rome," he remembered from some old history lesson. "Or do they just *roam*...ha, get it roam...*Rome*...uhm, maybe not. I think Billy Bartles has given me his brain drain."

As he walked, he noticed that the wound on his knee had entered the painful, scabby phase, stretching and tightening the skin. His instinct was to favor the sore with a limp, but, instead, he walked at an accelerated pace, determined not to let a little cut slow him up.

It was funny, but for the first time, in a long time, he actually knew that things were going his way. Compared to last night, the forest couldn't be any friendlier. It was daylight now, and streams of dappled sunlight pierced through the thick forest canopy. A slight breeze nipped his back, and as he walked further down the trail, Toby thought he actually heard the sound of birds singing in the distance.

Feeling a little smug, he proclaimed, "I think I'm finally starting to get the hang of this place."

Several surreptitious twists and turns eventually took him down a path that appeared to have seen its share of traffic over the years. A worn, dusty trail blazed down its middle, screaming, ***"THIS WAY ...TAKE ME...I'M SAFE!"***

There was no doubt left to chance. No unexpected demons lurking ahead...or behind.

"Yep, things are definitely looking up," he said. "Nothing but clear sailing ahead."

So, it seemed a bit peculiar that he chose, just then, to leave the path of certainty, and head off, inexplicably, back into the dark, unknown woods.

"Gotta go for it, Tubman," he said to himself. "This just feels right."

But what it actually felt like was a jungle...and Toby plunged into a wall of dead, stale air, wrapped in a wet blanket of heat and humidity.

He scanned the trees, expecting to see some sort of ape man, commuting on a vine.

"You Tarzan...me nuts...." he mused, but eventually determined: *no swingers...not today, anyway.*

Toby shrugged and decided to plow ahead. He figured, at best, the thick undergrowth was a challenge; at worst, a lethal error.

And it was definitely a struggle; an endless struggle, constantly pulling at vines and knocking back foliage, all the way. Every step brought another drop of perspiration, streaking his face and staining his shirt in a thick pattern of sludge.

Man, maybe this was a mistake. I could be lost in here forever. What made me think I'd find a stupid door way out here? Maybe I should've stayed on the path. I mean, if it was good enough for everybody else....

A horde of doubts cluttered his mind. "I gotta get out of here...be anywhere...but here," his breaths were short and erratic.

Just then, ready to give up, his desperation about to win, Toby spotted a small waterfall emptying into a pool of liquid salvation.

"It's like all you have to do is think about it...and there it is," he heard Billy say through a mouthful of burgers.

He grinned and approached the pool.

Several craggy outcroppings jutted from the pool's grassy banks and extended over shadowy areas that suggested a considerable depth. Toby walked out on one of these extensions and dropped to his knees.

"Ahhhchh," he had reopened his scabbed up wound. "Oh man...that hurts." He examined his knee and saw the beginnings of an infection starting to blossom. "This could get ugly."

He cupped his hand and scooped some cool water into his mouth.

"Whoa...does that tastes good or what. I can't remember ever being so thirsty."

The water ran from his palm, dribbled down his chin and onto his shirt. He took another handful and poured it onto his knee - "Man, that stings" - then sat back and enjoyed the tranquil effects of the waterfall.

"Now this is something I could get used to."

The cool spray carried on a freshening breeze and washed away his weariness; again, his confidence returned. He toyed with the idea of taking a dip and gazed into the pool's clear surface.

"I wonder how deep this thing really is."

Leaning closer to the edge, he noticed his reflection slowly taking form in the settling water - "Hey good lookin ...what's cookin?" - then fussed with his grimy hair. Only...the reflection that he saw, or thought he saw, was not exactly the one he had expected.

"Whosawhatsa!" His hands fell from his hair and grabbed hold of the rock. "Whatsawhosa!"

Instead of the familiar blue eyed mug that faithfully gawked back at him from the bathroom mirror on countless mornings, Toby stared into the face of someone else...someone older. Older than he was, at least. It was the face of a man; a face...filled with confidence.

Every muscle in his body froze, paralyzed by the startling image. Suddenly, his hand broke free and plunged into the water, stirring the surface into a broken mass of expanding ripples. When the water resettled he was relieved to see his own reliable, cautious face, creeping back over the edge.

"I must be thirstier than I thought," he said, and dunked his entire head straight into the pool.

Just then, the sack of keys awoke and filled his pocket with warmth.

Still submerged, inhaling a gallon of water, Toby opened his eyes, and gurgled, "Uh oh."

His eyes darted back and forth, scanning the pool's gloomy depths...*for what?* But he thought he knew. Then, he saw it...in the distance...a small opening; more hatch than a door, nestled in the far corner, a soft, green light, spilling from its keyhole.

"Double uh, oh." Toby yanked his head from the water.

"You don't suppose?"

A familiar bolt of light shot from his pocket and blazed into the pool.

Toby reached into his pocket, fumbled a bit, then finally, grabbed the sack.

"I do suppose." he said, feeling its amazing warmth. He opened the sack and removed a shimmering key.

"Owww...Hot stuff!"

The searing key singed his fingers and splashed into the pool; sizzling, it left a trail of phosphorescent bubbles in its wake.

Jumping to his feet, Toby followed the bubbles, anxiously watching the key - *his key* - sink deeper and deeper...slowly drifting away.

"I guess...it's everybody into the pool," he whispered, then executed a perfect dive.

Slicing gracefully through the surface, he squinted through the muted light and saw the escaping key, up ahead, still burning a bright emerald green.

Then, with one strong sweep of his arms, he waved the surrounding water aside, and without hesitation, grabbed the wayward key and smiled.

Toby located the small hatchway, a short distance away. Knowing what he had to do, he swam toward it, amazed he still didn't need to breathe.

He wasn't sure just how long this particular trick would last so he immediately inserted the key.

The hatch offered no resistance as it opened toward him. Still, not entirely convinced, Toby floated at the threshold and cautiously studied the opening.

He saw literally nothing on the other side.

I always said I wasn't afraid of nothing....

He heard his mother's voice correcting him. *Anything, Toby. You're not afraid of anything...not nothing.*

Same thing, Mom, it's still only nothing...right?

He nodded a silent affirmation and swam through. The door slowly closed behind him.

He emerged into a deep, inky darkness; the only sensation he felt was of a tremendous pressure building in his ears. He spun around in every direction, but, despite his inner panic, he remained calm.

This is not good. I'm still under water. In fact, way under water.

Needing to do something - anything - to relieve the awful pounding in his skull, he pinched his nose and blew out, making sure to keep his mouth tightly closed. But, it didn't seem to help.

I am definitely gonna drown here, although, surprisingly, he still didn't feel the need for air. Not yet, anyway.

But something was wrong. He was disoriented, finding it difficult just to find up. He was sure he had entered the hatch horizontally; it stood flat, against the bank. Yet, on this side, he had come out vertically; the hatch lay on the bottom.

Which way is up? It's all just one dark mess....

Then, staring straight ahead, he saw the flicker of what he hoped was daylight, rippling through the surface.

Doesn't take a genius to figure out that that might be the direction to go...at least for now.... Toby gathered himself, grabbed a foothold on the soft muddy bottom and pushed off. Then, keeping his cool, but conscious of the anxiety that threatened his plan, he forced himself to take slow methodical strokes, kicking his legs in strong rhythmic bursts.

I guess all those hours in the Y really paid off, after all....

He swam steadily for what seemed like miles, miles of nothingness; no fish, no rocks, no vegetation...not even a bubble. Through it all, he kept his focus square on the approaching light. And the closer the light became, the greater became his desire for air...until soon, he thought his lungs might actually burst.

So, this is what it really feels like to drown.

Then, suddenly, the light was everywhere, wrapping around him like a cosmic lifeline, drawing him to the top. Closer and closer...his body screaming for air...until....

...Toby burst through the surface, like a big clumsy fish. Long beads of water flew from his hair, streamed from his clothes, and glistened in the late afternoon sun.

"I made it." he gasped, flapping his arms and kicking his legs. "Gotta slow down...gotta rest...breathe ...again...."

Struggling, trying to regain his strength, he eased onto his back, and began to float. *Since when can I float on my back. I've never been able to float on my back.*

Stretched out like a pontoon he found a patch of lazy clouds, passing over head; a low, brilliant sun warmed his face...and he breathed...and he breathed...and he breathed....

After a short while, his heaving chest settled into an unconscious rhythm of inhale...exhale, inhale...exhale.

"I guess the first thing you should do is get out of the water, before you remember that you usually sink like a stone," he remarked to himself.

"My thoughts exactly, dear fellow," he responded in turn, then righted himself and slowly paddled over to the shore. A whiff of cool air skimmed the surface and made him feel alive.

From this point of view, he surmised that he was in the middle of some sort of large lake, or pond.

You know, there's something about this place...that seems familiar...too familiar.

Anxious to reach solid ground, he made a strong final push until his feet caught the pond's spongy bottom.

"At least now I have a leg to stand on, or at least something to stand my legs on...or something like that...but I babble."

Completely wiped, he dragged his waterlogged body onto a small strip of sand and immediately collapsed.

Suddenly, it dawned on him...*It's The Lake.* He sat up on his elbows. *I'm back at The Lake...again. But still, it's not exactly The Lake...is it?*

He had to admit there were *some* similarities, but this lake, besides being ten times larger, was surrounded by a series of soft hills, sloping swiftly upward toward the forest. Excepting this small spit of sand, the uneven shoreline consisted of a band of smooth, white, rounded stones.

Instead of toxic green, the color of the water was a clean sparkling blue...and there didn't appear to be any nasty weeds growing in it...or on it.

The sweet aroma of a wood fire drifted by. Someone was nearby, and while it was comfortable in the sun, Toby thought that a nice warm fire sounded even better.

He followed his nose toward The Lake's farthest corner, and he immediately saw a column of smoke rising against an endless sky.

Tracing the column down to its source, he thought he spied a small shack, or cabin. It was nestled on a hill, in a forested spot, just above the shore.

"Hmmmm...I think I'll go a vestigatin," Toby said. "Maybe it's another painter."

He stepped off the little strip of beach, on to the little white stones and set off down the shoreline.

Off to his left, back in the woods, he saw a rabbit scurry through the brush.

To his right, at the lake's shallow edge, he noticed a small school of fish, darting around a boulder.

Up above, a pair of black birds fluttered their wings, swooped by, and disappeared over the trees.

He wasn't sure why, but these simple little things made him smile.

The first of two thoughts suddenly hit him: his knee didn't hurt anymore; he still had the tiny tear in his jeans, but it seemed the wound had healed.

Maybe closing that door...left it all behind.

173

Then the second: *the trees were starting to shed.*

Somehow, the seasons had changed...right past spring, fast-forward through summer...and now...it was fall, with waves of colorful leaves, sailing to the ground.

"Awesome...I wish I had a football!" Toby said loudly.

"Well, well, well, what have we here? A visitor, I surmise. And a soggy one at that," said an unusual looking fellow standing up by the shack. "Come on up here, lad. Sit and dry yourself a spell. A little late to go a swimming, but I know the allure the pond can have on a body."

"Thank you," Toby said. He walked up the hill, back into the woods.

More woods...what's with the woods?

He found a small, handmade chair, next to a crackling campfire and sat. "This fire is great...toasty."

"I have a beauty of a hearth inside, too," the man boasted. "Built it myself. Kept me as warm as a bug, all winter. Kept the bugs warm too, for that matter. Nope, not a single complaint from any of my tenants. Yep, a fair landlord am I."

Toby smiled at the peculiar man with the wild shock of dark hair, sort of like that "Kramer" guy on TV. He was neatly dressed, although his clothes were mostly worn and strewn with tidy patches. The man appeared old to Toby, yet the sparkle of youth danced in his eyes.

The man put down his hammer and poured a strange, thickish liquid into a rough pottery cup. Toby hoped it wasn't targeted for him.

"Here you go, young man. Try some of this. Concocted it myself. Better than any coffee bean you've ever tasted."

"Uh...thank you," Toby said. He reluctantly took the cup, not wanting to offend his host.

"Go on boy, bottoms up. You'll warm to it in no time, as it warms to you."

Toby hoisted the steaming liquid up to his lips and blew.

I notice you're not drinking any. What are those...chunks or something...floating around in there, or what?

Cautiously, he sipped, and was pleasantly surprised by the sweet, smooth taste of the lumpy brew. He gulped a larger swallow.

"Whoa...slow down, Toby, or you'll scald your tongue. Then you won't be able to taste anything for a week."

"This is good stuff," Toby said. "What is it?"

"Oh, just a little something I picked up from some native writings I stumbled on in the local library. It's the Molasses that makes it just so...and...the price is right."

"*Come on down,*" Toby said, mimicking the television announcer.

The man twirled around, looking up toward the trees. "Where...who are you talking to? Who's up there?"

"Huh," Toby said. "Nobody's up there. You know, like the TV show."

"TV?"

"Never mind," He remembered where he was. "It's not important."

"Quite," the man said.

"Right," Toby responded.

"Of course, I don't usually do it with my clothes on."

"Huh?" Toby was a bit confused again.

"Bathe...in the pond. Swim...with my clothes on. I'm want to take many a dip, even at this time of year. But, never fully clothed. Though I suppose they could stand for a washing."

"Oh," Toby said. "I don't know. I guess something just told me to do it."

The man smiled broadly, "I understand."

He had the easiest manner of anyone Toby had ever known. Nothing seemed to surprise or bother him.

"How did you know my name?" Toby asked.

"Oh, I don't know. I suppose it comes with the territory."

"I suppose," Toby said.

"If you'd like, you can hang your belongings on the line. They'll probably dry faster. I have some spares."

"Uh, no thanks," Toby said, vaguely recalling a long ago dream. "I think I'll hang on to my clothes."

"Of course, suit yourself."

Toby took another gulp of the delicious brew, while all around, silence drifted to the earth on the backs of falling leaves.

"It's very peaceful here," Toby said. "I used to play here all the time, when I was a kid."

"Ah, then. So you're from the village."

"No, I don't think so," Toby answered. "I don't think I'm from anywhere around here."

"I see," the man said. "Well, I suppose the serenity of the pond is as much a matter of the mind, as well as its own natural beauty. Another pond may be just as serene to another man, as mine is to me. You might say there is a universal pondness."

"Right, a universal pondness," Toby repeated, with just a hint of amusement.

"On the other hand, another man...a man of industry, perhaps, may find my pond to be maddening and repulsive."

"If you say so," Toby said. Although he didn't quite understand the point the man was getting at. "Do you live out here...all alone?"

"Oh no, not at all. I have a great deal of company in my house, especially in the morning, when nobody calls."

"Ooookeeey," Toby shifted a little uncomfortably.

"I'm as alone as the loon in the pond, or as the pond itself for that matter," the man continued.

Toby nodded, beginning to understand. "Sometimes, I just like to think, too. Sometimes, I think I think too much."

"Ah, but you can never think too much," the man replied. "Most don't want to think at all; to experience; to discover. They just want it all to be as it is...stay as it was.

"Leave the thinking to the philosophers, they say. I have much too much to do, other than think, they proclaim!"

"You think so?" Toby smirked.

The man smiled back. "Yes, indeed I do. But all's the pity, I say. That much more for the rest of us to chew."

"Sometimes, I make myself crazy thinking...I don't know...crazy things," Toby said.

"Ah, well, the key, however, is not to let the thoughts do the thinking. Always make sure the mind is the master."

Toby thought of the painter. "But what about the heart? What about the...soul? Aren't those our truest feelings? Don't they control our thoughts?"

The man paused, considered his words, then answered. "But, isn't our heart...our soul, really just the deepest part of our minds, Toby. Why it's a true gift just to be able to understand that it exists.

"Some are never able to reach it. Others have the strength, to push through the clutter, but are afraid to tap in to its bountiful reservoir. It somehow seems untamed...unpredictable.

"Still, others make their peace with it. Some early...some later.

"That then, is the true gift. And those lucky ones...they are never alone."

"Go with the flow...bro," Toby said absently.

"Interesting," the man said.

"But, even this stuff...it's enough to make yourself a little loopy thinking about it."

"Loopy?" the man said.

"You know...a little nutty," Toby again thought of the painter.

"Only when we let our thoughts, take control, Toby. Only when we allow doubt and fear to take a foothold. Only if we stop...*believing*."

"In the gift...in our heart...our soul?" Toby asked.

"In ourselves," the man answered.

Toby turned and gazed deeply into the fire. "Far out," he whispered.

The man stoked the coals and sent a column of large orange sparks, soaring toward the treetops. He reached down and threw a handful of dry leaves onto the embers, instantly producing a blaze.

"Ah, nothing like the smell of burning leaves in the autumn to stir your senses," he said.

"It's against the law where I come from," Toby said. "Air pollution or something."

"Indeed," the man said. "Though I doubt it's leaves that's to blame."

"I guess. So what is it that you do out here in the woods...besides think, I mean?"

"Well, aside from tending to my everyday chores, which can keep a soul quite occupied, I might add, I put pen to paper quite often."

"You're a writer," Toby said, more as a statement than a question.

"I like to express myself...my thoughts. Perhaps I can humbly open a door or two for others...if they're looking, that is."

"Wow...I've never met a writer before, let alone a philosopher. What do you write about? Do you make lots of money?"

"Experience mostly. How I feel...about this place and other things. And no, not much at all."

"Not much of what?" Toby asked.

"I don't make much money from my writing. I've sold the occasional article, of course, but other than that...."

"Then why do you do it...why do you write?"

"Because I am a writer...it's what I do. If I didn't, I would burst from within."

"But don't you have to do some sort of work...you know, to make money...to make a living?"

"It's not money that makes a living, Toby. It's living that makes a living. Living is a full time job in itself. And one that is handled pretty shabbily by most, I'm afraid."

"Yeah but—" Toby tried to interject.

"I live a life, right here," continued the writer. "In fact, I consider myself to be the rarest of all things...*a happy man.*"

"But don't you want some money to buy things with? Stuff to make you more comfortable."

"I have mostly all that I need, right here, all around me. Those things, that nature can't provide, I obtain by teaching the land to say beans instead of grass...and then off to market I go. Occasionally, I lend a hand to a fellow farmer and receive compensation in the way of barter, and sometimes, cash."

Toby mulled this over but found it difficult to digest.

"Wait a minute. You mean that all you need to be happy is this little shack, a few beans and some books?"

"House, please...I prefer little house. You see, I think it best, in a simple world, to keep things...simple, simple, simple."

"That's three words," Toby interrupted.

"Ah, an observant lad," the man quipped.

"If you really want to keep it simple, why not say it once," Toby teased.

The man grinned.

"Sorry, I get a little carried away sometimes," Toby said. "Please go on."

"And, of course, I have all of this." The Writer spread his arms. "All that I see, I possess. What more can a man, ask?"

"Wide screen HDTV with surround sound mega bass stereo...anything with an "i" in front of it...whatever cool sneaker is hot...you know...stuff...."

"Toby, do you really think that it's *stuff* that makes people happy?"

"I don't know. It seems to make most of the people I know happy."

"What about you...do those things bring you happiness?"

"No, not really...I guess."

"Is it in the stuff that your friends find pleasure ...or is it *one upping* everybody else. Being the best on the block and so on."

"I guess that's most of it...yeah."

"So it's the competition...to do better...have more than everybody else?"

"I guess...but—"

"And how long does this kind of happiness last?"

"Until you find another guy doing better, jumping higher, running faster, blasting louder...than you."

"And how do you feel then?"

"Frustrated...lousy."

"And what feeling seems to last the longest...cut the deepest?"

"Lousy."

"Makes you think, doesn't it?"

Toby slumped back in his chair, "I think too much."

"Yes, you said that before. Do you think too much or...regret too much?"

"Huh?"

"You know, dwell on things long past, things that can never be again."

"I don't know, I—"

"Why look backward, where you've been, when there is so much to see ahead, where you're going."

Toby turned back to the fire. His head was starting to pound. He wanted to lie down for a while. He was so tired....

...He was startled out of his stupor by the sudden sound of hammering. He turned to his right, where the man had been sitting; it seemed, just a moment ago. Now he was gone.

Toby spun around and found the man sitting atop his roof, hammering away.

"Oh, sorry," the man said. "I didn't mean to startle you. You looked lost in yourself, so I thought it wise to let you chew for a while. I've got to tend to my leaky roof. Best to do it now, before the winter sets in. It comes fast to these parts."

Toby took a sip from the pottery cup and spit its icy contents into the fire. "Ugh...gross!"

"Doesn't taste as good once the heats gone from it, does it?" the man asked.

"No...no, it doesn't," Toby sputtered and spit some more. He got up, looking for something to rinse his mouth.

"Looks like your clothes have dried quite nicely too," the man said.

Toby reached down. *Bone Dry*, he thought. *Just how long have I been sitting here...chewing?*

He forgot the nasty taste in his mouth and walked up to the tiny cabin. It was in no way primitive; the man obviously knew a bit about carpentry.

"I used to love to camp when I was a kid," Toby said.

"And, you don't anymore?" the man asked.

"Well, I haven't gone in quite a while."

"I have a feeling you will again...if you want to."

"Maybe...someday," Toby said.

"Are you at all handy with tools?" the man asked.

"A little...if I want to be," Toby said.

"Well, climb up here then. I could use another set of hands...if you want to be, of course," the man shot back.

Toby smiled and jumped up the ladder and onto the roof.

The man once again hammered away wildly, "I'm not much of a skilled, artistic carpenter, but what I don't know, I beat into submission. I find beauty in function, not in form. Don't you agree?"

Toby watched while the man created a sort of patchwork design of shingles. "I suppose if it keeps you dry, who cares what it looks like?"

"Exactly," the man positioned another hand cut shingle.

"What do your neighbors think of you, living out here like this?"

"Oh, I suppose those that feel the need to voice an opinion, or hold a judgment, think I'm a bit on the odd side. That my time might be better spent securing some sort of future.

"I ask them...should I sacrifice a certain here and now, for an uncertain future?"

"What do they say?" Toby asked.

"Well, they merely huff and walk away, declaring me an idler and a shirker."

"I know the feeling," Toby said.

"Do you know what I really think bothers them?" the Writer said.

"What?"

"That I get away with it...survive...and they can't. Not that they couldn't."

"If they wanted to," Toby shot in.

"Exactly," the man said. "If they wanted to, they certainly could. But, they've convinced themselves that they *need*...as much as they can get."

"But don't people have different needs? Aren't we all different?"

"Of course...as different as there are stars. I would no more force my wants on another as I would have them force theirs on me."

"The...*key*," Toby interjected. "Is knowing *what* we need, and doing *whatever's* necessary, to make sure that we get it. As much or as little. No more...no less."

"Say," the man was clearly impressed with Toby's insight. "There is much evidence of a mind at work here."

Toby blushed but was prouder than he had ever been in his life.

"Most of my neighbors," the man continued. "Exhaust themselves from dawn to dusk...and then some more, in the pursuit of happiness. They think it's necessary to sweat in order to succeed. Well, I say, they must sweat easier than I."

"You must have a great antiperspirant," Toby interrupted.

"Interesting," the man said, then continued, "Some are strapped to the yoke of their ox, while others are strapped to the yoke of their greed. It's all the same.

"If they stopped to plow their minds, they might find that the happiness that eludes them, in fact, belongs to someone else. While all the time, their own, stood simple and true, before them.

"If the drum they tried a marchin to didn't match their stride, perhaps there was a different drum to be found."

Toby's eyes widened in recognition. "You mean it makes more sense to find our own rhythm, and then find the drum to match it."

"Exactly."

"But then, why do so many people follow the same path, the same old beat? Are they all wrong?"

"No, of course not," the man answered. "Who's to say that they aren't following the true course of their lives. I'm not speaking of those that are happy in their endeavors; and indeed, only they know if they are truly happy. I speak of the discontented. Those that lead lives of quiet desperation. Those that boast of happiness, but are resigned to the truth, in the emptiness of night...in the emptiness of their souls."

"Why do they do it...it all seems so obvious?" Toby asked. "Why do they deny the obvious."

"Because it's always safer to travel the known path. It takes a brave man to navigate the unknown. Fear can turn day into night."

"And the night can last forever." Toby said, quietly.

"If we all traveled, only by day—" the man started.

"—Then we wouldn't need light bulbs." Toby concluded.

"Interesting." the man said.

"How do we know if we're really happy?" Toby asked.

"How do we know if we're really hungry?" the Writer answered.

"It's that simple? Toby asked.

"As night turns to day."

A breeze stirred the treetops and Toby looked toward the sky; unsettled clouds had lumbered in, hastening the inevitable twilight.

Yet, Toby felt far from unsettled. It was all beginning to make sense. He was starting to fit the pieces together of what had been, up until now, his puzzling life.

"Speaking of night," the Writer said. "It looks as if it's fast approaching. I lose all track when I find a welcome ear."

Off in the distance, lightning pierced the darkening sky and the familiar sound of rolling thunder broke through the tranquility of the woods.

"Sounds like a storm's a brewin," the Writer said. "I think we best get off this roof and test our work indoors."

Toby sensed that his time with this wonderful man would soon come to an end. But, before it did, he was anxious to learn as much as he could; to greet whatever lay ahead; to find the next door. He was flowing with excitement.

"Tell me about your writing...what does it feel like...where does it come from...is it hard to do...what kinds of things do you write about...?"

"Well," the man stepped into the little house. "At the moment, I'm writing about a river trip I made with my brother, a few years back...you see...."

A trail of dust swirled on the wind and the man closed the door.

Chapter 22

The effects of Tkler's malady had clearly taken its toll; everywhere Malok and Musso turned they encountered undeniable evidence of the devastation of Keys.

Fields, once lush and fruitful, had grown brown and dry; crops, once bountiful and ripe, had withered and died.

The dusty roads they traveled were speckled with time weary farmers, who sat idly by on splintered stoops, counting regrets, lacking the strength to continue.

The weight of time had crushed them, robbed them of their will.

There was no purpose...no purpose to it, at all.

The worn out travelers absorbed it all yet remained steadfast in their task. Malok's condition had weakened considerably in the course of the journey, but he insisted that he be present when the King was told. After all, it was he, as well as Musso, who was entrusted with this very special assignment, by the King himself.

Overhead, storm clouds masked the skies and the ever present ticking, filled their lumberous ears.

"Come Malok, we're almost to the gates. I can see Tolmar ahead."

"Oh, the great Tolmar...the King's attendant, first musician of the Kingdom...and scholar of the Foretelling. Well, foretell this, Tolmar."

Musso cringed. "Malok please, he might hear you."

Malok merely sighed, "You know, Musso, I would have made a fine musician. I have always felt the notes in a way that most never do."

"Oh come now, Malok. You couldn't carry a tune in a basket, if you tried," Musso replied. "I've heard your song after a bit of brew confection. It's enough to make one of purpose cry."

"Exactly my point, Musso. I have the ability to move the soul."

"Malok, presently, you barely have the ability to move." Musso grunted, then placed his friend's arm around his shoulder and helped him to the gates.

"Greetings, Guidesmen," Tolmar spoke cheerfully, yet eyed the pair curiously. "How goes the most important assignment in all of Keys?"

"I'm afraid, Tolmar, we must see the King, immediately," Musso said.

"Tolmar, my good fellow...tell me. Do you not think I would have made an excellent musician? I mean, I know, now...it's too late...but given the right opportunity I—"

Tolmar's smile dropped from his face. He noticed Malok's graying pallor and covered his mouth with the cloth from his sleeve.

"He is infected, Musso...and you bring him to this castle. Isn't there enough sickness here, already?"

"Oh come now, Tolmar," Musso said. "You, most of all, know the disease cannot be transmitted. It must be directly assimilated...and then, there is the predisposition factor."

"That's what they say today," Tolmar said. "But what about tomorrow?"

Musso's eyes widened at Tolmar's temporal reference.

"Oh my!" Tolmar gasped. "I didn't mean that...did I?"

"Tolmar, you old crust of a— Take us to the King...we must report to the King." Malok announced.

"I'm afraid that will not be possible. The King is much too weak for visitors. Anything you have to report, you can report to me. I will see that he is informed."

"We lost the Queen," Musso said quietly. "And the girl...and the boy."

"The boy...the boy, Musso! You lost the boy!" Tolmar said.

"Not Toby, you old boneskull," Malok said, having been somewhat influenced by Billy Bartles, also. "The other one!"

"And Toby...what has become of Toby?"

"The Field of Doors," Musso said, holding his head high. "We took him to the Field of Doors."

"Then there is hope," Tolmar whispered. "Then there is hope."

Malok shook his head and eyed Tolmar with amusement. "He is just a boy."

"No," Tolmar said. "He is...*the boy.*"

The distinctive crack of thunder split the atmosphere and black clouds of doom, once again, rose over the distant mountains.

The three Keysians cowered and plugged their abundant ears, fending off sirens that began to wail throughout the Kingdom.

"Damn you Tkler," Malok shouted to the swirling skies. "You will not succeed...you will not have the boy!"

"Come...come in before it's too la—" Tolmar caught himself. "Come in. I will take you to the King. But I must warn you. He is not what he once was...it's rather...shocking...actually."

"I don't think any of us are what we once were, Tolmar," Musso replied.

"I was quite a tap dancer in my younger days," Malok said, cheerfully. "Why I could have been the premier tapper in all of Keys, if only—"

Musso threw up his hands. "Please Malok, not now." "We are going to see the King."

"Yes, the King," Malok said. "I'll dance for the King. I'll sing, too. I'll put on quite a show. Why there was a time I could have entertained a Kingdom."

"Hurry Tolmar, I think Malok is running out of ti—"

"Yes, Musso...I think we may all be."

Chapter 23

Lori slowly emerged from the serenity of her inner thoughts. She had never felt so at peace, yet, at the same time, she knew things were not quite as they should be.

Samira stood alone, by a withering tree, helplessly watching life evaporate from its mighty limbs.

She sensed that Lori had returned. "This tree had a noble purpose, Lori, but its true promise still lay ahead. This then is Tkler's curse."

"Samira!" Lori rushed to the Queen. "It was amazing. I was so...*content*. I was lying in a field of wild flowers...the sun was shining down...yet, it was as if *I* warmed the sun...*me*, from inside. It was like the last day of school and an entire summer lay ahead."

Emily yelped, "*Looooori*," then playfully folded into a ball and rolled to her friend.

A smile crossed Samira's lips. "Yes Lori, it is quite wonderful, isn't it. It really takes quite little to find serenity within. It's just a matter of knowing where to look."

"Man, that was great," Billy Bartles too had emerged from thought. "It was like I was locked in Mickey D's after closing...and all this food was cooked and ready to go...just sitting there...and you could eat anything, or everything, that you wanted...and all the video games were free...you didn't need any money or nothin...I'm tellin you, it was really amaz—"

Lori and Samira exchanged a glance and smiled at Billy's enthusiasm.

"Hey...what's going on here?" Billy asked. "Like, why is the great outdoors...indoors? Where the heck are we?"

Lori's smile faded. She suddenly recalled all that had happened.

"Toby...the Doors...the fire light...that terrible wind...Samira, what's happened to Toby?"

"Toby is safe within the Doors, Lori. Tkler can't reach him there. Not until he emerges. Then we shall see."

"How did we get in this place?" Billy asked. "The last thing I remember is the tornado...the ground shaking...and then...you know...Mickey D's heaven."

"Tkler's Hypo-spatial Transference," Samira answered. "The manipulation of not only time, but also space."

Billy scrunched his forehead with intrigue. "You mean he can just grab anything he wants, and take it?"

"I suppose it's all part of his ultimate plan, yes. But luckily, he still appears to be lacking the key to his fulfillment. Yet, I'm afraid his power grows every day, as ours weakens."

"Awesome," Billy was genuinely impressed by the possibilities of Hypo-spatial Transference.

"Billy!" Lori reproached.

"Sorry, Lor...but ya gotta be *wowed* with this guy Tkler. He seems to be putting a winning team together here."

"He won't win, Billy, he can't. Toby will help us."

"Lori...sometimes Toby can't even help himself."

"Billy, you *are* a horrible person."

"Just being realistic, Lor. I mean, I hope the old Tubman finds all the right doors and stuff...as much as anyone. He *is* my best friend, you know."

"Sometimes I wonder," Lori said.

"But, who knows what he's gonna run into out there. Who knows if he'll even go through with it...all the way? He could chicken out at any time. Who would blame him? Me ...I just want to go home...anyway I can."

"I know he will, Billy. I know Toby. I know what he has inside. He'll be back, and he'll have the key."

"Yeah, yeah the key. It's the stupid key that got us into this."

Just then, Tkler broke into the chamber. Billy and Lori stiffened.

"Ah, trouble in paradise, little ones. Things not going well?"

Lori and Billy gasped at the sight of Tkler's shadowy face. They were frozen by the sheer horror of it.

"Ugh...gross," Billy said.

"Samira..." Lori helplessly looked to the Queen.

"Don't let his vile appearance frighten you. It's merely a shield to keep others at a distance."

"At a distance from what?" Billy asked. "Who would want to get close to that."

"To shield his weakness," the Queen responded.

"I don't think this guy has any," Billy said.

Tkler bowed. "Welcome to Castle Endlum. If there is anything I can do to make your stay more comfortable, please feel free to ask."

Centurion burst through the portal, once again clutching his sides and gasping for breath.

"Ah, my good Centurion...lagging behind again, I see. Come, greet our guests. They were indisposed earlier, as you will recall."

"Remember the power," Samira said. "He cannot affect you if you use the power." But her words fell uselessly to the cold castle floor.

"I must say Samira. You underestimate me terribly. My powers can overcome any sort of mind trick you may try to hide behind. Why, don't you know, I have the power to move mountains."

The castle walls suddenly vibrated and cracked. Dust and rock tumbled to the surface. It seemed as if the whole world had suddenly shifted.

"Cool!" Billy cried.

"Yes," Tkler said. "Very *Cool*...indeed."

"What are you going to do to us?" Lori was trembling.

"Do...why would I *do* anything to you?" As he had done earlier Tkler lifted a long strand of Lori's shiny hair.

"Why I have only the best in mind for you, pretty little one. After all, you are the one who holds what is closest to the boy. You are the one who can access his heart...speak to his soul. For you, I have something very special in mind. Something I save for only those that are truly deserving. I am going to allow you to experience life...your life...*as it is...as it will be...as it might be*...again and again and again."

"Samira...what's he talking about?" Lori said. "Don't let him hurt me."

"Why, Tkler? Why must you derive your strength by making others weak? These young ones are meaningless to you. Why must you do this?" Samira pleaded.

"Oh come now, Samira. I think you know as well as I. What's important to the boy is important to me."

"His name is Toby. Why can't you bring yourself to speak his name?" Samira said sharply.

Tkler stared down into the eyes of the Queen. This time Samira couldn't bear it and turned away.

"That's so cool, Lori," Billy said. You get to experience your whole life. Don't you want to see how you're gonna turn out? Don't you want to know what it feels like to get old?"

"No...I don't. Not now...not this way," Lori said.

"Why not? It's not like you have to stay like that, or anything...you get to be yourself again. Right?" Billy glanced at Tkler.

Tkler's face was colored by an evil smirk. "Not quite, I'm afraid. You see, Hyper-Temprocity is quite irreversible. Old remains old...as remorse remains remorse."

"Ooooooh...not so cool," Billy said.

"Don't worry Billy. I have a much greater plan in store for you." Tkler enclosed his arm around Billy.

"Really...what sort of plan. Say, can I get me one of these cool looking outfits."

"Of course, Billy...anything you want. What color?"

"I think black is always cool, don't you?"

"Definitely...cool, Billy...definitely. Centurion...see that all is done." Tkler strode from the chamber with Billy under his fetid wing.

"Yes, my Lord," Centurion answered. "As you command."

"Samira," Lori cried. "Samira...."

Again, Samira stood silent, but a single tear fell from her eye.

Chapter 24

Toby sat by the warming glow of a plain, yet impressive hearth. The writer had prepared a simple stew, comprised of an assortment of nuts and possibly twigs...and some other ingredients that Toby didn't really want to know too much about. All that really mattered was that the food was hot, and it seemed to placate his angry stomach.

The storm continued to rage beyond the cabin's neatly constructed windows, but the patchwork roof repairs had done the trick and the rain stayed out, where it belonged.

After dinner, the pair sat, discussing sides and angles to issues that Toby had never dreamed existed.

I'm a long way from high school, he thought.

This fascinating man used his mind like the artist used his pallet. He was as comfortable discussing the human condition, as he was feeding a tiny field mouse, or watching armies of ants "fight to the death", as he put it.

"You can solve all of the mysteries you need, observing the brave battle of ants," he declared.

The Writer really did see the world in its simplest form. He took multitudes of man-made layers and simply peeled them away.

It was sort of like unraveling the mystery of a baseball. When you got to the middle, it really was just a cushioned cork center...like it always said on the outside cover, in the first place.

"Will you live like this forever?" Toby asked, putting his plate of stew to the side.

"Oh no, nothing lasts forever," the man replied. "I'll leave this place for the same reason that I came here. I suspect I have several more lives to live, and I don't want to miss them. When my time here is up...I'll know it. In fact, I believe it's not too far off."

Toby nodded in agreement.

Just then a strong gust of wind swept down the sturdy chimney and dispersed the dying embers.

"Well, it appears as if we need a bit more fuel for the hearth," the man said. "In my haste to repair a leaky roof, I neglected to re-stack."

"I'll do it." Anxious to repay his host in some way, Toby jumped up and grabbed the doorknob. "Which way do I go?"

The philosopher gave a crooked smile and replied. "Go confidently in the directions of your dreams, Toby."

Toby arched an eyebrow, "Uh, right. I'll just look around back."

Never expect a straight answer from a philosopher, he turned the knob and the wind caught hold of the door and whipped it open.

"Whew, a little gusty out there. This baby must have a good foundation." He scrunched his neck into his shirt and stepped outside.

Peering through the dark, he thought, *now, if I were a pile of wood where—* when suddenly, he heard the door of the cabin slam shut.

Toby spun around, "Hey...I don't see any wood—" and surprisingly - yet, not so surprisingly - the little house was gone...and with it, the man.

"—Out here," he quietly concluded.

Toby looked at the spot where the small cabin had stood. He had no regrets, only a deep satisfaction, and gratitude, for the hours he *did* spend with the writer.

"Time to move on," he said to no one in particular.

A voice echoed through the wind.

"Follow the direction of your dreams. Live the life you imagine...."

Toby smiled, then turned and walked confidently into the woods.

Chapter 25

Happy that the winds had finally quieted, Toby walked a mindless distance simply enjoying the serenity of the night. He reached around to his back pocket and felt for the small tube of blue paint. It was still there.

But what about the man by the pond? He hadn't taken anything to remind him of the Writer...*to prove that he was real.* But, then again, *I've taken more than I could ever hope to give back, haven't I?*

Up ahead, a tangle of trees opened into a clearing. A brilliant halo of light illuminated the space, and situated directly in its center, Toby spotted what he was apparently looking for: a semi-circle comprised of three individual doors.

He walked into the light and, immediately, the sack of keys began to glow.

"Gather round boys and girls. I think the fun is about to begin, again"

Inspecting the doors, he found nothing remarkable.

"I suppose the keys will tell me which one to choose." He removed the sack from his pocket, but this time, things were different...very different. This time, when he reached in to remove a key, he plucked out a tangle of three keys, each radiating with equal fervor.

"Oops, I guess I've got a case of the sticky fingers."

He tried putting the tangle back into the sack but the sack was having none of it. It was closed tighter than Billy Bartles' wallet.

"What's wrong with this thing? Come on you guys; this isn't how it works. This isn't fair."

But why did he presume to think that he knew how it worked? It seemed the only rule that mattered was the rules keep changing...all the time.

Toby studied the keys glowing in his sweaty palm. He hoped that one would eclipse the others...maybe shoot a beam into a keyhole.

Nothing.

"Ok...don't get crazy," he said. "Let's just keep it simple."

Now, the tranquility of the woods was far from comforting. In fact, Toby wasn't even sure he was *still* in the woods. He saw nothing. No trees, birds, rocks...nothing but the pervasive darkness outside the circle of light.

"Three doors...three keys...three choices. No...more like nine choices, dumbhead," he said, remembering his math.

"Oh man," he whined. "This isn't getting any easier. Isn't it supposed to get easier?"

A voice swirled through his mind, "*Which key...what door...Buckaroo....*"

Toby swallowed a deep breath and stepped toward the first door. Cautiously, he placed his hand on its rough wooden surface.

ZAP!

The jolt rocked him down to his socks. It stank of bad news and shouted loudly, into his soul: "*STAY AWAY TWERP ...YOU CAN'T SWALLOW WHAT WE'RE DISHING OUT! YOU WANT SOME TRUTH, BABY. WE SERVE TRUTH RAW ON A PLATTER...COME AND GET IT, PEEWEE...IF YOU DARE!*"

Toby backed away from the door, thinking the voice sounded strangely like that Nicholson dude.

In his palm, a single key now burned more intensely than the others; almost writhing like a snake.

Toby gasped, then grabbed the snake key and flung it into the darkness...outside the circle of light.

"No thank you, *Jack*. I don't think I'll be needing any today. Thank you very much, anyway."

Now, he approached the second door and laid his hand on *its* ordinary surface.

There was some sort of vibration, but it didn't seem to speak too loudly. In fact, it didn't seem to be speaking to him at all.

He backed away, then approached the third door and stroked his palm across *its* comfortable surface.

This time it felt somehow...right. He knew this was the choice.

One of the two remaining keys encouraged him, glowing brighter than the other. Toby smiled and inserted it into the keyhole.

"TOBY...HELP US...TOBY...PLEASE...!" another voice suddenly cried. It too was coming from the bad news door.

But it wasn't really a voice, at all; more like a feeling...a bad feeling. It was a chilling sense of...Lori, a terribly frightened Lori, screaming out...to him...for him. It was Billy, heading smugly into a world of trouble...and not even knowing.

Toby jerked the key out of the keyhole and its radiance extinguished.

He ran back to the first door and touched it again. His mind was flooded with images...of Lori...crying out in horror. Her face...distorted with intense searing pain...oozing from her pores.

Billy...walking in the shadow of darkness, with that stupid self-satisfied grin of his, spread across his face...except his face...his face had a cloud...a cloud of darkness...hanging from it.

Toby backed away. "Lori...Billy," he whispered. "The key...where's the friggin key?"

He looked into the blackness, "Shoot...smart move. Just throw it away, butthead," then approached its uncertain boundary, hoping that the key was within reaching distance from the light's circumference.

No such luck.

His mind, again, swam with images of Lori and Billy.

*Have to help them...have to find the key...*and without thinking Toby rushed from the light and into the darkness.

At first, his senses numbed, smothered by the emptiness.

He looked up, toward where the stars should have been.

Nothing.

He searched, hoping to see a glint of metal....

Something...anything. Just a reflection from the circle of light would do.

Nothing.

"Only if we let the thoughts do the thinking...." a voice said.

"Don't let the thoughts do the thinking, right...I'm doing the thinking, here," Toby willed himself to relax.

"I *will* find the key...I *will* find the key," he walked further into the darkness...then stopped.

Totally without sight, he reached down and picked up *the key.*

"Alright!" Toby bolted back into the circle of light.

Quickly, instinctively, he inserted the key into the keyhole.

"I'm coming Lori...I'm coming," he said, and the door slowly opened.

"Whoa...what's wrong with this picture?"

Toby spotted it immediately: this door was butt backward...it opened inward, dragging him across the threshold.

"Why does this worry me?" He wondered aloud, just as the door ripped from his hand and began pulling everything surrounding it into its insatiable vacuum.

Toby grabbed hold of the doorjamb and dug in with his heels.

"This is worse than Mom's Hoover on a Saturday morning," he cried.

Surrounding soil and rock swept through the opening, while breath rushed from his collapsing lungs.

His fingers cramped and lost their grip, then peeled off the wood one by one. His heels dragged across the dirt, desperately seeking something solid to jam against.

Until finally, he couldn't hold on any longer.

Toby fell through the door.

The circle of light went dark.

Chapter 26

From his viewing chamber, Tkler watched the scene unfold.

"Excellent...excellent work Engineer," he said with malignant glee.

"Thank you my Lord," Engineer said. "It was just a matter of acquiring the missing piece to the puzzle. It is I, who should thank you, for having the foresight to locate the missing piece."

"Do you hear that Billy?" Tkler sneered. "You're the missing piece to the puzzle. Without your connection to the boy, we should never have been able to intercede in the Procession of Doors."

Billy watched as Toby placed the key in the keyhole. It was as if he could actually reach out and touch him...as if Toby were standing in the room.

"Wow, this is better than 3D! You don't even need those stupid glasses. Way to go, Tobe, open them doors."

Had Toby really been in the chamber, he would have thought Billy looked ridiculous in a replica of Tkler's uniform of the day. A tad on the long side, the heavy black robes and flowing cape, draped over one shoulder, were constantly finding a home under Billy's stumbling feet.

"You see, my Lord," Engineer continued. "It was just a matter of adapting the principal of Hypo-spatial Transference to the inversion theorem of Counter-spatial Reciprocity. Once we had young Billy, here, it was just a matter of tapping into the brain connector patterns of—"

"Enough, Engineer...enough!" Tkler roared. "You are giving me a headache. Just deliver the boy to me."

"Well, my Lord," Engineer said. "He must still choose to open the...uhm...actual door itself."

"He will open it. Our friend Billy will see to it. Won't you Billy?" Tkler stared into Billy's mischievous eyes.

"Sure, no problem, Tk-man. Anything to get back home."

Billy closed his eyes and thought of Lori, thought of Toby, and thought of home. His thought patterns were scrambled, then re-arranged by Engineer. Finally, they were transmitted to Toby on the other side of the door.

Billy lurched. He heard Toby scream into his brain, "*I'm coming Lori...I'm coming!*" And it suddenly occurred to him, *Uh, oh...this might not have been such a good idea.*

Ashamed, he opened his eyes and saw his friend struggle, then fall, helplessly, through Tkler's trap.

"Toby..." Billy said quietly. "I'm sorry, man. I think I might have screwed up, big time."

Billy's thought link to Toby suddenly disconnected. The life like image sputtered and disappeared. Engineer frantically barked commands at the system and tried to override it manually.

Tkler rushed toward the control panel. "What is happening? Someone tell me...*what is happening?*"

"It's him, my Lord," Engineer waved his arms toward Billy. "He has managed to disconnect the system."

Tkler's eyes raged with fire. He marched toward Billy...raised his arm, and was about to strike.

"Such insolence from one so...so...so..." when he realized that Billy was his only hope of intercepting the boy. "...So strong of will. Really, one to be admired," Tkler concluded, bringing his evil hand to rest on Billy's head.

"Sorry Tk-man," Billy said. "I just got a little worried, for Toby. I wasn't sure I was doing the right thing and all."

"Yes," Tkler said, controlling his fury. "Doubt has been the undoing of many a genius mind."

"Wow...genius," Billy said. "Thanks, Tk. Nobody's ever called me a genius before."

"Indeed," Tkler replied. He turned toward the cowering Engineer.

"Where has he gone? Have we got him, or is he lost...again?"

"Well, my Lord," Engineer said, studying the scoping system. "I'm afraid...*not exactly.*"

"Not exactly what!" Tkler tried desperately to maintain control.

"Well, my Lord...you see we haven't exactly *lost him*...but we haven't exactly *got him*, either."

Billy wrapped the cape around his face, concealing a huge grin.

"What are you talking about?" Tkler approached the scoping system. "I swear, time is running out on my patience, Engineer. We don't want that to happen, now do we...*Engineer.*"

Engineer trembled. "No, my Lord. Certainly not, my Lord. If I might explain, my Lord."

Tkler pounded on the console. "That is what I have been asking you to do!" Once again, he fought to regain his composure. "Now then...proceed...*pleeeease*."

Engineer took a mighty breath. He sensed it could be his last. "You see, my Lord, when the boy, Billy, broke his thought connection with the other boy, we lost our ability to fully bring him through the Hypo-spatial barrier. He is here...in a sense...but not really here...in...another...sense."

"Sounds like a lot of *non-sense*, to me," Billy cracked.

"*Ennngineeeer*" Tkler sang out, impatiently glancing toward Billy.

"What I am trying to explain to you, Lord Tkler, is that the boy is here, but only inter-dimensionally. We can't quite get to him...and he can't quite get to us."

"You mean he's lost in a Hypo-spatial time distortion?" Tkler asked, disbelieving.

"Yes, my Lord...exactly. As we mark our existence with the tick of the clock...he exists in the space between the ticks."

"Awesome," Billy said. "We're ticking and old Tobe is tocking." Billy poked blindly into the air. "That you, Tobe...you out there, old buddy?"

"Quiet!" Tkler stomped over to Billy and shoved him into a nearby chair. "Children really should be seen and not heard...*don't you agree*?"

"Now that's very cold, Tk-man...very cold," Billy muttered. "Don't you agree?"

"Can we see him?"

"It depends on the strength of the connection," Engineer said. "The stronger the connection, with someone in our zone, the easier it will be to pull him through."

Tkler turned back toward Billy. "I'm not quite sure you're the one he's really looking for, young William. But, alas, you're the only one I can reach...*at this time.*"

"Billy or Bill...I hate William," Billy replied.

Chapter 27

It was as if his body had transformed into an immobile rag of exposed nerves; his brain, palpitated against his skull.

Toby sensed...*this is not a good thing....*

Then, the vacuum released and Toby found himself rolling like a runaway bowling ball across the cold, stone surface of Castle Endlum. If it weren't for the fact that he was actually *floating*, several inches above the stone, he would have taken a very nasty spill.

A hard, craggy wall of rock stopped his momentum and he flipped up to a sitting position. Cautiously, he scanned the dank, gloomy environment.

"Where am I...now?"

He staggered to his feet and after taking several small steps, looked down, "Wow...talk about light on your feet!" and saw his sneakers hovering and bobbing, several inches above the surface. Walking, usually an ordinary experience, had become a decidedly *non-ordinary* experience.

Working up a head of steam he ran down the hall and leapt high into the air. Incredibly, he soared about thirty feet then made an awkward landing.

"Wooooah...awesome!" he cried, until, suddenly, the sound of footsteps...large footsteps...echoed around the bend.

"That...does not...sound good."

His body seized with panic, then, frantically, he looked for a place to hide. He spun in the opposite direction, only to hear an equal amount of footsteps.

"Oh man, I'm gonna be a sandwich here," he shifted from foot to foot.

A group of, *some sort of soldiers*, he thought, whipped around the corner. They marched in a neat orderly formation and appeared dark, angry and mean. In their arms they carried a nasty, futuristic looking weapon. *Something of a cross-bow, with a kind of reddish blue neon light pulsating up and down the shaft.*

The light hummed with danger.

"Uh, excuse me," it was all Toby could think to say.

Behind him, the other squad of soldiers turned the bend and closed in.

"I seem to have gotten separated from my tour group...could you direct me to—"

The two squads converged and Toby struggled to keep his cool. The soldiers remained silent...deadly silent.

Toby closed his eyes and feared the worst. "Okay...I'll go peacefully." When he opened them, he was amazed to discover that the men, all of them, had passed right by...or through him, and continued on their way.

"Man," his eyes grew round with wonder. "I've been lost in a crowd before, but this is ridiculous."

He gathered himself and walked on, or floated on, further down the passageway. Not too far ahead, the corridor opened into a cavernous, circular hall.

"This must be the game room," he said, trying to amuse himself.

The large, open chamber was composed of dark, uneven rock formations that raced upward in a seemingly endless flight to infinity. Some parts of the room appeared to be weeping; a steady trickle of moisture leaked from within the stones.

Toby shuddered, *I'll never tell anyone to go to hell again...I think I've seen it,* then ran his hand along the craggy surface of the grieving stones. *They oughta think about some serious water sealer for this baby. No wonder this place is so moldy.*

Four soldiers stood guard by the entrances to four separate corridors. Without making a sound, Toby approached one of them.

Like before, the guard didn't seem to notice.

Toby raised his hand, inches from the guard's nose and waved it back and forth.

"*Yoo Hoo...I see yooo...do you see me?*"

He jumped up and down like a ridiculous jumping bean. "Wow, if I get me some nifty bandages and a cool pair of shades, I'll be just like that Invisible dude." Toby snickered at the image, then, suddenly, saw another, more unsettling image of those British guys with the big fuzzy hats, standing guard at that old palace in London.

All the dumb tourists get their jollies by trying to make those poor suckers laugh, or something. But those guys never budge...do they?

Toby looked into the eyes of the guard, "Are you like one of those guys, dark eyes?"

He backed off, thinking he should give this matter further consideration. Then he noticed something that might be important: their feet touched the ground...his did not.

Pleased with his astute powers of observation, he leaned against the wall, but stumbled when the wall didn't support his weight. Thinking he had somehow missed the wall, Toby shifted his weight forward, then overcorrected, backward, and finally, plunged into the wall itself and was encased in solid stone; as if he were actually a part of the stone.

"I don't think *this* is a good place to be," he said uneasily, then walked on, about five or six feet, until, to his great relief, he stepped out of the wall and into another room.

"So much for doors," he marveled.

He was in another chamber, one with a low ceiling. The walls were covered with some sort of long, clingy vegetation.

"Ugh, this place gives me the creeps," then he was suddenly struck by that overwhelming sense of Lori in pain.

His feet dropped, brushed the uneven surface, then rose again.

"Lori...I've got to get to Lori...and Billy. I've got to do something."

215

Though what, he didn't know.

He plunged back into the wall...slowly passing through...his molecules, again, mingling with the stone.

Nearing the final layer, that powerful sense of Lori in trouble returned.

His forward progress stopped. The stone contracted and grabbed him. Something was terribly wrong.

Toby gasped, his body was turning to stone...becoming the stone. He was stuck...helpless.

What's wrong...what's happening...why can't I get through?

The world bent in a distorted blur.

Lori...got to help...her...Billy...bonehead....

His eyes froze in place...his mind went dark...and his body stopped....

Chapter 28

"We've lost him...he's gone," Engineer said, clearly befuddled.

"What?" Tkler snarled.

"Whatever signal we had is completely severed. It's as if he never existed."

Tkler was careful. It could not be so easy. The boy...this *Boy* was supposed to be the one...the only one in his way. Could it be over so soon?

"Out of my way...show me the readings...I must see the readings."

Engineer punched several buttons and Tkler's eyes widened.

"You see, my Lord. There is no reading at all. No force...no will...at all."

"Yes, Engineer...as I always suspected...as I always knew."

Billy shuddered and closed his eyes, trying desperately to re-connect with Toby.

Toby...come back to us, man. I don't like what I'm hearing, here. Toby...you gotta help us...don't leave us here...Toby we need you....

Entombed within Tkler's Temprocity Chamber, Lori, or whatever remained of Lori, was overcome with a terrible feeling of despair. Something had happened to Toby. His presence was fading from her life, as if he never existed...as if she never knew.

She was too weak to scream, but her mind cried out in terror, *Toby...please I need you...don't go away...don't leave us alone...Toby we need you....*

*...TOBY, WE NEED YOU...*it was two voices, melded as one. Two voices, crying out a single thought.

And the thought rattled around Toby's darkened mind, poking and prodding through levels and levels of unplowed consciousness until, suddenly, the thought ignited a spark and exploded into a firestorm of raw emotions.

Lori...Billy...Lori...Billy...all of us...together....

The stone suddenly shifted and Toby spilled back into the circular cavern. Again, he floated inches above the surface. His lungs ballooned with air and his eyes popped open. Above him, the four guards continued their silent watch, still unaware of his presence.

"Maybe *I will stick* to doors," he gasped.

"*Toby*...." the voice cried in his mind.

"Lori...." Toby said in reply.

Suddenly, the circular cavern warped and bent...light fading in and out.

Toby's butt bounced hard to the stone surface, and then, bounced up again.

The guards stirred, detecting something peculiar in their midst. They saw a body flickering in and out of view. Two of the guards rubbed their eyes in disbelief, yet none were sure enough to act.

"Uh, oh, I think I'm starting to stick out a little, here."

The guards leaned forward, thinking they had heard something. Then they looked at each other...then they stared straight ahead.

Toby thought of Lori...heard her cry...and plunked back to the surface. He closed his mind...and rose back up.

Somehow, when I think of Lori...or Billy, in trouble, I become whole and visible. Otherwise, it's as if I'm not really here...or there.

He forced his mind to concentrate on finding Lori ...without feeling her sorrow. He had to shut off his emotions.

I know I can do that...I've had a lot of practice.

He stood up. It was working...the guards didn't stir.

Seeing his chance, Toby turned and bolted down one of the long narrow corridors. He tried hard to keep his focus, but that sense of Lori in trouble, hammered at his entire being.

"Toby...please...help...me...."

He saw Lori's eyes deeply entwined with his own. The searing heat of her anguish pierced his heart like one of Tkler's lightning bolts...and he ran faster.

The narrow hallways twisted and turned; again, a long forgotten dream. An eerie light flashed on and off and his sneakers skidded across the stone then skimmed back above.

Toby knew he was, somehow, racing against time itself. He slowed down...*it's a race I can only lose....*

His burning senses screamed to him: "*NO...TURN DOWN HERE!*"

He skipped and stumbled around the corner, his feet, once again, falling to the stone. He raced down another endless corridor lined with doors...*always more doors*. He thought his head might explode

Lori...where are you! he screamed with his mind.

"She's close...I know it...I feel it. Maybe behind one of these doors...which one, which one?"

The corridor stretched forever.

"I'll never get there in time."

In time for what?

"I have to focus...have to concentrate."

Then, up ahead, a great pair of wooden doors loomed heavily within the swirling hall.

"That must be it," his heart thumped madly in his chest. He put down his head, and ran all out. "I'm gonna bust right through them...can't stop...."

"*TOBY..!*" the voice in his head screamed.

Suddenly, his body re-materialized and his feet landed firmly on the surface.

He thought he heard the sound of cannon fire...then crumpled to the ground.

Brian Moloney

Chapter 29

Miles above, in the tower of Castle Endlum, Lord Tkler sat brooding in an oversized chair. It was a chair designed for a King...and Tkler was determined that it be just that.

The signal had returned. The boy had not succumbed after all. And Engineer's feeble excuses had put Tkler in a foul mood.

He should have known better. *It would not be easy...this boy.*

He had created a plan...an ingenious plan...harnessed and controlled the power of time itself.

Kingdom after Kingdom fell to his power and was his to command.

His plan was almost complete. All of the pieces, in place...except for this inconsequential spit of a Kingdom called Keys. But, without Keys his plan amounted to nothing; he would be nothing.

Everything hinged on the boy. Yes...the boy would be his doing...or undoing.

So now, the boy was back, and lost...again. And time...Tkler's time...was running out.

222

Centurion and Engineer burst into the darkened chamber, followed closely by Billy, who still found proficient *cape control* beyond his command.

"Man, why do these things look so awesome in the movies. They're just a royal pain in the butt."

"My Lord!" Centurion exclaimed. "We have word of the boy being sighted in the lower region."

"What!" Tkler spirits lifted. "He's been sighted...physically?"

"Yes, my Lord," Engineer boasted, eager to receive credit for the accomplishment. "Several of the guards have reported an apparition appearing in the circular cavern. Several reported hearing voices."

"Perhaps just a case of castle vapors." Tkler wanted to discount any possible explanation before he allowed his hopes to soar.

"No, my Lord. One of the guards reported hearing erratic footsteps crashing down a corridor. He followed in pursuit and spotted the boy running erratically down the Temporal Hall."

"Excellent!" Tkler said. "Then we have him."

"Not quite yet, my Lord." Engineer was again apprehensive. "It appears that the boy is still stuck, somewhere, between *here* and *there*."

Tkler looked toward Billy who continued the struggle with his cape.

"Hey, don't look at me, Tk-man. I had nothing to do with it."

"Young William is correct, my Lord," Engineer said.

"Billy or Bill," Billy corrected, irritably.

Engineer bowed in mock apology and continued.

"Apparently the boy is receiving a strong connection from the girl in the Temprocity Chamber."

"Ah yes, the girl," Tkler replied. "Of course, the girl."

"He seems to understand the significance of the connection and is trying very hard to resist."

"But he can't resist the girl, can he?" Tkler sneered.

"No, my Lord, his resistance appears to grow weaker the nearer he draws to the chamber," Engineer answered.

"That's where he is heading, my Lord," Centurion said. "I have already sent a deployment of guards to secure the chamber once he enters."

"Excellent...excellent," Tkler said. "Then we must go and greet our young friend. Come Billy. You may do the honors and introduce us. I'm sure the boy will be delighted to see you."

Billy stepped forward and, again, stumbled on the long end of his cape.

"Oh pick it up...pick it up, will you," Tkler said.

"Maybe I need a medium," Billy said. "Have you got this in a medium? I'll bet not in black."

Chapter 30

The taste of immovable door was growing on Toby; he seemed to be running into a lot of them, these days.

Sprawled on his back, still floating on the surface, he mumbled to himself, "Man, I hate when that happens." Then he checked to see that his nose was still centered squarely on his face. Assured that it was, he stood up and inspected the foreboding set of doors.

"I can do this," he said, and with confidence, passed effortlessly through to the other side.

"Yes," he whispered proudly.

He found yet another endless corridor stretching far into the darkness; the walls and floor vibrated with an ominous, low-pitched hum.

"*Toby...oh Toby,*" the voice murmured in his mind.

Once again, his feet fell to the ground, and his footsteps echoed up ahead.

On either side of the hall he noticed the walls were lined from top to bottom with large darkened windows. The windows consisted of some sort of dark translucent material and when he pressed his face directly against the one closest to him, he was unable to see through its inky blackness. Still, he sensed that someone, or something, was behind the barrier.

The dead glass hummed against his face. "Lori...Lori, where are you?"

Toby sighed, stepped away from the glass and resumed his cautious trek, down the hall. The uneasy sense of something ghastly behind the glass walked with him.

Did something move...or was it just a reflection?

He felt he was losing focus...becoming distracted by things he had no control over...not yet.

Have to concentrate...recapture the thing...the feelings, that led me here in the first place.

"Lori, ya gotta help me here...talk to me...anything...even a dumb story about your dad."

"Toby?" A frightened voice...only this time it wasn't coming from his mind.

Toby swung around and faced another darkened window.

"Toby...is that really you?" the voice said.

Suddenly, the window filled with light and a solitary figure stood silhouetted in its frame.

"Lori," Toby whispered, his mouth was dry as sand. He stepped forward and placed his palm upon the glass. "Lori...what's happened?"

Lori, her face concealed in shadow, also placed her palm against the glass.

"Toby, it's Tkler. He's taken us...using us, to get to you. You're not safe here. You have to go."

"I'm not going anywhere, Lori, until I get you and Billy out of here."

"No Toby...you don't...uhhhh...." Lori winced. Her eyes rolled into her head and her entire body shuddered. Something, deeper than pain, had seized her.

"Lori, are you alright...Lori what's happening to you?"

"Just life, Toby. My life is happening to me," Lori said.

"What do you mean...what do you mean...your life?"

Lori stepped into the light and Toby gasped.

It was Lori, there was no doubt about that. But it was a Lori from another time...a time fifty years from now.

Then, she changed again, aging before his eyes. Suddenly, yet not so suddenly, Lori was old...very old...and very frail.

Toby banged on the glass, but to no avail. "Lori!"

Lori was totally unaware, or merely too helpless, to do anything.

"She's living her life, Toby...over and over again. The joy, the sorrow...the happiness, the sadness...all of the experiences of life, concentrated in time...over and over again."

Toby turned and saw another window, across the corridor, also illuminate.

It was Samira; she sat on a solitary chair. Next to her, Emily lay on a table, heavily wrapped and restrained by a kind of body muzzle.

"*Tooooooobeeee*," she purred.

"Samira, what can I do...how can I get you out? I have to help Lori and...Billy...where's Billy?"

"You must go back to the Doors, Toby," Samira said gently. "You can only help us if you complete the Doors. You must fulfill."

"But it may be too late...I can't leave Lori like this."

"Toby, listen to Samira. You have to go back."

Toby spun. It was Lori. The Lori Toby knew....*but for how long?*

"Lori, I can't leave you like this."

Tears rolled from her vacant eyes, and Lori, again, grew old. She spoke in a tired, withered voice.

"Toby...it's horrible. My life has no mystery. I know it all. I've lived it a thousand times. It has no meaning anymore. Nothing to hope for...nothing to strive for...no mystery...anymore."

Lori dropped her eyes, again just a frail shadow of her youth, and the transformation continued. Her young life swallowed by the deep lines etching into her face.

Toby reached out and touched the glass but was startled by the crashing of doors. Tkler and his guards had entered the hall.

"Toby," Samira said, in a calm, steady voice. "You must use your mind. You must focus on the Doors. The only way to help Lori and Billy, is to complete the Doors. You have the key. You must use it."

"The key," he whispered. "Always the key."

Toby faced Tkler and his men; they were closing fast. Surprisingly, he was unfazed by Tkler's hideous presence

"So, that's what a Tkler looks like." He looked back toward Lori and again pressed his palm against the cold, vibrating glass.

"Lori, I won't let you stay this way. I promise."

"I believe you Toby...*I always have.* Please go."

Toby closed his eyes and focused on what he had to do...what he must do. Slowly, he rose above the surface and then...settled back.

"I believe in you, Toby," Lori whispered.

Again, Toby turned and confronted Tkler and his men.

"There he is," Tkler shouted. "Seize him!"

Suddenly, without thinking, and without knowing why, Toby ran right toward the oncoming crowd.

The guards stopped dead in their tracks, clearly not expecting this particular strategy.

"Making it easy on us, are you, boy?" Tkler said with disdain. "Think it will go better for you if you cooperate? *I don't think so.* Grab him!"

Still hugging the surface, Toby drew perilously close to his pursuers. He started wondering if this idea might have been a mistake after all.

Nah...gotta go for it, he thought, and his feet skipped off the stone.

Suddenly, he was taking long, bounding strides, and his form disappeared from view.

"What's happening?" Tkler cried. "We're losing him! Engineer do something!"

"The boy, my Lord. He must connect with the boy."

"Connect with him, William or I will connect with your head," Tkler said through clenched teeth.

Billy nodded, but the only thought he had was, *Go Tubman, go!*

Three long strides drew Toby within yards of the group. His image flickered and, suddenly, he materialized, inches from their grasp.

Tkler screamed, "GET HIM...GET HIM!"

One last stride catapulted him high into the air, vaulting the outstretched arms of the incredulous guards.

Everyone gasped, as they threw their heads upward to see the flying boy elude them.

"Whoa...Air Toby," Billy said with awe. "Very impressive, Tubman!"

He landed a good fifty yards away and waved to the astonished Tkler.

"Sound the alarm," Tkler said to Centurion. "I want him stopped."

"But my Lord, if we cannot see him. If he is between—"

"We will see him. Young William, here, will make certain of that." Tkler grabbed hold of Billy's cape and twisted it like a wet towel.

"You *will* heel to my every command, won't you William?" he said, yanking Billy behind.

Billy gagged and choked, stumbling to keep up with Tkler's furious pace.

"Billy or Bill," he sputtered. "I really prefer Billy or Bill."

Toby escaped from the chamber and ran back into the Temporal Hall. Its long row of doors seemed to mock him.

"Doors...doors...doors...I need a door. Come on fellas speak to me."

"*Toby help*," croaked the voice in his mind. "*He's killing me, man.*"

It was Billy...he could sense Billy.

No, have to focus...can't do anything until I complete, he shouted into his brain.

His feet skidded the ground and the guards closed quickly from behind.

"There he is, grab him, grab him, grab him," Tkler shouted, still twisting Billy's cape, drawing it even tighter around his throat.

"*Toby...Tubman...help*," the voice pleaded.

Toby skidded around the corner, trying to erase the voice from his mind. It sounded weak. It sounded as if it were dying.

"Billy, hold on, man. I can't help you just yet...please, just hold on!"

Another group of soldiers turned the corner from the opposite direction.

"There he is!" one shouted.

At the last instant, Toby closed his mind and rose off the surface, just in time to pass harmlessly through the rushing brigade. He could feel their grime crawling on his skin.

"Ugh...try using some soap, buddy."

The startled guards lurched to a stop.

"A door...I need a door. Any one of you guys will do...come on, speak to me...somebody."

"*Tubman...help....*" the voice pleaded again.

Toby's feet hit the ground and he stumbled on the stone.

"Billy, man, not you. You keep trippin me up here."

From everywhere, he heard the pounding of angry footsteps. He spun around, looking for another corner to turn...somewhere to go.

Got to concentrate, he thought. *Got to disappear*.

"*TUBMAN..!*" the voice boomed.

Toby grabbed his head, "Man, Billy, what frequency are you using?"

He staggered down the hall, desperately searching for a door among doors.

Nothing.

He tried to disappear.

Nothing.

"I'm doomed, here," he said. "We're all doomed here."

Suddenly...a burning sensation.

"The Keys!" Toby plunged into his hip pocket. "No...wrong pocket."

This time there was a different sort of warmth. It was coming from...

..."My back pocket." He quickly reached behind and pulled out the old tube of paint. It was glowing a vivid blue. Somewhere, from the corner of his mind, "*It can be whatever you imagine it to be.*"

Toby quickly removed the cap and released a large wash of cerulean light. The light pulsated into a column of brilliant blue sparkles and transformed into a large door, inexplicably embedded in the stone.

"Whoa, what's behind the blue door?" Toby filled with wonder.

The footsteps closed in.

"There he is!" Tkler spotted the mysterious door. "Don't let him escape!"

Confidently, Toby looked squarely into the face of evil as it approached with Billy in tow.

"Wait for me," Toby said. "Just wait for me."

The sack of keys jumped from his pocket. Quickly, he opened the sack, picked a key, and inserted it into the keyhole.

Toby looked back at Tkler, smiled, then leapt through the door and slammed it shut behind him.

Tkler's men converged but the brilliant blue door burst into a multitude of fiery sparks and disappeared.

A distraught Tkler approached and shoved passed his soldiers. With an indiscernible tremor, he touched the heat scarred stone where the door had been.

"Yes...I'll wait for you. Now...all I can do is wait," he whispered in return.

Chapter 31

Malok and Musso stood, stiff as wooden dolls, within the Royal chamber of the King of Keys. The atmosphere was thick with despair and the chill of lost hope bit deep into the bone. Buried in a mountain of thick woolen blankets and feathery pillows, the slight outline of a man was barely detectable.

Following Tolmar's lead, they approached the Royal bed and observed a living mummy fighting for every breath.

"My goodness, Tolmar," Musso said quietly. "I had no idea that he was in such a state. No one in the Kingdom is aware."

"No, Musso. The King believes he must continue giving the appearance of strength. His body is weak but his mind is strong...or stronger than appearances."

"Can he move...can he speak?"

"For Keys sake, Musso," Malok said. "Can't you see that he's barely able to move a finger without fear of it breaking off? The man has the constitution of a snowflake." Malok turned away. "There is nothing to be done. We are all finished."

"No, my good Malok," a voice rasped, barely above the softest whisper. "Put those sails, you call ears, to use and listen to what I have to say."

Malok stopped dead in his tracks. His large ears wiggled ever so slightly. Then he spun so quickly that he lost his footing and nearly stumbled onto the Royal bed.

"Your Highness...you have always been full of surprises. I should never have underestimated your resolve," he said with delight.

"My Lord," Musso said. "You can still speak."

"Yes...I can muster my strength for short periods...to...." The King trailed off into silence.

Tolmar stepped in and suggested they leave the King to rest for a while. "Perhaps when his strength—"

"No, Tolmar...I'll do it now," the King spoke again, gathering what remained of his strength. "I will see Musso and Malok alone. My words are few...and I have only enough to satisfy two sets of Keysian ears."

"As you wish, my Lord," Tolmar obediently turned and exited the Royal chamber.

Musso stepped forward and approached. Looking into the royal eyes he was pleased to find the sparkle of the man that was...before the battle began.

"I'm afraid...the situation is very grave, my Lord."

The King turned his sunken eyes toward Musso. He did not seem alarmed.

Musso continued. "The Queen has been abducted by Tkler...and, I'm afraid, the boy, Billy and the girl."

"They're safe...for now," the King said. "Lord Tkler needs them for now."

"There is good news, my Lord."

"Toby?"

"Yes, Toby. He has entered the Doors. He has chosen the Key."

"Yes...I knew he would. I have been aware of...changes."

"Your Highness," Malok interrupted. "The atmosphere in here is gloomy and dank at best. If I might suggest, perhaps a number - a musical number - might be in order to lighten the King's spirits. There's one in particular that I've always been partial toward. A one...a two...a one two three—"

Musso glared in horror. "Malok stop this nonsense at once! I know you're ill, but the King—"

"Ill? What do you mean, I'm ill, Musso?" Malok was somewhat puzzled and bemused. "Why, I've never felt better in my life. Why, you're just bitter that you don't feel half as good as I do. If you would only—"

A weak smile passed across the King's eyes. "Leave him be, Musso. He's experiencing the pleasant stage of the Tkler curse. It...gets much worse...I know...."

"Yes, my Lord," Musso said quietly, observing Malok walking away, bellowing out a song.

The King gazed into Musso's eyes and extended his hand. Musso grasped hold of it and was struck by *how terribly fragile* it was. He feared it might, indeed, crumble to dust under the slightest pressure.

"There is nothing to be done," the King whispered. "It is proceeding as it was written. Now, we must wait for Toby to play out his hand."

"My Lord?" Musso puzzled over the King's statement but suddenly jumped to his feet when Malok bellowed out another song.

"Come, Malok. We must allow the King to rest. We've done what we've set out to do."

Musso took his friend by the elbow and lead him to the chamber door.

The King whispered something indiscernible.

Musso turned. "What was that, my Lord. I'm afraid I didn't quite catch—"

The King had already shut his eyes and returned to his inner thoughts.

"Sounded something like, trick...knowing which key...what door," Malok said.

"How did you hear that?" Musso asked.

"I'm not sure," Malok replied.

"Puzzling indeed," Musso glanced back at his King.

The pair stepped from the room and closed the chamber door.

Chapter 32

The door vanished into a shower of infinite blue light. Toby raised the nearly empty tube of paint and turned it in the palm of his hand. "Thanks," he said, to no one...and everyone...in particular.

Gazing back at the empty space where the door had been, he thought of his friends...thought of his friends needing him.

He thought of Lori. He thought of Billy, ridiculous costume and all...and he thought of Lori, again.

He knew, now, for certain, that this - all of this - was not just for him. It was for all of them.

But then, *I knew that all along...didn't I?*

A quick look around told him he was in yet another cavernous space.

An auditorium of some sort...where...I haven't a clue...but who cares....

He was just grateful the floor was securely under his feet, and the walls weren't spinning like another weird, funhouse nightmare.

The pleasant sound of a guitar strummed across the room, coming from somewhere in the distance.

It was a simple tune comprised of only three or four easy chords, yet Toby found it hauntingly familiar.

"I think I've heard this before." Distant memories of rainy Saturdays, relics from the past, his dad's ancient record collection, clicked in his head.

The guitar playing continued, so Toby decided to walk toward the source.

"Hello...." Toby called out.

His voice echoed back in a rich resonant tone.

"Hellooooo...."

This wasn't just an auditorium. This was a place made for music...a concert hall. He spun around in circles, overwhelmed by its vastness. *Not just a concert hall either. This was* "the" *concert hall.*

Toby reached the stage and took in the full scope of the room. He could smell the artistry...the pureness of it. He inhaled and its effect was intoxicating.

From the shadows, the guitar strumming was joined by a solitary voice. The voice was alluring. Untrained, yet naturally pleasant. It stretched some of the notes beyond their limits; yet some raw, untamed quality screamed out..."*LISTEN TO ME...I HAVE SOMETHING TO SAY!*"

Toby recognized the song...though he'd doubted anyone else he knew would...or want to. It was what his dad once called a protest song, and it came from a time known ambiguously as "the sixties."

Off to the left there were steps leading up to the stage; Toby climbed up. The singer continued to play, and he continued to listen.

The man wore an old sport coat over a wrinkled denim work shirt, and a dark pair of pants, a little too snug to be comfortable. His brown hair was neatly slicked back, though without any apparent style. The man was a far cry from any rock n' roller Toby had ever seen.

Wanting to get a better look, Toby tried stepping closer, but his foot got tangled in a coil of cable and electrical wires. Hoping to remain unnoticed he quietly attempted to unhook himself, but yanked on the wrong cable and a microphone fell to the floor.

BANG! Wheeeeeeooooooo...the hall filled with feedback. The Folk Singer abruptly stopped playing and turned around.

"Mmman whose that...mmmarchin on...mmmy...mmmarchin?" he asked with a nervous stutter. The acoustic guitar resting on his knee looked like it had logged a lot of miles, and fought a lot of battles. Toby was hoping he wasn't about to start another.

"I'm sorry, sir," he answered. "I didn't want to disturb you. I was just listening and...well, I guess I wasn't watching where—"

"Wwell I'm glad...yyou weren't...trying to disturb me," the singer said. His stutter relaxed and the man filled the holes in his speech by occasionally strumming his guitar. "I'd hate...to see you try and get...mmy attention."

Toby approached the man. "Sorry. I know you. I used to listen to your records with my...Dad."

"Oh you were the ones, huh?"

"No seriously...My Dad said you were as good as the other guy...only with a voice you could listen to."

"The other guy had the real voice. Most say mine was just an echo."

"Not my Dad...he said that you remained true...that you didn't sell out."

"I couldn't sell out, Kid...nobody was buying"

"So...you were loyal to your audience, what's wrong with that?"

"Nothing, Kid...if it were true. Truth is...I did what I did for me...because I had to. I didn't give a damn about what the people wanted. I gave a damn about what I wanted...and what I wanted was never enough...for them...for me. Live with that. I never had enough...to sell out."

Toby took a step back from the Folk Singer. He hadn't expected to find such a bitter man. In fact, he thought there were *really* two men sitting there.

The pure artist, young and lean, ready to take on all comers; sensing wrong and emptying his soul to right it.

And the bitter man, a bloated version of the younger man. His eyes were raw and ran with anger. His vision badly skewed by those that preached change...but only looked to change others. They had plucked out his eyes and now, he only saw what remained...inside...and to him, it was ugly.

"But your music made a difference to people. You gave a voice to those that didn't know how to use their own," Toby protested.

The Folk Singer...the young and lean Folk Singer, looked down at his guitar and strummed a chord.

"The music was pure," he said softly. "The music ...the words...came from the heart. I always needed the music. I always needed the words. I didn't need people to listen...I just needed to do it."

"That's right," Toby agreed. "The music came from the soul."

"Yeah," the bitter man violently ran his pick across the strings. "But I wanted them to listen. I wanted them to believe I was the best there was. I wanted them all to listen. I wanted them all to know that I...could change the world...by myself. I wanted them, all of them, to believe I *was* Jim Dean and Elvis, all rolled into one...and they wouldn't...and they didn't."

"But you didn't have to be those people," Toby said. "In fact, *they* weren't even those people. Who you were...good enough...right enough. Who you were supposed to be. You can't change the world by yourself...nobody can. All you can do is the best you can do, with what you're given to work with. To find the place where your piece fits into the puzzle. The only failure is not trying. Giving up."

Toby suddenly stopped, cut by his own angry words.

Where was this stuff coming from? Who am I to tell this guy how to live – or should have lived - his life?

"Well," the pure Folk Singer said, gently strumming. "I guess it really wouldn't interest anybody—"

"...Outside of a small circle of friends," Toby completed.

"Far out," the Folk Singer said.

"Very far out," Toby said.

"What are you doing here, anyway, Kid?"

"I don't know," Toby answered. "I guess I'm where I'm supposed to be."

"I know what you mean. It feels good to be where you're supposed to be...and it fffeels bbbad to be where you're not."

The Folk Singer sang the last part of the statement finishing on an upbeat. Toby smiled at the tune, yet, felt sadness for the man.

"What are you doing here?" Toby asked, returning the question.

"Getting ready to put on a show...it's what I do. I've filled this place before and I guess I'll fill it again."

"Then you believe again...you believe in your soul."

"Oh sure, now I do...it's so clear now...so simple."

"Simple." Toby repeated, remembering the man in the woods.

"Of course, I've had some help from a few friends."

Just then, Toby heard the sound of an electric guitar belt out a few opening riffs. A tall thin man - sort of geeky looking, actually - stood fiddling with his guitar. He stopped to adjust an odd pair of glasses.

To the side of him another man, dressed in a bulky turtleneck sweater, tuned his acoustic guitar. A wild wave of hair topped his head and a permanent smirk etched his face

"It helps if these things sound the way they're supposed to. Right, Kid?" he threw Toby a sly wink.

"The others are just starting to arrive," the Folk Singer said.

"Wow," Toby said with reverence. "You guys must have a heck of a band."

"Hey that sounds like it could be a song or something."

"It was," Toby said flatly.

"Yeah, I think I might have heard it," the wavy haired man said. "Didn't think I'd be joining it so damn soon, though," he muttered.

Toby heard a clunk off stage and a white baby grand piano rolled into view, pushed by a familiar man with a beard and long hair, parted in the middle.

The bearded man was dressed in a white suit, and small wire framed glasses sat on his sharply defined nose.

He spoke with a somewhat amusing British accent. "You know it wouldn't kill us, you know, to have a few bloody toadies to give us a hand, you know. My bloody back is screaming bloody murder, pushing this bloody piano back and forth."

"Oh stop your bloody griping," the geeky man with the glasses mimicked. "It's getting bloody old. Very bloody old."

"So am I," the man in the white suit replied. "So am I."

The Folk Singer laughed at the exchange.

"Wow," Toby was clearly awed. "I hope I can stick around and hear you guys play."

"Sure, you can if you want. I'm sure you've heard it all before, though."

"I'll bet not like this."

Suddenly, the sack in Toby's pocket came alive, giving its own unique performance.

"Looks like something's trying to tell you something." The Folk Singer glanced at Toby's glowing pocket, then pointed toward the balcony.

Toby turned and detected the soft illumination of a door in the rear of the upper balcony.

"Well, I guess it's time for me to be moving on."

"I guess it is," the Folk Singer said.

Toby sighed, then turned, and slowly made the winding climb to the balcony...and the Door.

Occasionally, he'd sneak a peek back at the stage, seeing more performers walk out and take up their positions. He recognized some of them, some he didn't. Now and then, the hall rocked with laughter.

Finally, Toby looked down and whispered, "If only I could stay for just one song." But, the sack of keys burned adamantly in his pocket.

The Folk Singer gazed up, as if in reply, and waved a big good-bye.

Resolved to the choices he had made, and the new choices still to come, Toby selected a key and inserted it home.

He opened the door, stepped across the threshold...then shut it behind.

Chapter 33

Toby stepped from a shadow and found himself in yet another uncertain corridor...again, endlessly lined with a multitude of doors.

Behind him, ghostly echoes of music history leaked through the sealed portal, then slowly receded, *back where it belonged....*

"It feels good to be where you're supposed to be."

"And it feels bad to be where you're not," Toby said, as he backed away from the door. Finally, he took a look around.

"More doors. So what else is new?"

The narrow hallway was dimly lit. Small, eerie lights ensconced in the walls cast heavy shadows across the floor; much like the somber vestibule of a funeral home, Toby thought.

The walls were painted a dark hideous gray and its woodwork, trimmed in a garish red.

"Man, whoever decorated this place has a future in home mausoleum design. Excuse me sir, but where can I pick up my night vision goggles?"

At the far end he saw light flickering from a small room. In between his own slow, steady breaths, he heard, just barely, the muffled sound of something...maybe crowd cheers.

He approached the room and saw the door was slightly ajar. It seemed to be inviting him inside. His hand brushed the white enamel surface, and the unmistakable sound of hardwood against cowhide resonated from within. The crowd noise rose, then faded.

Toby eased the door open, not wanting to make a sound, but the painted hinges were stubbornly uncooperative. A solitary step on the tail of the door's uninvited squeak took him inside, and his eyes focused on a small black and white TV.

Man, when was the last time anybody watched one of those things? But of course he knew the answer.

Grainy images of baseball players, outfitted in baggy, woolen uniforms danced across the screen. They seemed different, older than the athletes he was used to seeing. Even the umpires appeared odd, wearing little caps and funny looking ties.

Toby's gaze led him away from the television and over toward a large, winged back chair propped in front of it. On the far side of the chair a small lamp illuminated the scene in harsh shadows; a solitary curl of smoke drifted toward the ceiling.

"The game had a certain innocence to it, back then, don't you agree, Buckaroo?" asked a familiar voice from within the chair. "No free agents...billion dollar players...domed stadiums...instant replay. They played because they loved the game...and the game loved them. Now, all they want is to take. Put in a few years and then live the good life, forever."

Toby thought he should be surprised. Thought he should go into some sort of shock or something; but he didn't. Instead, he never felt more at ease in his life.

"Yeah, but the best of those guys wouldn't have a chance against the players of today. They're worth every penny." He approached the chair and sat on a small footstool beside it.

"Oh, I don't know about that...Mays, Mantle, Aaron, Musial, Mays...."

"You said Mays, already."

"Well he was worth mentioning twice...he was twice as good."

"Say hey," Toby said.

"Say hey," the man answered with a crooked smile.

"Yeah but, that's the cream of the crop. Look at these guys," Toby pointed at the screen. "They're slower, fatter, and nowhere near in shape as the guys are today."

"Of course not," the man shot back. "They had to work for a living. They didn't sit around all winter, lifting weights and going to batting cages. When they played, their sweat had stink to it. Today, they sweat perfume."

"When those guys played, they just plain stunk, you mean."

The man smiled and took a deep drag on the cigarette he had burning. He sat back in the oversized chair and squinted through the smoke.

Toby looked down at the floor uncomfortably.

"Your mother was always after me to get rid of these things. I probably should have listened."

"I guess old habits are hard to break," Toby said.

"You know, when I was just about your age, I used to watch these guys lose...almost every day...a hundred and twenty times," the man said.

"That's about where they're at, right now," Toby said.

"But it's all different now, isn't it? Back then it was like watching a baby take his first steps. You know he's gonna fall more than he's gonna walk...but, sooner or later, it's all gonna kick in, and one step will follow the other, and the other...and then, before you know it...he's running marathons."

"I guess, but—"

The man continued. "A hundred and twenty days I watched, and every single one began with a clean slate and cup full of hope."

"And every single one ended with a loss," Toby answered.

"A loss in the standings...but not a loss in our hearts. Every single one ended with the joy of being in the game. And as soon as it was over, we had hope that we would win tomorrow."

"And forty two times you were right."

"It doesn't sound like a lot, but it was forty two days of pure satisfaction. Forty two days of joy turned to ecstasy. Forty two days I would never have had if I had just given up."

"Now it's kinda hard, since we've been to the top, won the series," Toby said. "Now we call em bums if they finish second or third, even if they win ninety games...but I don't really follow it too much, anymore."

"I think you will," the man said. "Once you get used to winning, it's hard to go back to losing. But if you strip away the disappointment and the hurt; if you strip it down to the purity of the game...the purity of hope...the purity of a fresh start...then you can face every day with a fresh chance to win. If you don't...you only lose...always."

Toby nodded and studied the face he hadn't seen in a while...his father's face. He thought about his words, and he knew he was talking about more than just a baseball game.

"You know, all I ever wanted was for someone...anyone ...to give me the instructions. I never got the instructions. If I had the rules I could play to win."

"Like what?" Toby's Dad said. "Like some sort of new video game?"

"Yeah...at least I'd know how the game is played. I'd know what to do. You didn't leave me the instructions ...nobody did."

Toby's Dad inhaled another long drag on his cigarette. The amber tip grew an angry red and long plumes of smoke sprang from his nostrils like dragon fire. His intense brown eyes squinted through the haze.

"Toby, there are no instructions, no rules to give. The only instructions are: there *are no instructions*. There is no right way to play the game. There are no guarantees. All we can do is play. All we can do is take a shot. There are no winners. There are no losers. Only players. And if you don't play the game—"

Toby shot from the small stool and turned angrily away. "Some things are just unfair! They don't make sense."

"It all makes sense, Toby. It doesn't follow a straight path. It takes turns and goes through dark places. If you keep pushing ahead, the light returns. If you stop ...you're lost, in the dark...forever.

"In the end, you'll look back and it *will* have meaning. It *will* pay for itself."

"Why did everything have to change?" A single tear ran from a pleading blue eye and streaked his cheek. "Everything was great. Why did you have to go?"

His father stood, brushed the tear from Toby's face and answered, "It had to change because it was time to change. It had to change because you had to change. I had to go so you could become the person you were supposed to be."

Toby returned to the small stool and sat down.

"The Kingdom of Keys was you. You made it up. You created all of this."

"No, Toby...not me...you. Without you, there wouldn't be a Kingdom of Keys."

"I...don't understand...what do you mean?"

"You will, Buckaroo. Someday you'll understand."

Just then a familiar beam of emerald light sprang from a small hatch tucked away in the corner of the room. Toby eyed it and looked back toward his Dad.

"I guess that's meant for me."

"It's all meant for you, Buckaroo."

"I wish I could stay a little longer. This keeps getting harder and harder."

"I know," his Dad said. "But I think you're learning the value of closing old doors behind...as well as opening new ones in front. Besides, I think there's someone down there you should really meet."

With a mix of emotions, Toby said, "Awesome," then, reluctantly walked toward the hatch. His Dad sat back in the chair, filled with pride, and watched as Toby knelt, selected a key from the sack, and placed it firmly in the keyhole.

A small brass handle was attached to the face of the hatch. Toby grabbed it and hoisted the door open. Inside, he discovered a rickety wooden ladder leading down into the darkness. Without hesitation, Toby stepped onto the ladder and turned back to his father.

"Goodbye, Daddy," he said, with the innocence of the child he had been...and the strength of the man he was becoming.

"Goodbye, son," his father answered.

Toby smiled and closed the door behind.

Chapter 34

At first, the ladder rungs bent and gave precariously under his weight. The darkness was overwhelming, but there was no place to go but down into the heart of it.

"You have to play the game if you want to have a chance to win it," Toby said out loud, keeping himself company.

The rungs became sturdier with every conquered step, and his mind began to fill with all the wonderful things that had occurred so far.

How long had it been since I opened the "Door to Nowhere"? How long since I first saw the painter on the hill?

He thought of the painter...the man in the woods...the Folk Singer...and most of all, his Dad.

Aren't they all telling me the same thing? Isn't it all so...simple?

"Believe...be strong...be pure...be fearless...be...to be...to be...."

"*Toby*?" rasped a weakened voice from somewhere in the darkness.

"Toby?" Toby repeated.

"*Toby*," the voice creaked again.

He looked down...still, only blackness. *I could be a foot off the ground...or a mile.*

The Wolfman appeared in his mind and he recalled how easily he had made him disappear.

"Believe...be fearless...." And with that, Toby released his grip and jumped into the void. Almost immediately, the darkness slipped away and was replaced by an ethereal, misty light. Within seconds his feet quickly, and solidly, hit the ground with a thud. "Yes!"

"Toby... I knew you'd come. I guess you always had to," the raspy voice said.

Toby peered through the fragile light and saw a very old man, lying in a large majestic bed; its huge, fluffy mattress and mountain of pillows almost swallowed him whole.

"You've been waiting for me?" Toby approached the bed. "I guess I don't find that too surprising, anymore."

The old man seemed as frail as a broken bird.

It's been a long time since this guy has flown, Toby thought.

"Please, forgive me. I'm not as strong as I once was," the man said. "Would you mind giving me a hand? I'd like to sit up. Don't worry, you won't break my arms off or anything. And if you do, so what. They're not good for much. I'll just be an armless old Venus."

Toby smiled and thought of Billy. "I think sleeveless sweaters are pretty cool, myself."

"There you go."

He found the old man's manner of speaking odd, yet, not entirely unfamiliar.

Gently reaching under the man's arms, Toby pulled him to an upright position. The old man was, indeed, as light as a feather.

Toby straightened out his pillows and stepped back.

"You're a regular Nightingale," the old man said, meeting Toby's eyes, directly, for the first time.

Toby gasped. The wind rushed from his body and he thought sure his knees had buckled.

This man...he knew this man...he knew this face; although he had never seen it...before...like this.

His eyes...the old man's eyes...deep, piercing blue eyes...an exact reflection of his own.

"What's the matter...never seen a King before?" the man said.

Toby stared deeper into the old man's familiar eyes...his eyes.

"You...me...you're the King?" he whispered. "I'm...you're the King of Keys?"

"At your service...or out of service is more like it...at the moment. But I'm hoping that will change now."

"How can that be? How can this be? How can any of this be?"

"It can be anything you imagine it to be...Toby," the King replied.

Toby plopped on the edge of the bed and nearly jostled the old man off the pillows. Toby reached out and stopped his fall.

"Nice save," the King chuckled.

Suddenly, Toby's face lit with recognition. "Does this mean I've finished? Have I finished the Doors? Am I done? Have I achieved...found purpose?"

"Only you know the answer to that, Toby. What do you think?"

Toby pondered the question.

"I think there's more to do...to get Lori and Billy back...to stop that Tkler guy," he answered.

"Yes, Lord Tkler...the keeper of time. The Demon of Doom. The darkness that steps with me...with us, like a shadow."

"Who is that guy, anyway? Where'd he come from?"

"He came from me, Toby. He came from us. He's the dark side to our light. He's the gloom that fills our mind in the silence of night. He creeps like a wet, enveloping shroud, permeating every fold and crease in our being. He dampens our mind and smothers the promise...the promise deep inside."

"Wait a minute," Toby's face twisted in confusion. "Tkler is you...Tkler is—"

"Yes...the dark side...the ugly side. He is fear, a fear so great it cannot be considered, let alone confronted.

"Oh yes, we have woven him strong...so strong.

"But, loose ends exist, Toby...you know them...where to find them...to unravel the strands."

"Me...why me? How will I know where to find them?"

"I'm old and weak, Toby. You're young...you're strong."

"How did you know I would come? How did you know?"

"It was written, Toby. You'll know that...someday. The Foretelling has it all. We've always known. Always...the Foretelling."

"What is this Foretelling...why is it so important ...where did it come from?"

The old King mustered a toothless smile, raised his withered hand and pointed to a small, decrepit cupboard in the wall.

The cupboard was shuttered with a slab of dry, rotted wood. A badly rusted keyhole sat directly in its center and the corroded, green remains of a solitary key lay broken in its lock.

Toby instantly swelled with a sense of mystery, and, with reverence, he approached the vault. He reached out, touched the fragile door and it immediately crumbled into a mush of rot and dust. The remains of the brittle key struck the floor and shattered.

Toby peered inside the dusty hole and saw a thick coat of spider webs encasing a pile of loose, dry fragments, of something that looked like a manuscript.

The delicate condition of the aged brown pages was beyond time itself.

It was the *Foretelling*.

Toby took a deep breath, then carefully reached in and removed the ancient tome.

"Bring it to me, please," the King whispered.

Cradling the desiccated parchment against his breast, Toby felt it charging him with life...the same life it brought to The Kingdom of Keys...the same life he brought to it....

Pieces of the fragile pages broke away and fell unceremoniously to the floor as he handed it to the King.

"This is the result of Tkler's work. With every new conquest - as he gains strength - the Foretelling is diminished.

"Unless Tkler is destroyed, the Foretelling will never be. And quite simply, without the Foretelling...there is no Kingdom of Keys."

"But this is nuts," Toby's head spun with paradoxes. *"There is a Foretelling.* It's a little on the seedy side, but there it is. It's already written. *There already is a Kingdom of Keys.* It exists...I'm sitting in it. Others have come...it's helped so many...it's existed forever."

"I know it's difficult for you to understand in your terms, Toby. But remember, in a timeless world—"

"I know...it can be anything that I imagine it to be."

"Toby," the King said. "You hold the key to Tkler's demise. You can save the Kingdom of Keys."

"How?" Toby asked. "Why do I have this wonderful honor?"

In answer, the King slowly raised the tattered cover to the ancient manuscript and Toby read the words that changed his life forever.

All at once, his senses numbed and his face drooped like rubber.

Toby spoke quietly. "I think you'd better start explaining this Foretelling stuff to me...in a *timeless* way."

"Yes," the King replied. "I think you're ready now."

258

Chapter 35

High above the noxious caverns of Castle Endlum, Lord Tkler sat upon his darkened throne. Discontentment dampened his thoughts while he weighed the dubious direction his fortunes had recently turned.

He had worked too hard to let it *all* slip away...simply slip away, because of...*the boy*. The cursed *boy*!

Already, signs of decay had manifested at the very core of Castle Endlum. At first the slow moving tremors were no more than a whisper. No one seemed to notice the tiny vibrations, the minute ripple of the glass. But Tkler noticed. Oh yes, Tkler was aware.

I will be ready for him, he thought. *After all, he* is *just a boy. A mere boy....*

"My Lord," Centurion entered Tkler's chamber. "I have taken care of the piggish boy, Billy, in a manner that I believe will please you."

"There is only one thing that would please me now, Centurion, and that is to get on with it."

A massive vibration abruptly shook the chamber and it rumbled in a most distressing manner. Centurion shifted his eyes to the floor, troubled by the undulating stone beneath his heavy boots.

Tkler remained seated, unfazed by the disturbance, but Centurion, out of character, relented and fell to his knees in search of a stable piece of furniture to hold on to.

"Oh, get up. Get up you sniveling idiot. It's just a little thunder."

"Thunder, my Lord?" Centurion sprang to his feet. "I think it's more than just thunder. Why, thunder would never—"

"Oh, shut up...shut up, will—"

Again, the chamber shook. Large slabs of stone chased a blizzard of mortar and crashed to the floor in a series of slow sickening thuds.

Off to the side, Tkler's surveillance equipment collapsed in a tangled heap of smoke and sparks. Once again, Centurion shuddered and crouched on the floor.

"Thunder, My Lord?"

A low nauseating rumble rose from below as a thick cloud of dust rushed from the circular shaft and swirled through the room.

Centurion cowered and choked. Tkler refused to budge.

As if challenged by his obstinacy, the rumbling intensified until at last, a final, overpowering force rocked Tkler from his throne.

"*Yes...thunder!*" Tkler's legs scrambled every which way, struggling to find a foothold; his eyes blazed a fiery red and pierced his shadowy mask.

"Yes, my Lord...thunder," Centurion said, reassuringly. "We could use a bit of rain, my Lord."

"Oh, shut up... shut up!" Tkler cried.

The quaking receded to a whisper.

"Yes, my Lord," Centurion said.

Tkler rose from the floor, ignoring the layer of chalky dust clinging to his cloak. He walked slowly into the shadows and fell back upon his throne.

"It's the boy," Tkler said gravely. "He has discovered the secrets of the *Foretelling*. With his growing strength, I become weaker. Show him to me. I must see what he is doing!"

Centurion faced the smoking heap of equipment that had crumbled to ground.

"I am afraid it will take some time, my Lord, for Engineer to repair the system, and locate new tranceptors."

Tkler turned to Centurion. A hollow gaze draped his sallow face and he spoke in a wilted tone that chilled the soldier's bones. "I am afraid time has turned against us, Centurion. Time is slipping out of our domain."

Pools of shadow filled the creases surrounding Tkler's eyes.

He turned and settled back into his beloved darkness.

****

Miles below the swaying tower, in the bowels of Castle Endlum, the quaking reached a merciless intensity. Seeping through the darkened crevices of Tkler's keep, the echoes of suffering and fear flowed like a perpetual river of despair.

Motionless, upon a simple wooden rocker, a very old woman sat, her crooked hands folded quietly in her lap.

It was Lori.

Long, flowing, chestnut hair now transformed to white, ragged straw. Her tired face, deeply lined with the residue of life; but, most of all...her eyes...her eyes were vacant...eyes without hope.

She had lived a thousand lifetimes. She had died a thousand deaths. Now, she sat, and wondered at it all. Now, she sat, and waited for the end.

In one way, she wanted it to end.

Yet, in another, she knew, now more than ever, life was a wonderful gift; the happiness and the heartache; the triumphs and the tragedies.

She thought of the million or so events that were necessary to create...*her*...only *her*...exactly *her*. The million or so circumstances that had to fall *just right*. The miracle of it all. The mystery of it all.

But, it was enough for *one* lifetime, not a thousand.

Still, there was Toby. Throughout *all* her lives, she had never lost Toby.

Her eyes brightened, and her soul stirred with hope.

She believed...in *Toby*...and she knew...*he* needed *her*...to believe.

Lori gazed into the adjacent chamber. She saw Billy, Toby's best friend, bound and wound in a ridiculous fashion; strapped to something that looked like a barbecue spit, wearing nothing but his undershorts.

Around and around he spun, like a bizarre roasting pig at some sort of insane luau.

Lori was certain, if it were not for the large apple that protruded from his mouth, Billy would have plenty to say about this *porcine* state of affairs.

Across the way, Emily slept, still wrapped in her peculiar restraining device, while Queen Samira sat quietly within her thoughts. She felt Lori's gaze and opened her eyes.

"Do you sense the change, Lori? Can you feel it?"

Lori knew the Queen wasn't speaking of her physical changes.

"Yes," Lori said, in a time worn voice. "I can almost inhale it."

"He's coming...he's coming because *you* believe."

"No," Lori said with a crooked smile. It was the smile of ancient wisdom. "He's coming because *he* believes."

Samira returned Lori's knowing gaze. "Yes."

Billy continued to turn on the spit, suspiciously eyeing the pile of wood stacked beneath him.

They wouldn't actually light this thing, would they? Man, if I could only sink my teeth into this apple....

Chapter 36

Tolmar and Musso stood amongst the sea of stricken faces.

As far as the eye could see, citizens of *Keys* lay wasting away. Their cries of desperation drained the tears of the healthy.

Tkler's evil hand leaned heavy on their fading souls, their broken hearts...their lost lives.

Musso lowered his eyes to his friend Malok. He lay upon a harsh thin mat, resting - or what resembled resting - upon the cold barren ground. A coarse woolen blanket covered his now wasted form, but comfort was not Malok's concern any more.

"How can we leave him lying here on the ground," Musso said.

"This is the place for him, now," Tolmar replied. "He will not suffer alone."

Musso was not so certain. He scanned the sickness surrounding him. "No, Tolmar. They may all be here in body...but they all suffer alone."

Just then, a young *Keysian* boy scampered toward the pair. His youthful exuberance and wide-eyed innocence in the face of such devastation struck Musso with a deeper sadness.

Would no one escape Tkler's curse? he wondered.

"Tolmar!" the lad cried. "The King has sent word to fetch you and the Guidesmen to his chamber."

Tolmar eyed Musso, then tweaked the young one's still developing ear. "Is that what you hear, little pip? And how did the King, who can barely lift a finger, send this word?"

The young *Keysian* merely shrugged.

"Come, Musso," Tolmar said. "I find this curious. I think we should investigate."

Just then there was a slight tug at the leg of Musso's trousers. It was Malok, beseeching him with half opened eyes. Musso dropped to his hands and knees and leaned toward Malok's withered lips.

"Yes Malok, what is it I can do?"

Malok took a shallow breath that Musso feared might be his last. With much effort, Malok exhaled a voice barely loud enough to hear, even by the most substantial of ears, *"Believe...Musso... Believe...."*

Tolmar and Musso dashed through the twisting castle corridors until, at last, the massive doors to the Royal Chamber stood imposingly ahead. Fueled by a hungry curiosity, the eager pair met them head on and burst into the room...where they were struck motionless.

"What's the matter, never saw a King before?" Toby said, in greeting.

Musso and Tolmar's eyes shifted from Toby, to the King. From The King, back to Toby.

"Toby!" Musso exclaimed. "You've returned. You've completed the *Doors*."

Toby smiled. "Not quite yet, Mus. I think I've still got a few things to take care of, first."

"You mean *this* is still a part of the...*Doors*?" Musso asked.

"Incredible," Tolmar said. "As it was Foretold...*there would be doors within doors...dreams within dreams*."

"Yeah, sort of like holding a mirror up to a mirror," Toby glanced toward the King. "It *can* get a little confusing."

Tolmar approached the King and smiled. "Your Highness, you appear stronger. Is it true?"

"Yes Tolmar, it's true. Toby, I'd like you to meet Tolmar. He's been invaluable in interpreting many aspects of the *Foretelling*."

Toby extended his hand in greeting. "Hello, Tolmar."

Tolmar took Toby's hand and felt the strength...the power that had grown within. "It is truly my honor, beyond bounds," he said, bowing with reverence.

"No, please," Toby said uncomfortably. "Trash the bowing. You're as important to *Keys*, as I am. You shouldn't bow to anyone."

Tolmar peered into Toby's knowing eyes. "Yes...you *are* ready for Tkler. You *can* destroy the beast."

Toby turned to Musso. "Where's Malok? How's that allergy of his."

Musso's eyes dropped. "Toby, I'm afraid Malok has fallen victim to Tkler's curse. He lies among the fallen."

"*Tkler*..." Toby said in a quiet curse. He glanced toward the King. "I'd like to see him. Can I see him?"

Tolmar fussed, "I don't know if it would serve any purpose to take you there, among the hopeless."

The King responded. "I disagree, Tolmar. It would serve *every* purpose. Take him."

"Yes, my Lord," Tolmar said obediently.

"Thank you," Toby said to the King. "Thanks for everything."

"No, Toby," the King replied. "Thank *you*...for everything."

Toby nodded. "I'll take care of this...and then I'll be back."

"I know you will," the King said.

"This way, Toby," Musso stepped toward the doors. "I'll take you to Malok...if he's still—"

Toby placed a comforting hand on Musso's tiny shoulder and walked with him through the Royal Chamber Doors.

Left to ponder his thoughts alone, the King laid a weary head back on his mountain of pillows and closed his eyes. *Yes, it would take all of Toby to win this one.*

Still, he believed in the *Foretelling*. He believed in *Toby*.

Chapter 37

"Malok...Malok, wake up. You have a visitor. A special visitor."

"Musso...I can barely see you...I can barely hear," Malok croaked.

"You must try to gather your strength, Malok...you must see." Musso scampered around and boosted his friend to a sitting position.

"Ugh...Musso, must you continue to torment me? Isn't it enough that my inners rot from my *own* torment?"

"Please, Musso, be careful...don't hurt him," Toby said, crouching toward Malok.

"Toby?" Malok whispered. "Do I hear Toby? Surely I'm hallucinating."

Toby reached out and grasped the little man's wasted hand. "It's me, Malok."

Malok's mouth opened wide. A flush of color washed over his face and a spark leapt from his eye. "Toby...you have completed. You have achieved...it is done."

Toby looked toward Musso and smiled. Musso nodded back.

"Thanks to you, Malok...it's almost done. You helped get me here...this far. You got me to *Keys*...to the *Doors*."

"You made the choices, Toby...you chose to come."

Toby nodded and said, "Yes, I did choose...I chose to play. I chose to believe."

As Toby spoke, the surrounding sound of anguish began to subside. Musso looked on in amazement, sensing hope among the hopeless.

"Tkler tried to slow you down. He tried to stop you by infecting you with his disease."

"I don't think I was singled out," Malok said. "Merely a matter of chance."

"No, I don't think chance had anything to do with it, Malok. Tkler knew that *you* had the strength to reach me; to get me through the doors. So he needed to stop you...slow you down.

"But, you were too strong, Malok. You were infected, but you didn't give up. You defeated Tkler in your own way...by fulfilling *your* purpose."

Malok's eyes opened even wider. Strength appeared to return. "Then, I have done it. It is done, Musso. Do you hear...*it is done*."

"Yes Malok," Musso said, clearly pleased. "*It is done*."

Musso gently helped Malok lay back upon the tattered mat.

"*It is done*," Malok said quietly.

Musso touched Toby's arm. "Come Toby, we must leave him now."

"You have *all* the keys now, Toby...use them wisely," Malok smiled.

Toby smiled back, "Use it or lose it...that's the deal."

And with that, a warm, comforting wind swept down from above. Toby looked up, toward the breeze, then, back to Malok. All color had left the tiny man's body; the *Keysian* was fading right before his eyes.

Malok winked and his essence mingled with the wind. Then, like a fading shaft of moonlight, Malok disappeared.

"Malok." Toby gasped. "Musso, he's gone."

"No, Toby," Musso said with a comforting hand. "He's fulfilled *purpose*. He has moved on to the *next*. There is more for Malok, on the *next*."

"But I don't—"

"I know Toby. None of us really do. Malok spent a lifetime trying to achieve. Through you, he finally has. He beat Tkler's curse. He found his *purpose* and fulfilled. Now, he's moved on."

"But what about you? You did as much as Malok. Why didn't you move on?"

"Oh, Malok was our driving force. He was always the steady one, with his eye sharply focused. He had the true strength...and now, I will, hopefully, inherit that strength.

"I sense there is much more for me to do. You see, one *knows* when one has *truly* fulfilled."

"Well," Toby said. "I guess we better get started then."

"Started?" Musso questioned.

"Yep," Toby said, looking to the empty mat where Malok had been. "We better get started taking care of this Tkler thing."

"We?" Musso was incredulous. "Surely, you don't intend to take *me* along."

"Yes, I do...and please, don't call me Shirley."

"Excuse me?" Musso was flabbergasted.

"Forget it...just an old joke."

"Indeed," Musso said. "An old joke, indeed."

In the tower, high above Castle Endlum, evil Lord Tkler perceived the rancid taste of bile rising in his throat.

Was this the taste of fear?

Doubt flooded his mind in waves.

I must prepare. He is coming....

Chapter 38

"Certainly, Toby, I will only slow you down. You'd be better served— Why, I'm not even sure if it's permissible for an outsider to participate in someone else's *Doors*. I must consult the *Guidesman Handbook*."

"Relax, Musso, this is sort of a *Door add on*, anyway. Throw away the rule book. This is `No Rules Doors'. Anything goes."

"Oh my," Musso said.

Toby and Musso had retreated to the lowest reaches of Castle *Keys*, searching for the door that would lead them to Castle Endlum.

"This isn't getting us anywhere," Toby said. "So much for short cuts. Maybe if I—"

Toby opened the sack of keys, looking for a clue. There was none, and his selection was dwindling.

"It's me," Musso said. "I'm hindering the process. The *Doors* won't accept me."

Toby cinched the sack of keys and returned it to his pocket. "What happened to all this strength you were supposed to inherit from Malok?"

Musso dropped his eyes. "You're right, Toby. I'm ashamed of myself. What do you need me to do?"

"Well, for starters, you can help me find a way to this Castle Endlum place. Is there a way we can get there over land?"

"Yes, but it's a significant journey, over difficult terrain, not to mention Tkler's forces that stand in between. And then there is the...*Dark Territory*."

"*Dark Territory*...what's that?"

"No one knows for certain," Musso's voice was tinged with fear. "It's the area that surrounds all of Tkler's domain. No one who has entered has ever come back. It consumes everything, even light and sound."

Toby recalled the dark void surrounding the circle of light where the door -Tkler's *Door*- had stood. "I think I've been there. I lost something in there...but I found it."

"Incredible!" Musso said.

"I don't think I can wait to get this done. Lori and Billy need me, now."

"Then perhaps we should continue searching for a Door," Musso said with a smile.

"That may be like trying to put toothpaste back in a tube. Hey, wait a minute!"

Toby reached around to his rear pocket and pulled out the tube of paint he had stashed away earlier. "This could do it...it worked before!"

"An empty tube of paint?" Musso said.

"Not *just* a tube of paint. A special gift, from a friend," Toby said.

"What do we do...paint a picture of a door? My word."

"Something like that," Toby flipped the tube in his hand..."There's not a whole lot left, but here goes nothing..." and removed the cap.

Suddenly, a brilliant blue light burst from the tube, swirled into a tight twinkling ball, then expanded into another perfect doorway...hanging in mid-air.

"Here goes everything," Musso gasped.

"Going up," Toby announced. He inserted a key and opened the suspended door. "Third floor...ladies lingerie. All aboard."

"Ladies lingerie...indeed," Musso said, then stepped into the dazzling light.

In the large circular cavern, far below the tower of Castle Endlum, four familiar, stone faced guards, stood at the entrance to four familiar corridors.

Suddenly, a blinding burst of blue light split the sordid atmosphere. A large, vaporous swirl flooded the cavern and immediately dulled their senses. The guards remained motionless, yet followed the swirl with roving eyes. The vapor lulled them, confused their reality with their dreams, then concentrated in the middle of the empty chamber and transformed into an impossible blue door.

The guards rubbed their eyes; their mouths fell slack. Then, the door opened...and a boy emerged...*the boy*, accompanied by a strange, little man with excessively large ears, and a round bulbous nose.

"Everybody out," Toby said, then grabbed Musso's arm and jumped from the doorway.

The guards didn't budge...still numb, still staring in disbelief. They had heard of the magic door- how the boy mysteriously escaped through it. Now, he had come back....right into their hands.

"Hi guys," Toby said with inspiring cool. "Long time, no see."

Musso gulped, yet marveled at the unruffled control Toby exhibited in this most precarious situation.

Behind them, the brilliant blue door once again dissipated into a thousand sparks of light. Unhappily, Toby watched it disappear.

"Well, there goes our ride home"...and his cool was somewhat less inspired.

The sudden disappearance of the blue door snapped the guards from their stupor. They advanced toward the center of the room.

"Seize him!" one shouted.

"Alert Lord Tkler!" shouted another.

Musso, having full confidence in Toby, bravely stood his ground. "Well, what's the plan...do we vaporize them?"

"Great idea," Toby said. "Pass me the vaporizer."

"Oh my," Musso said. "You mean we have no plan."

"Sure we do...here's the plan...."

The guards advanced, readying their laser loaded cross-bows.

"...*Run for it!*" Toby shouted...and he did...running straight into the semi-circle of guards, again hoping to catch them by surprise. But this time the surprise was his, and he was brusquely thrown backwards onto the hard surface of stone.

Musso, more diminutive in size and lower to the ground, managed to squirt beneath their scurrying legs. "Run for it...that's the plan...? That's *no plan!*"

The guards instinctively spun in unison and aimed their weapons at the little Keysian. They fired, and angry bolts of searing light instantly sliced the air. They missed Musso by inches as he wildly zigged and zagged down the corridor.

Small size, it seemed, had its advantages.

The endless streaks of fire continued to rip toward Musso.

"*NO!*" Toby screamed, and with that, the guards viciously hurdled onto their backs, as if they'd been snagged by some sort of an invisible lasso. Their weapons suddenly jumped from their hands and rocketed through the infinite shaft that reached past the upper limits of Castle Endlum.

"Did I do that?" Toby marveled. "Wow...this stuff *really* rocks!"

The guards rose and charged as one, screaming in rage.

Toby observed their advance then willed them to halt...and they did, somehow frozen in time.

"Awesome!"

The guards shuffled - obviously, he needed to work on his concentration.

Musso sensed that the danger had subsided and sneaked back into the chamber. He saw Toby single out one of the guards, then focus his ice blue eyes.

Musso's jaw dropped with amazement - and more than a little amusement - as the guard rose from the ground, twirled in mid-air, and spun, head over heels, at a steadily increasing rate.

Toby faced another guard and willed that soldier hoisted up by his feet. The incredulous guard turned white with terror, fruitlessly grasping for something to hold on to. Suddenly, his head bounced to the ground, and then bounced up, bounced down, bounced up and down, like a yo-yo man.

The third guard flipped into the air and rotated like a giant helicopter, while the last was merely catapulted and pinned, like some grotesque butterfly, high upon the wall.

"My goodness, Toby," Musso said. "Where did you learn all of *this*?"

"I'm not sure." Toby stood in the center of the circular cavern, arms folded, admiring his handiwork. "Maybe something I read."

"Indeed," Musso replied.

"Come on...Lori and Billy are down this way. So's Queen Samira."

"Oh my," Musso said. "I'd nearly forgotten about the Queen."

"I'll tell her you said that," Toby responded with a smirk.

"I wish you wouldn't," Musso said, then followed Toby down the corridor to the *Temporal Hall*.

Behind them, the swirling and whirling guards crashed to the stone in a tangled heap of twisted arms and legs.

Toby and Musso turned back, just in time to see their tail ends disappearing around the bend.

"*Runawaaaaaay...!*" Toby shouted.

Musso agreed, "Yes, indeed," then repeated loudly, "*Runawaaaaaay...!*"

"Come on," Toby smiled. "Down this way."

Engineer sifted in vain through the rubble of Tkler's sophisticated electronics, trying, desperately, to rig something that would satisfy the increasing rage of his Lord and Master.

It was difficult work, especially since the Tower had become an increasingly unstable environment for concentration. Piles of stone lay everywhere...mortar dust blew in waves. Castle Endlum was clearly falling to pieces.

In his darkened corner, Tkler paced a circular path, over and over again. The fine white dust had now settled into every fold of his long black robes and he constantly flicked and flecked at the garments like a flea infested animal.

"*Engineer!*" he roared, stepping out of the shadows. "Engineer, I must see him...*NOW!*"

Engineer cautiously looked up and inwardly gasped at what he saw.

Tkler, the dark hollows of his face encased in dust, looked frail and weak. In fact, if it weren't for the dust, Engineer believed that Lord Tkler might *actually* be transparent. Still...this *was* Lord Tkler, transparent or not.

"My Lord," Engineer said meekly. "I'm afraid it is useless. It will take time...much time to make the necessary repairs. And the dust...it's just impossible...."

"*Wrong Answer!*" Tkler screamed. "*Your time is up, incompetent fool!*"

Tkler raised his black draped arm and pointed toward the astonished Engineer who indeed endured an endless moment of time - "*No my Lord, please...no,*" - and a violent flash of light shot from Tkler's sleeve.

"No...." Engineer whimpered, cowering into a ball.

But the intense streak of light merely dispersed in mid-air, blossoming meekly, like a firework on the Fourth of July.

"*Ahhhhhhrgh!*" Tkler roared. He was losing it all.

Then a clatter emerged from the endless circular shaft as objects unknown streaked past like comets.

Tkler turned. *What commotion is this*?

He ran to the edge, seeing more of the objects fly into the night. One of them struck the wall, rattled around, and fell back.

Tkler reached out and grabbed the object before it passed.

"A guard's lightning-cross...from where?" he asked, puzzled, yet afraid to guess the answer. Cautiously, he leaned over and peered into the darkness.

Just then, Centurion burst into the chamber.

"My Lord, the b—" he glanced curiously at Engineer, who still cowered in the electronic rubble, then continued. "My Lord, the boy...he's back. The guards have encountered him...but I'm afraid unsuccessfully. He appears to have...powers."

279

Tkler stiffened and turned to face Centurion. Whatever color remained, now drained from his countenance entirely.

"So, the boy has returned," he said quietly. "Of course he has. And is he with us completely, or between time again?"

"He appears to be solidly among us," Centurion answered. "He has one of the *Keysians* with him."

"How bold," Tkler whispered.

Centurion looked on with concern while his mighty Lord walked meekly to the tower window. He expected the Master to spring into action and storm into battle. Instead, Tkler surveyed the surrounding landscape, as a condemned prisoner might study the clouds before stepping into the noose.

Engineer rose to his feet and exchanged troubled glances with Centurion.

"My Lord," Centurion said. "Shall I assemble a detail?"

Tkler remained silent, continuing to stare deep into the night.

Engineer again glanced at Centurion and shrugged, yet neither dared approach.

Suddenly, an amber aura of light enveloped Tkler's form. His black robes puffed, filled with the light, and shed an avalanche of dust to the floor.

Tkler stepped back from the window and turned.

"My Lord!" Engineer and Centurion gasped.

The strange amber light coursed from within, flowing through Tkler's entire being...from his eyes, his nose...even his ears.

Slowly, the aura subsided and retracted to Tkler's evil core.

At last, he had renewed his strength...become whole again...and was ready...for *the boy*. Ready for battle...the final battle.

Tkler sneered and returned to the window. With an intensity of purpose, he raised his arm and unleashed a solid beam of fiery light, racing into the night.

Tkler smiled.

Engineer cringed.

Turning again, arm still extended, Tkler faced his faithful Engineer. Their eyes locked instantly.

Centurion sensed what was about to transpire and quickly stepped to the side.

Tkler snarled, "I think not," and lowered his lethal appendage. "I shall not waste an ounce of the power on the likes of you. I believe I will need *all* that I possess...later."

Engineer slumped and released a sigh of relief.

Centurion studied the walls and ceiling. The quaking had ceased. The tower had stopped its incessant swaying and the mortar dust had finally settled.

"Come Centurion," Tkler, strode down the long circular ramp that would lead him to the boy. "There is work to be done. Gather your men. The time is *NOW!*"

"Yes my Lord," Centurion said excitedly. His Lord Tkler had returned...ready to battle...powers intact.

Still, it was the boy...and the boy had discovered...his own....

Chapter 39

The massive doors that marked the terminus of the *Temporal Hall* loomed before them.

"This is the place," Toby said. "They're in here."

Musso cringed, "Oh my," and the little man took a giant step backward.

"I know," Toby said. "You can feel it, can't you? It's even worse inside. It's like...this room...is somehow the heart of it; the agony...misery and despair, all concentrated, here. But we're gonna change all that...real soon."

"Toby, how will we get past these doors. They appear to be securely bolted, and quite impenetrable."

"I know. Last time I was here I was able to just step through them."

"Step through them?" a befuddled Musso said.

"It's a long story," Toby answered. "Let's see, if I were me...what would I do? Wait, I know...I almost forgot."

Toby closed his eyes, then scrunched his face into an intense mask of concentration.

The wooden doors rattled, ever so slightly. Musso took another step back, but watched the proceedings with wonder.

Toby opened his eyes, "Hmmmm, this stuff is a little trickier than I thought," then closed his eyes again.

Need to sharpen my focus...even more.

He thought of the doors. He thought of Billy...and of Lori.

He heard Billy's frantic screams. He saw the haggard pain, thriving on Lori's face, the hopelessness in her eyes...

...And the doors suddenly exploded into a million shards of kindling and dust. Instantly, a nightmarish wave of putrid air rushed from the opened crypt and swept the length of the Temporal Hall. Musso covered his prodigious proboscis and turned away.

Then the loathsome wind slowly receded and Toby opened his eyes to a pile of splinters and a gaping hole where the once impenetrable doors had stood.

"Far out," he said in awe.

"Very far out, indeed," Musso replied. "Masterfully done, masterfully done, indeed."

"I just blew them suckers away, Mus. Did you see it?"

"*Mus?*" Musso said uncomfortably. "Yes Toby, I did ...and I smelled it too. He wiped his nose with an extra-large handkerchief he had pulled from his trousers. "You certainly did...blow them suckers away."

Toby smiled at the little man. "Come on Mus, this way."

"*Mus?*" Musso repeated, clearly befuddled, and followed Toby into the darkened room.

Toby took small, deliberate steps and studied the familiar hall, lined with the mysterious, translucent panels.

Again, he sensed the torment that resided here, quietly marking time. Only now, it was *more* than a *sense*...he could *feel* it too.

Toby glanced toward Musso who was also visibly shaken.

"Toby, what is it? Where are we?"

"It's some sort of dungeon...only worse, somehow...only worse."

"Then we must keep moving, Toby. We must—"

Toby ignored his external senses, and looked within. Slowly, the darkened panels illuminated. Musso shuddered, frozen by the sight, but managed to grasp hold of Toby's arm. Now, he understood.

Behind each panel, encased in rows of bare narrow cells, indescribable creatures writhed in torment...writhed in fear.

Toby's head spun in circles...everywhere...all around him...pathetic creatures...extended long, sinewy arms that merely suggested human form. Alien mouths stretched in tortured submission, filled his head with deafening wails, within the silent room.

"What is this...who are they?" Tears threatened to stream from Toby's eyes.

"Lost souls...of hope and dreams. Tkler's work I'm afraid."

"I know them," Toby said in a whisper. "They're like the creatures who gave me the sack of keys, at the tree...the *Elephant Tree*."

"Yes, I know," Musso said quietly. "I know. Come, Toby, let's proceed. There is nothing we can do for them, now."

"I want to help them...I have to...I.—"

"You will Toby...in fact, you've done more for them than you know."

Then suddenly, Toby saw them, the cells...the cells that contained Lori and Queen Samira. And he needed to be there...now!

What if they weren't there? What if Tkler had moved them...or worse?

"*No!*" he screamed. He had to remove all doubt from his mind. *They* would *be there*...and a burst of unbridled energy propelled him down the hall.

Musso struggled to keep pace, valiantly working his tiny *Keysian* legs.

The illuminated windows streaked by in a series of peripheral blurs. Faster and faster...Toby ran at break neck speed....

...Until a somewhat familiar sight...caught his eye....

"*Billy*," he shouted. "*What the—*"

Toby's eyes widened like a pair silver dollars. It was Billy Bartles...spinning and spinning on a barbecue spit, with a big fat apple lodged, firmly in mouth.

A small chuckle escaped Toby's lips. "Taking a little spin, Bill?" He couldn't resist.

Billy muttered something; his eyes bulged, and his face flushed a brilliant red. It sounded like, "*Tbmnn!.*"

"*Toby?*" croaked the slightest whisper of a voice. "*Toby...have you come back for us?*"

Toby spun toward the whisper, then returned to the *Billy Luau*, "I'll be back in a jiff with the pineapple, Bill. Don't go away," then he ran to the adjacent window.

"Lori," he said. "Lori hold on...I can fix it. I can fix everything."

"I know Toby," Lori said enigmatically. "I always knew, Toby."

Toby smiled, but his heart was battered by the decomposing figure sitting before his eyes.

Lori had grown *more* than *old*. Her beautiful hair - he could still smell its comforting scent - had been replaced by desolate bunches of brittle white strands.

Her face had collapsed, as if the very bones beneath, had caved into her skull. Her body was consuming itself. She was turning into one of *them*...those creatures. He was losing her.

Musso finally caught up and stiffened at the sight of Lori.

"Musso...my dear Musso. I knew you would come," said a sweet, gentle voice from behind.

Musso spun, "Queen Samira!"

Samira sat in her cell, still ever peaceful and composed. Emily, still restrained, purred acknowledgment.

"Samira, what is happening...what—?"

"Believe, Musso. You must believe in Toby."

"Yes, Samira. I do believe...in *this* one," he said, turning back.

"It is all as it was *foretold*. Is it not, my Guidesman?"

"Incredibly so," Musso answered.

"Still, there is much to be done...much to be fulfilled," Samira said.

"Lori...." Toby placed his hand against the glass.

"Toby," Lori replied with an empty grin. Unable to rise from the rickety old rocking chair, she struggled to lean forward and placed her desiccated palm against his.

Suddenly, the glass hummed with a powerful warmth. Slow rivulets of viscous liquid streamed to the floor, formed a puddle at their feet, until finally, Toby's flesh was touching Lori's, and the barrier melted away.

"Lori...." Toby stepped into the cell and, carefully, carried Lori from the rocking chair. He was afraid she might crumble in his grasp.

She did not.

Slowly, Lori slipped from Toby's arms, stood unsteadily and faced him.

"I knew you'd come back for us," she croaked. "Everything will be alright, now. I know it will."

Toby wrapped uncertain arms around Lori's frail body and felt something he had never known before: a wholeness deep inside.

For the first time in all this craziness, Toby knew. It was near. He was close.

"Everything *will* be alright," he whispered into Lori's ear. "I'm certain of it now."

Their embrace strengthened and an inner light encircled them, finding life in their unity. When it disappeared, Lori was as young and as radiant, as she had ever been before.

To Toby, *she was* magic.

Across the way, Samira and Musso witnessed the transformation and smiled. Musso brushed a tear from his eye and blew his nose. *HONK...!*

Lori, jumped, then nervously giggled.

"Well, Mus, I see you've inherited *something* from Malok, after all," Toby said.

A flush of red bloomed on Musso's face. "Mus...?"

Toby then took Lori's hand and led her away from Tkler's evil influence. Together, they approached Samira.

Toby inspected the panel enclosing the Queen. "I think I have the key for this," and placed his palm on the glass. It too evaporated, just as before.

Toby stepped into the cell and bowed. "It can be whatever I imagine it to be," he said, cryptically.

She bowed her head in return and smiled a knowing smile.

Toby helped the Queen to her feet, then unbuckled the restraining device encircling Emily.

Emily purred. "*Tooooobeeee...beeeleeeeve.*"

"Yes Emily," he answered. "Toby believe."

Emily popped to her two hind legs and placed her paws on her hips. She almost appeared to smile. "*Gooooooooood.*"

Toby laughed and rubbed her pointed head. Lori entered the cell and immediately snatched up Emily and hugged her.

"*Loooooori,*" Emily purred.

""Hi Emily," Lori said with a huge smile. "I missed you."

"*Miiiiisssssyoooooootoooooooo.*"

Toby then stepped from the cell and marched over to Billy.

288

"Well, what have we here...*Barbecued Bartles*?" he grinned.

Billy mumbled something unintelligible, while large veins emerged on his forehead in frustration.

"Nice undies," Toby teased, clearly enjoying the moment. "When did you give up the teddy bears?"

"*Mmmmmmmphgfhre!*" Billy squirmed and moaned, still struggling with the rotating spit.

Toby closed his eyes and the glass melted with a splash.

Toby opened his eyes and saw the apple pop from Billy's mouth like a cork. "*POP!*"

Without missing a beat, Billy immediately started babbling. "Come on, Tubman. Get me off of this hibachi before I get roasted. That Tkler guy is nuts...you don't know."

Oh I know," Toby said. "Believe me, I know."

Again, Toby concentrated, and the spit disappeared, dropping Billy onto the unlit woodpile like a stone.

"*Ohmmmmph!*" Billy cried. "Couldn't you at least be gentle about it? How'd you do that anyway?"

"Magic," Toby answered.

"Yeah, well believe me, you're gonna need all the magic you can muster against this Tykguy."

"I know," Toby whispered. He gathered Billy's clothes from the corner.

"Hey, pass me my pants, will ya."

"Why should I. You wouldn't give me mine when I needed them," Toby said.

"What are you talking about," Billy muttered. "Come on it's gettin drafty in here. Where've you been, anyway? How was it, was it cool? I bet it was cool. You know I'm gettin a little hungry. Did you see where that apple went to?"

Toby shook his head - some things, it seemed, never changed - and threw Billy his clothes.

"Get dressed, will ya. You're not a pretty sight."

Toby turned to join the others.

"Hey Tobe," Billy said.

"Yeah?" he answered, turning back.

"Don't I get one of those magic hugs, too?"

"Try it and I'll kick your butt," Toby said with a big smile.

"Yeah...right," Billy said, and jumped into his jeans.

Toby returned to the group.

"What happens now Toby?" Lori asked. "How do we get out of here?"

Toby looked at Samira and Musso. "Well, I think we have some business to finish up before we leave."

"Tkler?" Lori said.

"That's the guy," Toby answered.

Billy stepped into the mix and added, "You know, maybe it would be a better idea if we just tried to find a back way out of this place and left while the leavin is easy. Know what I mean?"

"Come on Billy B," Toby said. "Where's your sense of adventure?"

"I think I left it in your closet."

"Well, I think you'd better run along and fetch it."

"Believe me, nothing would please me more than to walk back through that old *Door to Nowhere*, right about now."

Emily stood on her hind legs and placed her paws on her hips again. "*Yoooooogooooofeeeeetch*," she snarled in Billy's direction.

"Not the mutt again," Billy sighed. "Come on, let's get out of here...somewhere ...anywhere. This place gives me the creeps."

And with that, they banded together and began the painful journey...back through the corridor of forgotten dreams.

The relentless suffering, again, bogged the hall and shackled their every step.

They tried averting their eyes, quickening their pace, hurrying to reach the exit...but there *was* no escape.

Billy's eyes, despite all efforts, kept drifting back to the windows. "Man Toby, we have to do something for these guys. This is the most horrible thing I've ever seen."

"I know, Bill. I just don't know what to do."

Musso shouted back to the two boys. "Please we must continue. There is much more to be done. You can't help them now, Toby."

Toby and Billy acknowledged Musso's plea, but were unable to dismiss the agony. Lori joined them.

"What can we do," she whispered. "Toby you helped us, maybe you can help them too."

Musso reached the doors, or where the doors once stood, and stopped, frustrated by the others who lagged behind. His oversized ears twitched with the sound of rushing footsteps...angry footsteps, very nearby.

He looked toward Samira. She too looked concerned.

"Please Toby, we must go immediately!" Musso shouted.

"Hold your pits, short stuff!" Billy returned. "We're trying to think here."

Toby studied the luminous panels and closed his eyes. Instantly, the panels popped and transformed into extravagant webs of cracking glass.

"Yeah, Jiffy Pop em, Tubman...way to go," Billy said.

Suddenly, the glass shattered and crashed to the ground in a blizzard of sparkling shards. Then, the noxious wind returned. It rushed from the cells and overwhelmed their senses. Billy and Lori turned away. Toby remained motionless, oblivious to it all.

Then, as suddenly as it began, the wind abated...gathered itself...and reversed direction, rushing back through the corridor in a gentle curl.

It was no longer threatening...evil and stale. Rather, it was fresh and comforting...somehow...alive.

Billy and Lori smiled, while Samira, Musso and Emily approached in silent awe.

Toby opened his eyes, and the creatures began to transform. Their suffering was in retreat, smothered by the renewing breeze. No longer horrible, inhuman things; now, they were people...smiling...happy...at peace...with themselves, filled with the wonder of life.

But the evolution was not yet complete.

"Toby...look at it...do you believe...?" gasped Lori.

Thousands upon thousands of minute sparkling balls, slipped from within their mellifluous forms. Then a glittering light enveloped their souls in a tranquil, metamorphic swirl, until at last, their substance...their very essence rose on the sparkling light.

The corridor filled with the ethereal presence...it surrounded the group with gratitude.

Lori reached out to touch it, but it passed through her fingers like stardust. Billy gaped in awe...spinning and turning...trying to follow its flight.

Toby smiled and the sparkling light diminished then, slowly, disappeared.

The corridor was empty now, except for the mounds of broken glass that lay across the floor.

"Toby, what happened? What happened to all of those people?" Lori asked.

Toby turned to Samira and Musso.

"They are free now," Samira said. "They were on the brink of achieving when Tkler stepped in and robbed them of their lives. He imprisoned their souls and tortured them with the knowledge that achieving was within their grasp, but never fulfilled. Now, they have been released and will achieve their purpose. They are truly free."

"You have already scored a great victory, Toby. Tkler is greatly diminished," Musso said with a broad smile.

"Come on, Tobe. Let's go finish off that dark eyed nitwit," Billy said with new found confidence. "Let's kick some Tkler buttsky."

Toby glanced at Lori and smiled, then turned toward Billy and hugged him.

"Here's that hug you were looking for bonehead. Thanks, I need your help."

Toby expected some sort of wise crack from Billy, some sort of verbal shield. Instead, Billy hugged him back and said, "You got it Tubman. You always have."

Toby opened his arm and Lori stepped into the circle.

Samira and Musso smiled. Emily gently purred.

High above the circular cavern, footsteps raced forward at an angry pace.

"I want him...I want him this time. Do you understand, Centurion. I want him...*STOPPED!*" Tkler raced down and around the circular ramp that led to the lower reaches of Castle Endlum.

Centurion furiously shouted orders into a small communications device that was woven into the fabric of his cloak.

"Yes, my Lord, you shall have him. I've sent an advance detail ahead to intercede. They should be coming upon them momentarily."

"Excellent," Tkler sneered. "Then he shall be mine."

"I'm afraid there is a new development, my Lord," Centurion said cautiously.

Tkler stopped dead in his tracks. "What sort of development, Centurion. Tell me, will this new development displease me, Centurion?"

Centurion swallowed deep and relayed the news. "It appears that the boy has accessed the *Temprocity Chamber* and—"

"Yes...what Centurion...he what...?"

"He appears to have liberated the *enslaved*."

"*Impossible...!*" Tkler roared. "*It is impenetrable...the process is immutable...it is as infinite as time itself!*"

"Never the less, my Lord," Centurion said with trepidation. "It is done...I'm afraid."

Strength washed from Tkler's face. His eyes deadened. "What sort of boy is this? What am I up against? How could this be?"

But Tkler knew, all too well, how it could be. Tkler too, knew the *Foretelling*.

"Come Centurion," the evil Lord gazed over the circular ramp, into the dark abyss below. "We have nowhere to go but down. Down, to meet our destiny."

Centurion stiffened.

Did, indeed, these words ring true...truer than the Master did intend?

Chapter 40

At times they were certain they had been running around in circles. One after the other they confronted an endless maze of twisting hallways and darkened corridors.

Billy hunched over, hands on knees, and gasped for breath.

"Man...I'm sure I've seen...this exact same...rock ...about a hundred...times now, Tubman."

"Well, you're the one who's supposed to know his way around. *You* had the run of the place."

"Well, I was sort of kept on a short leash...if you know what I mean."

"Yeah, I think I remember," Toby said. "By the way, I don't think black is your color. I see you more as a *Spring/Summer* type."

The others finally caught up.

Musso also gasped for breath. "Toby, where are we running to? It feels as if we've been running down one dead end after another."

"The little guy might be right, Tobe," Billy said. "Maybe were forcing the action. Maybe we should let the game come to us."

Toby smiled at Lori, who was still carrying Emily. He couldn't help but be reminded of Dorothy and Toto, although this was indeed a very strange version of *Toto*.

He guessed that, in a way, this was their *own* version of *going off to see the wizard*...in a *very* strange *Ozzian Oddity*, kind of way.

"How you holding up, Lor?" he gently swept a wayward strand of hair from her eyes.

"I'm okay," she said with a smile. "How you doin?"

"Never been better," he answered.

Billy inspected the multiple trickles of water that seeped through the subterranean stone. "Man this place is gonna flood up the kazoo at the next—"

Suddenly a bolt of white hot lightning smashed into the rock next to Billy's extended hand. Billy instinctively fell back and the corridor exploded into a storm of flashing light.

Musso pulled Samira to the ground and threw himself protectively over her back.

Mortar and stone flew wildly...searing beams of fire crashed from every side.

Toby spotted a small alcove set into the stone to his left. He wrapped his arms around Lori and Emily and jumped in. Billy remained crouched on the ground covering his head.

"Billy, over here," Toby shouted.

Billy nodded. He grabbed Samira by the arm and rushed through the maelstrom of lethal light until, finally, they collapsed into the safety of the hollow.

Toby reached out and pulled them further inside.

"Thank you, Billy," Samira said. "That was most unselfish."

"Ah, it was nothing I wouldn't do for any other Queen," Billy smiled and winked at Toby. "Hey, what happened to the *half pint*?"

Lori giggled and Samira turned to reveal Musso, spread eagle, across the back of her gown, his eyes, clamped shut, and his teeth, clenched in a rattling grimace.

Billy tapped Musso on the shoulder. "Hey, little guy. You can let go now. We're out of the storm."

Musso sheepishly opened his eyes, released his grip on Samira's gown, and slowly slid to the floor.

Queen Samira turned and knelt to Musso's eye level. "You protected me with your life, my Guidesman. I will be eternally grateful for your noble and heroic deed, as will the King."

Musso beamed with pride. "At your service as always, my Queen."

Billy patted Musso on the back, "Nice job, big guy," then walked away, leaving a big dirty hand print behind.

Toby peered intently around the corner. The firing had stopped, but he knew that Tkler's soldiers would be coming for them.

Lori stepped over to Toby and said, "What do we do now? We can't stay here for long."

"Look." Toby noticed that the laser blasts had badly damaged the walls. The little trickle of water was, now, a mini waterfall.

"There must be some sort of underground stream, or something, that runs through here."

"Great," Billy cracked. "What are we gonna do, swim out?"

"Billy, be quiet, Toby's thinking," Lori said, impatiently.

"I've got a plan," Toby said.

"Yeah, me too," Billy said. "Let's get out of here."

"We need to draw them out, into the corridor. We need to set up a decoy."

"A decoy!" Billy exclaimed. "Don't look at me. Send the mutt."

"*Illlgoooo*," Emily said bravely.

"No, not you Emily, I'm afraid you're a little too small to be noticed. No, we need someone bigger." Toby stepped toward Billy. "Someone louder. Someone with a big mouth, whose used to attracting attention to himself."

"Sounds like a perfect fit," Lori snickered.

"Yeah, well fit—"

"Come on, Bill," Toby cut in. "I won't let anything happen to you. I promise."

Billy looked at his friend. "Alright, Tobe. Whatever you need. What do you want me to do?"

"Just step out there and make them notice you. Get them out in the open."

"Toby, why don't you merely deal with them the same way you dealt with the earlier guards? That seemed to be quite effective," Musso asked.

"There's too many of them now, Mus. And I don't have surprise on my side anymore. They'll be looking out for tricks."

"I see," Musso said. "*Mus...?*"

"Go on Billy," Toby said. "Get them out in the open."

"Here goes nothing." Billy took a deep breath and jumped out into the unprotected hall. "*Hey...Hey over here. Your Tkler wears army boots!*"

The corridor remained silent. The soldiers were apparently wary of some sort of deception.

"I guess that won't work," Billy whispered from the side of his mouth. "I forgot...he does wear army boots." Then, Billy stepped further out into the corridor.

"Hey, what's the matter...you guys afraid of a little action?"

The soldiers responded with a barrage of laser fire. Billy jumped two feet in the air, then covered his head and dove back into the alcove.

"Nice plan, Tobe," he said, gasping for breath. "What's next? Would you like I should light myself on fire and run screaming down the hall?"

"Sorry, Bill," Toby said. "I guess that plan only works in the movies."

"What movies are you watchin?" Billy said.

The torrent of fire stopped and the corridor grew eerily silent.

"This is creepy," Lori said.

"Yeah, it's as if they're just waiting us out or something," Billy said.

Toby glanced at Samira and exchanged a knowing look.

"They're waiting for Tkler to arrive," he said flatly.

"Well good," Billy said. "That's what we want, anyway...isn't it?"

"Not like this," Toby answered. "We don't want to be backed into a corner."

"Sssssssshh," Lori said. "I have an idea."

"Oh great," Billy muttered.

Lori shot him a threatening look.

"What is it, Lor?" Toby asked.

"Just keep quiet and be ready to do, whatever it is you're gonna do," she said decisively.

Lori crept up to the edge of the tiny alcove. She gathered herself, then croaked into the silence with a weak and dying voice.

"Help...help...me. They're all dead....you killed them all...you killed everyone. Toby's dead...the Queen...now, Billy too. Help me, I'm hurt...dying."

There was no response. Only the sound of water, pouring into the hall.

"That's your plan?" Billy mocked. "Where'd you see that...*Winnie the Poop Poop*?"

"Help...please...somebody." Lori croaked, shooting another threatening look Billy's way.

Suddenly, the heavy shuffling of boots approached down the hall.

"Whoa...way to go *Poop Poop*," Billy said.

Lori stuck out her tongue, then carefully peered around the edge. "They're coming," she whispered. "There must be twenty or thirty of them."

"Are they all out in the corridor yet?" Toby asked.

"Uh, huh...all of them."

301

The squadron of Tkler's soldiers cautiously marched down the passageway. They had heard of the boy's powers and they were still on their guard, ever alert.

Toby turned his blue penetrating eye on the seeping wall. He focused on the small flow of water running from the blasted hole...he imagined the massive pressure on the other side...building up against the thick, yet ancient stone...he imagined the power of all that water...rushing at once...against the solid surface....

...Suddenly, the stone exploded and a torrent of water gushed into the corridor...as if Toby had unleashed the power of Poseidon. The soldiers were immediately swamped by the water and panicked. Some turned to run, but were viciously swept away by the flood.

Billy followed the others into the corridor, and admired Toby's style.

"Excellent plan, Tubman," he said with a huge grin. "Really excellent! What flick did ya see that in?"

"Ten Commandments"

"Yeah, that Huston dude was cool."

"Heston."

"Yeah, right."

"Come Toby, we must keep moving," Musso said.

The group retreated down another twisting corridor.

Up above, Tkler continued his spiral decent to the circular cavern below. Time, it seemed, was escaping.

Chapter 41

Another series of endless halls and corridors...another series of dead ends.

This time it was Toby who pulled up and clutched his aching side. Leaning against the cold stone, he gasped for air and said, "This is crazy, Billy. All we're doing is chasing our own shadow."

"Yeah well, what else are we supposed to do? If we're gonna take care of Tkler, we have to find him...unless...."

"Unless what?" Toby asked.

"Unless he doesn't want to be found. What if he's already cut his losses and high tailed it out of here? What if he knows he can't win?"

Toby sucked some wind and considered Billy's statement. "Nah...guys like Tkler don't run. It's all or nothing. If he were gone...we'd be gone too. All of this would be gone. Something tells me we should go back to that circular cavern place. I think that's where it all goes down. Everything begins and ends there."

"How do you know that?" Billy asked.

"My heart...my soul...they're telling me. I'm listening to my heart and soul."

Again, Billy's face developed that question mark and he placed his ear against Toby's sweaty chest.

"All's I hear is your heart pounding a mile a minute. Just like mine. What's it, some kind of Morse code thing you got going there?"

Toby pushed Billy away. "Get away from me, knucklehead, before I do something I might regret...or worse...I might not regret."

The two buddies chuckled and waited for the others to catch up.

"What are you two guys amused at now?" Lori asked.

"Nothing, Lor," Billy said. "Just guy stuff, you wouldn't understand."

"So what else is new?" Lori said with mock exasperation.

Toby and Billy giggled again.

"You know, I don't think I'll ever understand you two."

"I know, Lor," Toby put his arm comfortably over her shoulder. "That's okay. I don't think we will either."

Musso cleared his throat, feeling uneasy amidst the frivolity. "Really Toby, don't you think we should get to wherever it is we're going?"

"Indeed I do, Mus...indeed I do."

Musso grimaced again at the sound of his newly acquired nickname.

"Come on short stuff, lighten up." Billy chided. "Toby's zoned now. He's marchin to the beat of his heart."

"Exactly," Samira said, smiling at Toby. "It makes all the difference."

"Now you're gettin it, Billy boy," Toby said with a smirk. "There might be hope for you yet."

"Huh," Billy said. "What'd I say? I said somethin ...what?"

"Where're we going, Toby?" Lori said, ignoring Billy.

"I think we need to get over to that circular cavern place. You know, the one with those four passageways, and that weird air shaft or something, shooting up to who knows where."

"Yes, Toby," Samira said. "I believe you are correct. That would be the logical place. It's the heart of Castle Endlum. It's where it all begins and ends."

"Yeah," Billy said smugly. "That's what we we're saying earlier, right Tobe."

Toby shook his head in amusement. "That's right, Billy. Whatever you say."

"Toby, I believe it's in that direction," Musso said. "We've gotten twisted and turned a bit, but I'm fairly certain."

"I think you're right, Mus," Toby answered. "Come on let's get going."

Taking Musso's lead they traveled down yet another narrow corridor until, Emily, wiggling and a waggling behind, stopped dead in her unusual tracks. Intuitively, her needles bristled and pointed toward the approaching corner.

"*Daaaaangerrrrrrr*...." she growled.

"Did you say something?" Billy asked Toby.

"Not me. You're hearing things."

"Great."

Just then, they stepped around the bend and walked straight into another hale of laser fire, heavier and more intense than before.

"Man this is so getting old!" shouted Billy.

The two boys crouched in unison and froze near the wall. Lori, hidden around the corner, reacted quickly. Without thinking, she quickly reached out, grabbed both of them by their collars, then yanked hard. The three of them fell backwards together, crashing one on top of the other in a jumble of arms and legs.

"Geez, that was close," Billy scrambled to his feet. "What's with these guys?"

Toby sat up and looked at Lori. "Thanks, Lor. I think you might have saved our lives."

Billy glanced at Lori, but his attention was focused on what was about to come around the corner. "Yeah, thanks, Lor."

"No problem," Lori said, matter of factly, smiling at Toby. "Just returning the favor."

Toby smiled back, then turned to the sound of rushing footsteps. A powerful burst of fire soon followed.

Musso and Samira had already doubled back to select an alternative route.

"Come on, I think we're taking a detour," Lori said.

"Quickly, this way," Musso shouted over the roar of the laser blasts.

Toby helped Lori to her feet and they quickly followed Billy down the corridor. Behind, Tkler's soldiers turned the corner and

306

unleashed a storm of destruction. Stone and mortar disintegrated. Entire sections of corridor collapsed.

Shielding their eyes from the flying rock, the three friends frantically followed Samira and Musso around another bend.

"Man, I think these laser boys have stepped it up a little," Billy said, running three steps ahead of Toby and Lori.

"You think?" Toby panted. "We must be pissin them off."

"Don't you think it's time to hit em with another one of your special effects?" Billy took another look back at the soldiers. "Maybe a hoard of locusts or something."

"Yeah, Toby," Lori said. "Let em have it."

"I need to concentrate," Toby said. He was struggling with the frenzied pace that Billy was setting. "I have to stop and focus...and I don't think that's a good idea about now."

Up ahead, they could see Samira, Musso and Emily. They had stopped running. In fact, they were standing still as stone.

"What's the matter with them...why're they just standing there like statues?" Billy asked. But all too soon, they found out.

"Oh no!" Lori cried. "What do we do now?"

"We're doomed here," Billy said.

They had run into another dead end. An empty cul-de-sac that led nowhere. Toby turned back and saw the guards closing in, laser's blasting.

"This is not good," Toby said. "This is definitely not good."

"Toby you can handle this," Musso said. His little legs trembled as he eyed the approaching storm.

"Right," Toby said. "I can handle this."

And with that a bracing wind suddenly rose from the surface. It gathered itself and gained momentum, swirling round and round the semi-circular room.

Toby stood in the eye of the gale while the others huddled together against the wall. The wind accelerated, sweeping faster and faster around the cul-de-sac, until finally, as if on command, it exploded into the corridor and walloped into the oncoming soldiers.

The gust impacted like another ruinous tidal wave, picking the guards up and throwing them maliciously into one another. Everywhere, ragged soldiers lay scattered and bent in all directions.

Centurion, had taken leave of Lord Tkler and come ahead to lead the capture. As soon as he turned the corner the veteran commander spotted the swirling dust and immediately threw himself down along the edge of the wall and waited out the tempest. Then with an evil calm, Centurion raised his weapon, fingered the triggering device, and took aim at the skinny boy that had created all of this ruckus.

How easy it all seems, he thought. *What, after all, is this fuss about? He is just a boy.*

Centurion steadied the weapon. The low angle of trajectory and awkward position of the boy would not allow him to make a direct hit. A carom shot, off the wall and across the rounded ceiling, would have to suffice.

Just as well, Centurion thought. *Tkler wanted the boy in one piece, anyway. Look at him, standing there, eyes closed, so confident in himself. It is all so easy...indeed.*

Centurion fired.

Toby stood transfixed in concentration. He opened his eyes and saw the swirling wind sweep into the hall and blast the soldiers away.

About to say something to Billy, he abruptly froze when he spotted the bolt of lightning streak over his head.

Lori cried out, "Toby watch—"

In an instant the blast hit the wall, bounced up and hugged the domed ceiling. Then, swooping around, it took direct aim at Toby.

"Tobe!" Billy shouted.

But it was too late. The deadly light crashed into Toby's chest and immediately encircled him like an unearthly cocoon.

"Toby!" Lori tried running to him but was repelled by the unnatural force emanating from the light.

Then, the light consumed itself and disappeared.

Toby crumbled to the ground.

"*No!*" Lori screamed, and feverishly scrambled to his lifeless form. "*Toby no....*" her voice trailed to a whimper. Samira and Musso recoiled in horror.

Two soldiers rushed into the room and took aim on the fallen boy. They wanted to finish him off and be done with it.

Lori, reacting swiftly and instinctively, flew off her feet with a ferocious scream and flung her body lengthwise into the two assailants.

Billy couldn't believe his eyes. It was all happening so fast, yet he saw it all in slow motion. Every subtle detail burned into his brain.

Lori plowed into the soldiers, throwing them back against the wall. One of their weapons discharged into the ceiling and the laser bounced wildly around the room.

The other soldier dropped his weapon and it skidded off to the side. Billy saw his chance and dove to the stone surface.

"Lori, get out of the way!" he shouted, and snatched up the unusual device. He saw a trigger and pulled.

The powerful recoil caught Billy by surprise. The weapon let loose a horrific combination of light and sound and Billy was blown backwards, into the wall behind.

The vicious blast encircled both soldiers at once. Their faces froze in the beginnings of a terrible scream. The light swirled, seem to grow hotter, and then, devoured the soldiers completely.

Lori hurried back to Toby, while Musso and Samira, along with Emily, crouched by his side.

"He's still breathing," Lori said. "It didn't—"

"No," Samira said. "He merely appears to be stunned. He'll wake up soon."

Musso turned and approached Billy, who was still propped against the wall, staring at the spot where the soldiers had been.

"You had no choice, Billy. You did what you had to do."

"But I meant to put...you know...lasers on stun...not melt down."

"You did what was necessary...no more...no less."

Billy continued to stare at the charred stone.

"Man, I just wanna go home."

"Soon," Musso said. "Soon, my boy."

Billy tossed the lethal weapon to the side and stood up. "How's Toby?"

"He'll be fine."

They rejoined the others just as the brigade of Tkler's guards rushed into the room.

"*Seize them*!" Centurion shouted. "There will be no more tricks from this one, for a while." He marched up to Toby and prodded him with his heavy boot.

Centurion turned and noticed the blackened spot where two of his men had been *dealt with*. He turned back, without compassion or concern. He smiled. "Lord Tkler will be very pleased. Take them to the circular cavern. We mustn't keep the Master waiting."

Billy looked at Samira and said, "I think it's game time...and our quarterback is down."

Queen Samira nodded. There was no sign of her usual inner calm. She looked concerned...very concerned.

The guards rumbled in, plucked Toby from the stone and wrapped some sort of mysterious restraining line around his slackened body. Satisfied that this *"Wonder Boy"* was sufficiently bound and rendered harmless, they dragged him out of the hall.

"Don't hurt him," Lori cried. She was brusquely shoved into formation with the rest and led away.

Lord Tkler approached the circular cavern and stopped.

Perhaps...just perhaps, he thought quietly...and waited...waited for his time.

Chapter 42

An unpleasant jarring motion bounced around inside Toby's head. *What the heck's going on*, he thought. *Mom, vacuuming under the bed, again?*

A whirl of bizarre signals raced madly through his brain. He couldn't move his arms...or his legs, for that matter. *Was he paralyzed?*

Slowly, his eyes began to focus. An array of strange looking lights flew overhead, one after another.

I've been captured by space aliens!

The sound of heavy footsteps...heavy boots, crashed and echoed through his skull. The dampness and cold...that saturating cold...wrapping around every muscle, every bone.

He was being dragged, in some way...somewhere...by someone. The floor was rough, *hard cobble stone or something*. The walls consisted of large gray rocks, *like some sort of medieval basement*.

Toby shook his head, desperately trying to clear it...bring some sense to it. Actually, he was grateful just to be able to move it...to move anything.

He tilted back, trying to snatch a look from behind. The world was upside down. *Ain't that the truth*, he thought.

There were men, of some sort, uniformed...oddly uniformed men.

There was a brilliant, radiant light. Most of the men held the light. It hummed back and forth in their arms.

Maybe I really have *been captured by space aliens!*

He pulled his head back up; saw a group of people. Their faces were unclear...fuzzy. He tried to sharpen his vision, squinting his eyes and scrunching his face.

"*Bonehead Billy*," he murmured. "*He's been captured by the aliens, too...hope they have enough food to keep him quiet.*"

Toby's vision cleared a little more.

He saw a woman, also in the group. Very pretty. She held her head high, like a queen, yet there was an emptiness in her eyes.

A strange little man walked beside her. He had the biggest ears and nose that Toby had ever seen. He too looked sad.

Maybe somebody died....

Behind the woman and the little guy, there was another, more familiar face. A face he had seen for years, yet had just begun to know.

"*Lori*...," he whispered. "*Lori...Tkler...The Kingdom...of Keys!*"

He studied the strange bands constricting his movement. Then he flipped his head back, again, to see the soldiers...Tkler's soldiers.

This is wrong...all wrong. It's not supposed to be this way...it's not supposed to....

Or is it...will it?

"It can be whatever I imagine it to be," he said quietly.

His mind flashed to this incredible journey he had been on; how, *really*, his whole life was *supposed to be* just one incredible journey. He just never knew it.

All the *doors* were his to open. All the *keys* where his to use...*always*. It was always *his* choice. It will *always be*...his choice....

There was just one piece of unfinished business to take care of...and then....

"*It can be whatever I want it to be...whatever I imagine it to be.*"

The soldiers hauled Toby the remaining fifty yards and dropped him in the center of the large circular cavern. Then they herded the remainder of the group around him and waited.

Centurion approached. With a gloved hand, he reached down and grabbed Toby's uppermost restraint and jerked him to a standing position.

"On your feet...*boy*," Centurion snarled. "We've waited *ages* for this moment."

Toby stared into the eyes of Centurion. Smelt his foul breath. Sensed the emptiness of his soul.

"Please to meet ya," he said. "I'd shake your hand, but I'm a little tied up at the moment."

Billy rolled his eyes at Toby's corny response, but was happy that Toby had the cool to crack wise.

Centurion stared blankly into Toby's smug expression. Then, a crooked grin spread across his face.

Toby wanted to think it was a sign of appreciation for his wry sense of humor, but was afraid it might really be a sign of something much more threatening.

Toby swallowed, then looked up through the spiraling tower that led past the upper reaches of Castle Endlum.

Funny, he thought he saw stars...though he found it unlikely.

Centurion suddenly raised his lightning-cross and pointed it at Toby.

Billy turned his head while Musso's mouth fell open.

"*No!*" Lori screamed. She fell over, shuddering in sobs.

Centurion glanced at her, then turned his attention back to the boy. Slowly, he fingered the trigger.

How easy it will be. I'll write my own conclusion to the Foretelling. *Over and done...the end. And they all lived happily ever after....*

Deliberately, he began to squeeze....

"*No! You Fool!*" Tkler burst into the chamber. He yanked the shaft of the lightning-cross straight into the air. A brilliant streak of crimson blue shot through the tower and into the darkness.

Toby exhaled a squeak. The others, including the guards, stood silent.

Tkler plucked Centurion by his cloak and heaved him across the stagnant cavern.

"I have waited...all of time...for this moment, and *you* would choose to squander it *all*...for what? To add some noble worth to your meaningless existence. To take it upon *yourself* to write the final chapter. To end it *all* in a way that *you* see fit."

"But my Lord," Centurion said, struggling for his footing...struggling for existence. "But my Lord...I thought only of you...of—"

"*I think not!*" Tkler raised his lethal arm and, without thought, instantly dispatched Centurion with a searing bolt of white flame.

The soldiers stirred, yet no one said a word.

Tkler turned toward Toby. Rage exploded from within the shadow that concealed his eyes.

"Forgive the interruption," he said in mock politeness. "My associate sometimes suffers from the occasional lapse of protocol in these situations."

Toby surveyed the scorched outline of Centurion's form. "I don't think he'll be suffering from much, anymore."

"No...his time is...*UP!*" Tkler deviously popped the final P.

Toby glanced toward Lori and Billy. They were standing together, looking for strength. Emily rubbed passively against Lori's leg, while Queen Samira allowed Musso to hide behind a length of her gown.

"Let them go," Toby said flatly. "It's not about them, now. It's me you want. It's me you *need*."

"Oh, I could certainly dispatch them in the same manner as my brave and noble Centurion...if you wish," Tkler said with sinister delight.

"No...just...let...them...go," Toby said evenly.

"Don't worry, my boy. They are of no use to me. Their wellbeing depends on you...now doesn't it?"

Toby focused cold blue eyes on the shadow surrounding Tkler's face. They pierced the darkness, entered Tkler's dead, evil eyes...and awareness filled his soul.

"But, I have been so rude, now haven't I," Tkler continued. "Allow me to introduce myself. I am—"

"I know who you are," Toby said. "I've known you all my life."

"Yes," Tkler mused. "I suppose you have, haven't you?"

"I'm as much a thorn in *your side*, as you are to me," Toby said.

"Yes...I suppose you are. But, then again, you're just a boy."

"But, then again...I'm *the boy*.... The one you've always dreaded."

"*I dread no one!*" Tkler's face flushed a dark, evil shade of gray.

"Who am I?" Toby asked. "*WHO AM I?*" he screamed.

"You are the boy," Tkler answered, brusquely turning away.

"Say my name," Toby commanded.

Lori and Billy watched the confrontation with eyes, wide open...mouths, horribly dry. Neither seemed to breathe; neither seemed to want to.

"*I know your name!*" Tkler screamed. Then muttered, "I don't need to speak it."

"*My name is Toby*...do you hear me Tkler...*I am Toby...I choose to be...Toby*!

"You can't say it, can you, Tkler? You can't say my name. Toby, Toby, Toby. I can say your name, Tkler," Toby jeered. "I can say yours. *Tkler, Tkler, Tkler!*"

Tkler covered his ears and closed his eyes.

"*Silence!*" Sharp bolts of fire exploded from his deadly orbs and streaked over the heads of Lori and Billy, who abruptly panicked, ducked, and shrieked.

"I will take pleasure in turning your little friends into melted blubber, while you stand helplessly by, watching their useless lives digested by the stone."

Suddenly, the mysterious bonds ripped from Toby's body, as if they were made of the driest straw.

"You're not hurting anybody," Toby said, and boldly stepped forward, catching Tkler by surprise.

Forcing all of his will into pure concentrated energy, Toby stared directly into Tkler's eyes and blasted him against the wall, ten feet high.

Tkler splattered against the unforgiving stone, arms and legs at odd dangling angles; then he fell like a sack of melons to the surface.

"Way to go Tubman!" Billy shouted. "*The Incredible Tubman Rules Again!*"

The soldiers moved uneasily. They didn't know if they should run or advance.

"Stop him," Tkler croaked. "I want him stopped."

The guards began to advance. Emily tried to shoot a wad of needles into the pack, but they kicked her harmlessly away.

Toby faced the guards and they screeched to a halt.

"Stop him...I command it," Tkler said, weakly.

Toby turned back to the evil Lord and Tkler, again, flew off the cobbled surface. Toby focused and Tkler spun...then twirled...bounced back to the ground...up again...then flipped to the center of the room.

He was helpless.

"That is like so awesome, Tubman," Billy shouted. "You gotta teach me this stuff."

Tkler crumbled to the stone and extended his weakened arm for mercy.

Toby approached.

It was all so easy. So easy to make him go away...just like that, he thought.

Toby inspected the pathetic, outstretched arm, searching for a trick.

"Please, help me...I think I'm dying," Tkler moaned.

Toby was surprised by Tkler's meekness.

This guy's just a paper tiger, after all....

He actually felt compassion and, instinctively, reached for his hand.

"Toby, no!" Lori shouted. "It's a tri—"

Suddenly, Tkler grabbed Toby by the arm and viciously flung him over his shoulder like an old discarded towel.

"I don't believe *he* fell for that one, too" Billy shouted. "*No one* falls for *that one.*"

"Ha! Compassion is a weakness, boy...and *your* down fall."

Tkler sprang to his feet and centered on Toby. The evil light blazed in his eyes, then violently streaked toward its prey.

Toby looked up just as the fire shot from Tkler's eyes. To his surprise, his own eyes countered with their own fiery light and it met Tkler's head on, in the center of the room.

Lori gasped.

The dual beams of concentrated heat filled the cavern, an enormous inferno, raging in midair.

Billy stepped back, "Wow...talk about turnin up the heat...."

Then, the beam that shot from Toby, engulfed the one flowing from Tkler, and forced it back into its source...back into Tkler's eyes. Finally, it snapped, and Tkler was blown to the ground.

"Yes!" Musso exclaimed.

Tkler shot an evil sneer in the tiny man's direction and Musso again ducked behind Samira.

Toby focused. This time, the beam shot under Tkler's beaten form.

"That's it, Tobe...burn his butt!" Billy shouted.

A wary Tkler reached for something to grab while he floated off the stone.

"Ha!" Billy shouted. "Why don't ya grab this, Tkman...."

"Billy!" Lori reproached.

"Sorry."

Then, with the force of a rocket, Tkler was catapulted through the vast tower of Endlum, into the void.

Tkler's soldiers instinctively readied to attack...stopped...considered it for a moment...then broke ranks and ran away.

Toby turned, re-focused, and the guards suddenly clumped into a solid mass of arms and legs. The clump levitated, spun wildly in the air, then separated into smaller clumps and followed Tkler through the tower, miles into the night.

"Alright Tobe!" Billy said. "You did it!"

"Toby," Lori said, rushing into his arms. "He's gone...you finished him for good."

Toby looked into the knowing eyes of Queen Samira.

"I don't know, Lor...that was a little too easy...I'm just not sure at—"

Just then a fiery blast shot down from the tower.

"Look out!" Billy shouted as he saw Tkler descend on a cushion of intense orange flame.

"*I'm baaaaack, boys and girls...you didn't think you'd be rid of me so easily, now did you?*" he spoke with an evil frivolity.

Toby spun away from Lori and glared up at Tkler, hovering ten feet above. Again, Toby focused his thoughts and his own cushion of thrusting fire suddenly appeared beneath his dirty sneakers. The fire slowly raised him off the surface until, once more, he stood face to face with Tkler.

"You and me," Toby said. "Just you and me...the others are out of it."

Tkler studied Toby's blank expression, trying to grasp an insight, a handle on his foe.

"Agreed," Tkler said. "You and I...the *final chapter*."

Toby's gaze drifted to his friends below. They stood, frozen in time, like mannequins gaping skyward at some unearthly spectacle.

Would they ever be freed from this moment...again?

He looked at Tkler and nodded.

Then together, they rode the powerful flames upward, through the vast tower of Castle Endlum and into the surrounding void.

Their eyes never wavered...never blinked.

Chapter 43

They emerged beyond the reaches of Castle Endlum and passed into a darkness that transcended night. No light...no sound, only the void of hopelessness that surrounds a stolen dream.

The fiery pedestals, on which they stood, provided their only source of illumination...their only source of life. They circled, dissected their prey, searched for weaknesses, but found none.

Tkler marked his time, waiting for Toby to falter. *Everyone cracked,* he thought. *Everyone gave in, sooner or later. They always gave in. Soon, the boy would grow anxious. Make an uncertain move for the sake of movement. Make a sound to break the silence.* Then, Tkler would measure him, take advantage of his uncertainty...and crush him. It would be...*so easy.*

Toby hovered, still circling; not making a move...not making a sound. He was filled with confidence...the confidence of *knowing*.

No, he wouldn't give in. He wouldn't crumble under Tkler's icy stare.

They remained this way for what seemed to Tkler an eternity; in fact, it may have been. Finally, it was his own patience that wore thin and Tkler broke the silence...took the initiative.

"It will do you no good to stare me down, boy. As long as you breathe, I will be by your side. As long as you desire, I will be there to whisper *treachery* in your ear."

Toby smiled but said nothing, hovering...circling ...feeling his foe.

Tkler was uneasy, unsure how to proceed. He couldn't afford to make a mistake. He must be certain...to win. Everything was at stake.

Toby, however, had found a calming peace. He was concerned *only* with the battle. The outcome didn't matter...only the fight. The fight was *now*.

He focused all his energy on that singular thought. If he controlled the *now*...the outcome would take care of itself.

Tkler spoke again. "You *are* the impertinent one, to think *you* might match against *me*, boy. Others have tried, and all have failed."

Toby answered. "That's a lie. You thrive on lies...on deceit...on treachery. You try to cheat us of our lives...of our *purpose*. You try to fill us with doubt...uncertainty. To crush us with the weight of our empty souls. Then, you feed on it and become even stronger.

"You're not satisfied until we lock up our hope...our dreams...and throw away the *key*...forever."

Tkler smiled, he sensed weakness in the boy's passion.

"It's oh so *easy*, boy. You have no idea how *easy* it all *really* is. In fact, most are more than eager to do the dirty work for me."

"No, you're wrong. I know...I know how easy it is...to give in. I know how easy it is...to lose. But now...."

Tkler eyed the boy suspiciously. "But now...*what*?" The pedestal of fire beneath his boots suddenly bobbed and dipped as the flame sputtered and coughed.

"Now...I know how *easy* it is...to *win*," and with that Tkler plunged into the void, unable to control his fall; his flaming pedestal, no more than a spark.

Toby smiled, but he knew the fiend would be back. No, he hadn't finished with him yet. *But, score one for the home team.*

Tkler screamed, plummeting head over heels, helplessly dazed and confused. *What was this boy that opposed him? What power did he hold over him?* He thought he might know the answer. Worse, he thought the answer might know him....

At last, he gathered himself and centered on his *own* mighty powers. He knew what he held within. Yes...he had his *own* secrets, too.

His flame roared with a vengeance and Tkler stormed back through the dark.

Toby saw Tkler's flame re-ignite and steeled for his counter attack.

How would it come? Would he be able to withstand it?

Questions flooded his mind. One small victory, it seemed, did not bury doubt.

Tkler's head suddenly swelled to hideous proportions, like some sort of grotesque balloon.

"Wow...is it Thanksgiving already?" Toby calmly remarked, trying to suppress his fear.

The massive head raged from above and filled the darkness with its evil countenance.

The head bellowed and its foul breath melted Toby's confidence.

"You are nothing to me but a stupid, silly boy, who trembles at the unknown, the uncertain!"

"I'm everything to you," Toby countered, unevenly. Now, it was his pedestal that bobbed and dipped with a sputtering flame. "Without me, there wouldn't be a you...I hold the *KEY!*"

"*LIAR!*" Tkler roared. "*YOU HOLD NOTHING...YOU'LL WISH YOU NEVER FACED THE LIKES OF ME...I OWN YOUR HEART...YOUR SOUL...I OWN THE KEY, BOY!*"

"*NO! NOT IF I DON'T ALLOW IT,*" Toby shouted, then found refuge within an inner calm. "*Not if I don't want it.*"

Tkler's enormous face reddened with frustration. He puffed his hideous cheeks, then released a fetid wind that raged amidst the void. Toby covered up and steadied himself against the evil gale.

Tkler commenced a ghastly cackle. "Look at you, boy. So terribly weak, and so easily frightened...and *YOU* will control me...*I DON'T THINK SO!*"

"I'm not afraid of you," Toby boldly declared, staring into Tkler's massive eyes.

"You should be," Tkler sneered. *"I'M YOUR WORST NIGHTMARE!"*

And with that, Tkler puffed and exhaled another malicious gale. The powerful flame beneath Toby's feet again sputtered and this time nearly extinguished. Suddenly, Tkler blew again and Toby was savagely thrust miles into the blackness...miles into the unknown.

Tkler laughed wildly. *"So easy...oh, how so easy!"*

A swarm of black thoughts raced to control Toby's mind as he plunged helplessly through the stillness. He knew that once there was a Toby that would have been happy to continue this journey into nothingness; to hurdle limply out of control.

But, not now...not anymore. He knew...there was strength in the *knowing*. It was a strength that could conquer worlds, conquer universes. And he was certain it could take care of an annoying little bug like Tkler.

Toby's flame suddenly re-ignited.

"Nice play, Tkler," he said defiantly. "It's all tied up, but there's a lifetime left in this game. My lifetime...not yours, *Melon Head!"*

Tkler's hideous cackle abruptly ceased. He spotted the spark of light re-ignite in the darkness and his head abruptly deflated back to its normal size.

"That wretched boy," he muttered, with just the hint of a whimper.

Toby roared over Tkler's head, his fire, now, more powerful than ever.

Tkler spun and quickly pursued Toby's streak of light, roaring in the distance.

"What *is* he up to?"

Toby soared for miles, testing the outer edges of the darkness...the unknown; and with every inch, his strength increased, gobbling up his fear.

Tkler didn't like this. No...he didn't like this at all. He didn't know what the boy was doing. All he saw was the powerful light, swooping and soaring, retreating further into the distance.

Perhaps the boy had cracked, after all, he thought. *Perhaps he was frantically searching for an escape.*

"Ha! You will never escape from me, boy...never," Tkler said, boldly. Then, from nowhere, Toby suddenly swooped out of the darkness and zoomed around the unknowing Tkler.

"I think you've got it a little mixed up, *Tk-a-babe*. I think you're the one whose gonna want to find the escape hatch, here," he said, and with that Tkler suddenly began spinning, feverishly, like a top.

"You know," Toby said slyly. "I used to get sick on the merry-go-round. But this...this seems a bit more intense, don't you think, *Tk-arooski?*"

Finally, at Toby's command, the spinning ball of Tkler slowly spun to a halt. Toby swooped down to gather what was left of the gelatinous figure of Evil Lord Tkler, but suddenly pulled up.

"What!"

Tkler was gone...completely gone. All that remained was the vile remnant of his long black cape, about to slip into the void.

Toby reached out and grabbed the tattered cloak.

Suddenly, a violent crack of lightning ripped across the vacant atmosphere. Toby turned and saw his foe, hovering up above, both palms extending outward. Suddenly, malevolent streaks of fire burst from their core, and Tkler stood boldly, on high ground.

"*Tk-arooski* is it?" Tkler crossed his palms and the two flames merged to produce a single violent beam. The powerful blaze streaked toward the cape and ignited it.

Toby instantly threw the fiery cloak from his grasp.

"What's the matter, boy...can't stand the heat?"

"No," Toby replied. "Can't stand the cook."

And with that, Toby spun, head over heels, and again flew off into the darkness. This time, Tkler was prepared to follow.

Together, they soared through the wasteland, further and further into its tyranny, both with the knowing...*only one would return.*

Again, Tkler crossed his palms and shot a bolt of deadly fire.

Toby dove, then swooped behind in an expertly executed defensive move, designed to turn offensive. He crossed his own palms and - not really to his surprise - the same deadly fire emerged, approaching target Tkler.

Tkler skidded to a stop, defensively maneuvering on his own. Then, the two hovered and faced each other, once again.

Toby was reminded of every old cowboy movie he had seen on TV, as a kid. The ones where the sheriff and the bad guy meet for the final showdown. *Two guns drawn...one left standing*, he thought.

"Make your move, Tkler," he drawled; arms hung loosely at his side.

"Move? Move what?" Tkler asked impatiently.

"Uh, nothing," Toby said. "Sorry...I get carried away sometimes."

Tkler suddenly raised both arms and said, "*Try carrying this!*" and another massive bolt of fiery light burst from Tkler's palms.

Toby countered with his own blast of lightning and deflected Tkler's evil barrage upward. There, the two fiery shafts locked together and, at first, opposed each other - right against wrong...life versus death - until, suddenly, the two powers combined, forming a united beam; its brilliance was blinding.

Toby and Tkler struggled. With every ounce of power they possessed, they struggled, while the penetrating beam forged an insurmountable bond between them, as if their very souls were, somehow, melding together.

Neither dared to blink.

The combined beam of light intensified, raging from within, until, with a power never imagined, the beam exploded into the void and savagely ripped a hole across the darkness.

Both combatants gasped in wonder as a swirling maelstrom of color and light filled the void.

Then, the stillness surrounding them moved, as if something was awakening. The hole within the darkness had begun to consume the very emptiness that surrounded it...and slowly, began pulling the evil Lord Tkler and Toby toward its hungry center.

The end was coming. They both knew it. *Two guns drawn...one left standing.* Their eyes locked, revealing secrets forever clutched inside.

Tkler released first, trying to catch Toby by surprise. He withdrew his fiery light for just a fraction of a second...but that was all it took. Toby saw it...Tkler blinked.

In a single, timeless moment, Toby swooped his fire downward and undercut Tkler's legs. Lord Tkler broke contact with the powerful blaze that sustained him...and, as simple as that, it extinguished.

Caught in this endless second, Tkler glared at Toby with horror raging in his eyes. It was the horror of *absolute certainty*...the inevitable certainty of the *end*.

Then, slowly and deliberately, in an act of cosmic redemption, the vacuum began its chore...inhaling Tkler into its terrible abyss.

Tkler reached out to Toby, in one last, desperate act of submission. A weak, wavering beam of light emerged from his foul hand, dragged it back to its opposite...and they grasped.

Tkler grasped for survival...Toby, for a reason unknown.

The swirling light summoned, the vacuum relentlessly tugged...and Tkler looked into Toby's piercing eyes.

Then, within the strange, churning mass, the shadows, surrounding Tkler's own pleading eyes receded and revealed another exact blue reflection...of Toby's.

"You need me, boy...I'm your *out*...your *excuse*."

Toby returned Tkler's stare. "You're my *nightmare*...you said it yourself."

"Nightmares are just dreams, boy...I'm *real*...very *real*."

"No...you're just a dream, gone bad...a lie...to myself...I can *make* you go away."

"You can't *make* me go away, boy...I'll always be there with you...I live in your heart...I'm as much a part of you, as your soul...your soul *is my soul.*"

"You don't have a soul, Tkler. You're just a shadow...an illusion...mirrors and light. Do you know what happens when you shine light on a shadow, Tkler...*do you know?*"

Toby loosened his grip and Tkler swung precariously over the edge.

"*No!*" Tkler screamed.

"*It disappears...poof...it disappears,*" Toby said with venom.

"*No! Don't let me go! You can't believe that you can be rid of me!*"

"I believe I created you," Toby said, bravely. "I created all of this. *It's whatever I imagine it to be.* Yes Tkler, it's oh so *easy.*"

"*No!*" Tkler wildly kicked his legs above the swirling mass.

"...All I have to do...."

"*Noooo!*"

"...Is let...you...go...."

"*NOOOOOOOO*ooooooooooooooooooooooooooooo...!"

Toby released his grip and Tkler was sucked into the abyss. The raging sea of color and light hungrily raced to consume him.

Toby winced, yet felt a decided satisfaction, when the vacuum turned Tkler inside...then out. With a sudden...*POOF!*...he was gone.

The hole in the darkness healed itself closed.

Toby smiled. It was done.

Chapter 44

The darkness had abated, replaced by a beautiful azure sky. Toby smiled as he slipped through layers of delicate clouds, felt life renewed in their moisture, and soared into the tower of Castle Endlum. There, he found his friends frozen in time, exactly as he had left them. His fiery pedestal gently lowered him to the surface and disappeared.

"*Toby...he's getting away*," Billy screamed, pointing toward the empty tower.

"*Toby—*" Lori shouted, she too, looked up into the, now, vacant space.

"He's gone," Toby said, quietly from behind.

The astonished group abruptly spun around in unison.

Toby approached Lori and hugged her. Reaching out, he also put his arm around Billy. "It's done."

Queen Samira smiled broadly while Musso breathed a large sigh of relief. Emily squealed happily.

"But how?" Billy's question mark returned. "A second ago you were...just...up...now, you're—"

"Don't ask," Toby said with a crooked smile. "It's a long, long story."

Lori squeezed Toby firmly.

Suddenly, the very foundation of Castle Endlum began to crumble. Entire walls and ceilings rattled, then collapsed.

"Come on." Toby shouted. "We better get out of here, fast."

"Toby, which way do we go?" Musso shouted. "There are four ways to choose."

Toby knew whichever passage he chose...would be the right one.

He selected one of the four and, without looking back, led the group down its dark, twisting halls. Behind them, the narrow corridors crumbled into a coarse rain of sand, nipping at their heels, until finally, they escaped into the bright warmth of sunshine and the safety of a flowering hill.

Suddenly the sky erupted with the roar of finality and Castle Endlum imploded into oblivion.

"Now, it's really done," Toby said.

Lori took his hand. "Let's go home."

Toby smiled, "I'm ready."

Billy sighed, "It's about time."

Chapter 45

The celebration was already in full swing when they had returned to the *Kingdom of Keys.* News, it seemed, traveled fast in this timeless land.

Reveling in the clean, crisp, revitalizing air, the happy *Keysians* danced and sang their peculiar songs. Dark, threatening clouds no longer loomed in the distance, having been replaced by colorful, birdlike creatures, chirping and swooping playfully about. Large, *Keysian* ears no longer twitched at the sound of deadly thunder and the incessant ticking it conveyed. Instead, they captured the beautiful rhythms of their strange exotic melodies.

"*Hello good-bye...Hello good-bye,*" the merry makers sang, over and over and over.

"Man, push the advance button on that, will ya," Billy said, stuffing a giant drumstick, of some kind, into his mouth.

"Oh, come on, Billy," Lori said playfully. "They're honoring you. They think you're some sort of a hero. Why don't you show them your nice black cape?"

"Shhhh!" Billy's eyes darted back and forth. "I wouldn't want that stuff gettin around. You know, somebody could get the wrong idea or something."

"Right," Lori answered, tickling Emily behind her pointed ear. "We wouldn't want that to happen, would we Emily...no we wouldn't."

Emily's needles bristled and marked Billy.

"*Heel...heel that mutt*," Billy said nervously. Lori and Emily squealed with delight.

Toby and Queen Samira also laughed. "I guess some things never change," Toby said.

"Sometimes for the better," Samira answered.

Musso approached the group, accompanied by a handsome, vigorous man. The man's vibrant, penetrating, blue eyes brimmed with confidence and knowing strength. He walked with a majestic presence.

Samira smiled as the man approached.

Toby also smiled, though he still felt somewhat disconcerted in his presence.

"Say," Billy said to Lori. "Isn't there something about that guy with the half pint, that seems...you know...familiar?"

"I know what you mean. I can't quite put my finger on it, though. It's his eyes...it's as if I *know* him from somewhere...or maybe *I will*...someday."

"Yeah, right...exactly," Billy said, scratching his head.

"Toby," Musso said proudly. "The King would like to express his gratitude."

Toby motioned for Lori and Billy to join him. Billy brought his half-eaten drumstick along.

"Lori...Billy, this is our host...the *King of Keys*."

Lori smiled bashfully and nodded, while Billy extended his greasy hand.

"Have we met before, somewhere?" Billy asked.

The King accepted Billy's outstretched hand with his own, then smiled as he wiped off the residue on his tunic.

"Ooops, sorry about that, chief...uh King," Billy said sheepishly.

Toby smirked and said, "You know, Billy, I can't take you anywhere."

Lori giggled.

"It's my extreme pleasure to meet all of you," the King said. "You're all a delight, just the way you are...please don't change a thing."

Billy nudged Lori and whispered, "See, I'm a delight."

Lori nudged him back.

"I see you're feeling better, since the last time we spoke," Toby said.

"Yes, thanks to you, Toby. I...we owe *everything* to you."

Toby smiled. "I think I finally understand what you mean."

The King smiled back.

"Well, there's one thing I don't understand...about all of this" Billy said loudly.

"Billy!" Lori said.

"No, that's fine," the King said. "What is it, Billy?"

"Well, if you guys always had this *Foretelling* thing, all along...why were you so concerned about how this was all gonna end up? You had to know ol' Tubman here was gonna win. It's all written down."

"That's a fair question," the King said. "You see, while it's true that the *Foretelling* has always been with us, I'm afraid that it had never been complete...or resolved...until now."

"Huh?" Billy said.

The King continued. "The *Foretelling* tells of events that have taken, are taking, and will take place. But the conclusion...the conclusion can never be assured...until the path has been decided. Choice is a *key*...and choices must be made, and keys must be used. It was up to Toby to write the final chapter. To unlock the door and choose his path. Now, he has."

"Oh...yeah, right," Billy said, scratching his head again.

Toby laughed. He put his arm around Billy and knocked on his head. "Hello, anybody home in there."

The others joined in the laughter.

Lori leaned over to Billy and whispered, "Don't worry...I don't really get it all either."

Toby draped his arms comfortably around the shoulders of his friends and said to the King, "I'm ready to move on now."

"Yes," replied the King. "I'm certain you are."

"*Yes!*" Billy exclaimed.

The surrounding crowd of *Keysians* began to sing, "*Hello good-bye...Hello good-bye....*"

Toby knelt and shook Musso's tiny hand. "Hello good-bye, Mus. Thanks for your help. I couldn't have done it without you...and Malok too."

Musso smiled warmly. "Thank you, Toby. I was just doing what I was *supposed* to do...what I was *meant* to do."

"What about this *purpose* thing...haven't you done enough by now to...you know, move on?"

"Only when it's time, Toby. Oh, I can only *imagine* what's in store for me. There must be great things ahead."

"Yeah, I know what you mean," Toby said with pride.

"Be good...*Tubman*," Musso said with a giggle, then covered his mouth with embarrassment.

Toby laughed and stood up. Samira approached and embraced him. "Hello good-bye Toby. You were everything we knew you *would* be...and *will* be."

Toby kissed her softly on the cheek.

Lori hugged Emily and rubbed under her needled neck. "Bye bye, Emily. You be a good girl now...bye, I'll miss you."

"*Hoooologoadbooooy...Hoooologoadbooooy*," Emily sang.

Lori stood up and hugged Samira. "How can I ever be the same after all of this?"

Samira smiled and said, "Not to fear, Lori. This will all live, merely as a seed, in the back of your mind."

"Oh, man," Billy said disappointedly. "How come these things always end up like that? You know...."

A large wooden doorway suddenly appeared before them. Grasping hold of each other's hands, the three friends approached the door together. Toby took the small canvas sack from his pocket and removed the final key. Without hesitation, he placed it in the lock, turned it, and the door swung open. This time Toby removed the key and placed it in his pocket. Then he turned to the smiling crowd and waved.

Further back, on a distant hill, he saw another boy, looking down...at him. The boy seemed lost...frightened...alone.

Musso and another Keysian Guidesman approached the hill to greet the boy.

Toby smiled and dropped the empty sack.

He won't be alone for long.

With his friends in hand, Toby stepped through the door and closed it behind.

Epilogue

Inside, behind closed doors and windows, propped up on a mountain of pillows, a young man slept peacefully in his bed...until he was jarred awake by the sound of another hurricane, blowing wildly through his room.

This time, however, it was only *Hurricane Mom*, feverishly toiling at her appointed *Road Runner* rounds. Shades were flying upwards, windows were opening, and clothes swirled madly about. *Beep...Beep!*

"Toby Pierce...do you know what time it is...it's almost noon, on the most gorgeous spring day you've ever seen...and you're *still* lost under the covers...I swear this boy will never change."

Toby rubbed his eyes, desperately trying to make some sense of where he was. He felt like he'd been asleep for years.

"Mom, please, you're killing me here...and I thought yesterday was the most gorgeous day of spring." he croaked.

"Let's go. The storm's passed and the world has returned to the living."

"The storm...." Toby said, suddenly throwing the covers aside. He jumped out of bed, fully clothed, muddy sneakers and all.

"*Tobias Pierce!*" Mom shouted. "*What on earth are you doing in bed...with all of your clothes on?*"

"Not taking any chances, I guess," he answered cryptically, then scampered frantically around the room, looking for the sneakers that were already on his feet.

His mother stood dumbfounded, watching her only son dance like a maniac.

Toby suddenly stopped, in front of the "*Door to Nowhere*", and inspected the wide crack that ran around its painted seal.

Was that the faintest trace of glittery green dust around its edges?

A mess of muddy footprints led away from the door...*into* the room.

"Toby, this room looks as if the storm began and ended in here. What were you up to last night?"

Toby planted a big kiss on his Mom's cheek.

"Toby, are you okay? Let me feel your forehead."

"I never felt better," he answered. "I gotta go out for a while, Mom. I'll see you later. Okay? Love ya...bye."

"Love you, too," Mom murmured, watching this stranger run from the room and down the stairs. Shaking her head, she turned to change the bed and noticed a small object tucked under the covers. Picking it up, she discovered an old, tightly rolled tube of paint. It was blue.

"Where does that boy find this stuff?" she mused, then tossed the tube into the garbage pail.

Toby raced down the street, toward the corner, hoping to find somebody...anybody...but, mostly Lori.

The sun was high in the sky, diligently making fast work of the large puddles that remained from the storm. Everywhere, scattered branches cluttered the sidewalks and blocked streets. The intersection was empty and a long cable lay across the way, hanging from a familiar pole.

No wiffle ball game today. Still called on account of sewer.

Toby made a beeline for Lori's front porch and quickly took the steps two at a time.

Lori's Dad answered the door. "Hi, Toby, how you doing today?" He eyed Toby's muddied clothes. "Say, that was some storm last night, wasn't it? What've you been doing, jumping in puddles?"

"Hi, Mr. McSwain," Toby said, impatiently bouncing from foot to foot. "Nope, just the usual post-apocalyptic horde of malevolent drivers running wild through the streets, splashing innocent pedestrians. Got to watch where you're going. Is Lori home?"

Mr. McSwain couldn't help but chuckle. "Yes she is, Tobe, she's upstairs. I think she slept in pretty late, today."

"I know the way. Mind if I go on up...thanks" Toby didn't wait for an answer. He quickly scooted by Mr. McSwain and bounded up the steps.

"Say, how do you think that team of yours is going to do this year?" Mr. McSwain said with amusement.

"Just take em one game at a time," Toby answered. "One at a time, and count em up at the end."

Mr. McSwain shook his head and smiled. He hadn't seen Toby exhibit this much energy in years. *Must be spring*, he thought. "*Hmmmmm....*"

"Lori are you decent?" Toby yelled, hoping, maybe, that she wasn't quite.

"I'm in here," Lori croaked from her bedroom. Toby found her sitting at a small, white table, brushing her long brown hair. She was dressed in a clean blue T-shirt, with a picture of Dorothy and Toto on the front, and fresh jeans, frayed at the knees. Toby noticed a pile of dirty clothes lying in the corner.

"I slept in those things, last night. Don't ask me why, because I haven't a clue."

"I know the feeling," Toby answered. "Lor, are you all right? You look pretty tired."

In fact, Lori *did* appear as if she hadn't slept in days.

"I feel like I've lived a thousand lifetimes, in a single night."

"Wow!" Toby said. "I'm pretty tired too...but I feel great...you know...inside."

Lori smiled. She was happy to see Toby happy.

"That's great, Toby. I hope you stay that way, for a while."

"I think I will. I feel like things might be a whole lot different now. I don't know why...I just do."

Lori stopped brushing her hair, gazed at Toby and smiled. She didn't know quite *what* to say, so she said, "Have you seen Billy and the beastie boys? They were out front a while ago. Billy was making a speech about some weird dream he had last night. He was hanging out with some sort of *Darth Vadar* guy or something."

"Ah, that nutcase watches too many movies," Toby said with a dismissive wave of his hand.

"Tell me about it," Lori said. She got up and shuffled over to the window. Toby was struck by just *how* pretty she *really* was.

He approached her and quickly...awkwardly...kissed her. His clumsiness rewarded him with a half lip, half cheek combo.

Now, Lori was *really* stunned, and stood as if frozen in time.

Toby tried again, and, this time managed a soft, gentle kiss, full on the lips. *Bull's-eye!*

Now, to his surprise...Lori returned the kiss. Then, she caught herself, blushed, and nervously turned away. "Toby, my father is *downstairs*!"

"Good," Toby replied. "Let's hope he stays there."

Lori giggled and playfully pushed Toby away.

Oh well, Toby thought. *One game at a time.*

Awkwardly changing the subject, Toby asked, "So, where did those knuckleheads go to, anyway?"

"Down to *The Lake*."

"*The Lake*. They haven't gone down there in years."

"I heard Herbie saying, that the *Elephant Tree* had gotten blown right out of the ground, last night."

"Why do I know this?" Toby wondered.

"They said the roots look like some sort of monster or something...so off they went. You know...*children*."

"Right...*children*," Toby agreed.

The two shuffled a bit.

"*You wanna go down and see?*" Lori asked.

"*You bet!*" Toby said with enthusiasm.

"Toby...there's only one thing."

"What's that?"

"I don't remember any storm last night...do you?"

"Not really. Not clearly anyway."

"Oh...."

"Yeah...oh."

Toby looked out the window and saw the big pine tree standing guard outside. He noticed several small branches were snapped and bent. Also, more muddy footprints remnants were slightly visible on the roof.

"Hey Lor, you been out climbing down this old tree or something, lately?"

"What, are you crazy? I haven't done that in years. I might break my neck or something."

"Yeah...break your neck...right," Toby muttered, eyeing the footprints.

"Besides—"

"*Let's do it!*" he shouted excitedly.

"*Toby!*" Lori exclaimed. "*My father is* right *down stairs!*"

"Right, he'll never see us. It'll drive him nuts, just like old times. Come on, what do you say? Down the old tree, for old time's sake."

"Oh...that," Lori said, flushing a bright crimson. "Toby, we'll.—"

"I know, *break our necks.* We won't...I promise. I won't let it happen. I'll carry you on my back."

Toby bent over and tried to pull Lori over his shoulder. Lori screeched hysterically.

"*Ahhhhhhh...Toby stop! You'll hurt yourself!*"

"Lori," came the anxious voice of Mr. McSwain, from the bottom of the stairs. "Why don't you and Toby come down stairs and play, now."

Lori choked back a giggle. "Be down in sec, Daddy," she called.

"Come on," Toby said. "Old times."

"And *new times,*" Lori said. She leaned forward and, once again, gently kissed her *old buddy* on the lips.

"*Yeah...new times.*" Toby said. He stepped back numbly and opened the window.

Effortlessly, the pair slithered onto the roof and skillfully tackled the big evergreen. Within seconds they hit the ground running and spilled out to the street, full of mischievous giggles. Puffing with energy, the two *old buddies* slowed to a downhill walk in the direction of *The Lake*, comfortably holding each other's hand. Toby absently reached in his pocket and pulled out a small brass skeleton key.

"What's that funny key for?" Lori asked, seeing it glisten in the palm of his hand.

"*Everything...*" Toby answered.

* * * * * * * * *

It was the second *real* cliche' of spring. Up above, in budding trees, robins chirp a knowing song, inspired by the scent of fresh mown lawn.

Somewhere, in a place without time, a King opens the door to a newly constructed vault. Taking the freshly restored manuscript, written in an *other* time, he reverently returns it to the place where it belongs.

Glancing at its rich leather cover, the King reads the words that changed a life forever:

The Foretelling

of

The Kingdom of Keys

By

Tobias Pierce

The King smiles, closes the door and turns the key.
Click...click....

Brian Moloney

Acknowledgements

Inspiration for *The Kingdom of Keys* was derived from the many fanciful tales and images of my youth. Part Star Wars...part Wizard of OZ...part Lord of The Rings...part Peter Pan...and part just about anything else that allowed a young boy's imagination to lock on and run away with it for a while. In that way, it's a story that's been with me from a very young age, patiently waiting for the day I would finally open my own "Door to Nowhere" and step through....

Learn about the fascinating life of Vincent van Gogh by picking up a copy of Irving Stone's, "A Lust for Life".

For more of Henry David Thoreau's unique thoughts and meditations check out a copy of "Walden", his best known work that describes his time living alone in his small, hand built house in the woods, overlooking Walden Pond, in Concord Massachusetts.

And for insight into the brilliantly talented yet complicated mind of 60's folksinger, Phil Ochs, read Michael Schumacher's biography, "There But for Fortune: The Life of Phi Ochs"...and give a listen to some of his music, much of which is more than relevant today.

Thanks to Joelle Wilson for her great selection of cover photos and for putting up with my endless requests...and to "Forever Friend" Pami Kientz Cowan, a special thanks for the use of the keys and your keen copy editor's eye. I owe all my closed quotes and restored punctuation to you. Any missed are strictly on me for not following your notes, properly. And yes...I'm still looking for your roller skates.

And, of course, thanks to all of you, for taking the time to read my story—even the boring acknowledgments. I hope it was worth your while....

About the Author

Brian Moloney (that's me) has worked in the fields of Advertising, Film and TV on both the commercial and corporate sides, since 1978. He (still me) began freelancing as a writer in 1992, when he discovered he could type on a computer without the need of whiteout to hide all his mistakes; a process he found extremely messy and time consuming. In addition to "The Kingdom of Keys", he's also written a children's Christmas Story, entitled "The Little Red Christmas Ball", which he hopes to publish in the very near future; preferably around Christmas, because to publish it for the 4th of July would be just silly. In addition, he's currently at work compiling a collection of essays from his bi-weekly humor column "The Freelance Retort" which he threatens to finish and send out soon...very, very soon.

"The Freelance Retort" can be found at
http://freelanceretort.blogspot.com/
"Like" the FLR on Facebook...along with all the cute cats and everything else....
Email the Author: freelanceretort@gmail.com

Made in the USA
Middletown, DE
20 December 2018